P9-CKQ-623

ATTACK!

Time stopped and war came to Brady Field. The
pilot of a World War I fighter plane fired on the
control tower and then dipped around and
strafed the sleek modern jets jerked lazily on
the runway. Three of the F-105 Starfires burst
into flames as their fuel tanks of jet fuel ignited.
Again and again, the bright yellow flying
antique with the black Maltese Cross soared
over the field, spitting a leaden stream of destruction.

In the control tower a sergeant lay on the floor,
looking dazedly at a red trail of blood that
oozed from his chest. He crawled across the
floor to his radio and reached the microphone.

"MAY DAY! MAY DAY! This is Brady Field.
We are under attack."

THE
MEDITERRANEAN
CAPER

Bantam Books by Clive Cussler
Ask your bookseller for the books you have missed

ICEBERG
THE MEDITERRANEAN CAPER
NIGHT PROBE!
RAISE THE TITANIC!
VIXEN 03

THE MEDITERRANEAN CAPER

CLIVE CUSSLER

BANTAM BOOKS
TORONTO · NEW YORK · LONDON · SYDNEY

To Amy and Eric,
long may they wave.

THE MEDITERRANEAN CAPER
A Bantam Book | published by arrangement with the author

PRINTING HISTORY

Bantam edition | December 1977

2nd printing .. December 1977	8th printing ...... August 1978
3rd printing ...... January 1978	9th printing .. November 1978
4th printing ...... January 1978	10th printing . September 1979
5th printing .... March 1978	11th printing . September 1979
6th printing .... May 1978	12th printing .... February 1980
7th printing .... August 1978	13th printing .... July 1981

*All of the characters in this book are fictitious,
and any resemblance to actual persons,
living or dead, is purely coincidental.*

All rights reserved.
Copyright © 1973 by Clive Cussler.
*This book may not be reproduced in whole or in part, by
mimeograph or any other means, without permission.
For information address: Bantam Books, Inc.*

ISBN 0-553-20320-7

Published simultaneously in the United States and Canada

Bantam Books are published by Bantam Books, Inc. Its trademark, consisting of the words "Bantam Books" and the por-
trayal of a bantam, is Registered in U.S. Patent and Trademark
Office and in other countries. Marca Registrada. Bantam
Books, Inc., 666 Fifth Avenue, New York, New York 10103.

PRINTED IN THE UNITED STATES OF AMERICA

22 21 20 19 18

THE MEDITERRANEAN CAPER

PROLOGUE

It was oven hot, and it was Sunday. In the air traffic tower, the control operator at Brady Air Force Base lit a cigarette from a still glowing butt, propped his stocking feet on top of a portable air conditioner and waited for something to happen.

He was totally bored, and for good reason. Air traffic was slow on Sundays. In fact, it was nearly nonexistent. Military pilots and their aircraft rarely flew on that day in the Mediterranean Theatre of Operations, particularly since no international political trouble was brewing at the moment. Occasionally a plane might set down or take off, but it was usually just a quick refueling stop for some VIP who was in a hurry to get to a conference somewhere in Europe or Africa.

The control operator scanned the large flight schedule blackboard for the tenth time since he came on duty. There were no departures, and the only estimated time of arrival was at 1630, almost five hours away.

He was young—in his early twenties—and strikingly refuted the myth that fair-haired people cannot tan well; wherever skin showed, it looked like dark walnut laced with strands of platinum blond hair. The four stripes on his sleeve denoted the rank of a Staff Sergeant, and although the temperature was touching ninety-eight degrees, the armpits of his khaki uniform displayed no

1

damp sweat stains. The collar on his shirt was open and missing a tie; a custom normally allowed at Air Force facilities located in warm atmospheres.

He leaned forward and adjusted the louvers on the air conditioner so that the cool air ran up his legs. The new position seemed to satisfy him, and he smiled at the refreshing tingle. Then, clasping his hands behind his head, he relaxed backward, staring at the metal ceiling.

The everpresent thought of Minneapolis and the girls parading Nicollet Avenue crossed his mind. He counted again the fifty-four days left to endure before he was rotated back to the States. When each day came it was ceremoniously marked off in a small black notebook he carried in his breast pocket.

Yawning for perhaps the twentieth time, he picked up a pair of binoculars that were sitting on the window ledge, and surveyed the parked aircraft that rested on the dark asphalt runway stretching beneath the elevated control tower.

The runway lay on the island of Thasos in the northern part of the Aegean Sea. The island was separated from the Greek Macedonia mainland by sixteen miles of water, appropriately called the Thasos Strait. The Thasos land mass consisted of one hundred and seventy square miles of rock, timber and remnants from classical history dating back to One Thousand B.C.

Brady Field, as generally termed by the base personnel, was constructed under a treaty between the United States and the Greek government in the late nineteen sixties. Except for ten F-105 Starfire Jets, the only other permanently based aircraft were two monstrous C-133 Cargomaster transports that sat like a pair of fat silver whales, glistening in the blazing Aegean sun.

The sergeant pointed the binoculars at the dormant aircraft and searched for signs of life. The field was empty. Most of the men were either in the nearby town of Panaghia drinking beer, sunbathing on the beach or napping in the air-cooled barracks. Only a solitary MP guarding the main gate, and the constant rotation of the radar antennae atop its cement bunker offered any form of human presence. He slowly raised the lenses and peered over the azure sea. It was a bright, cloudless day, and he could easily recognize details on the distant Greek mainland. The glasses swung east and gathered in the horizon line where deep blue water met light blue sky. Through the shimmering haze of heat waves the white speck of a ship resting at anchor came into view. He squinted and adjusted the focus knob to clarify the ship's name on the bow. He could just barely make out the tiny black words: *First Attempt.*

That's a dumb name, he thought. The significance escaped him. Other markings also darkened the ship's hull. In long, heavy, black lines across the center of the hull were the vertical letters NUMA which he knew stood for the National Underwater Marine Agency.

A huge crooked crane stood on the stern of the ship and hung over the water, lifting a round ball-like object from the depths. The sergeant could see men laboring about the crane, and he felt inwardly glad that civilians had to work on a Sunday too.

Suddenly his visual exploration was cut short by a robot-like voice over the intercom.

"Hello, Control Tower, this is Radar . . . Over!"

The sergeant laid down the binoculars and flicked a microphone switch. "This is the Control Tower, Radar. What's up?"

"I've got a contact about ten miles to the west."

"Ten miles west?" boomed the sergeant. "That's inland over the island. Your contact is practically on top of us." He turned and looked again at the big lettered blackboard, reassuring himself that no scheduled flights were due. "Next time, let me know sooner?"

"Beats me where it came from," droned the voice from the radar bunker. "Nothing has shown on the scope in any direction under one hundred miles in the last six hours."

"Well either stay awake down there or get your damn equipment checked," snapped the sergeant. He released the mike button and grabbed the binoculars. Then he stood up and peered to the west.

It was there . . . a tiny dark dot, flying low over

the hills at tree top level. It came slow; no more than ninety miles an hour. For a few moments it seemed to hang suspended over the ground, and then, almost all at once, it began to take on shape. The outlines of the wings and fuselage drew into sharp focus through the binoculars. It was so clear as to be unmistakable. The sergeant gaped in astonishment as the rattley-bang engine sound of an old single seat, biwing airplane complete with rigid, spoked wheel landing gear, tore the arid island air.

Except for the protruding in-line cylinder head, the fuselage followed a streamlined shape that tapered to straight sides at the open cockpit. The great wooden propeller beat the air like an old windmill, pulling the ancient craft over the landscape at a tortoise-like air speed. The fabric covered wings wavered in the wind and showed the early characteristic scalloped trailing edge. From the spinner enclosing the propeller hub to the rear tips of the elevators, the entire machine was painted a bright and flamboyant yellow. The sergeant lowered the glasses just as the plane, displaying the familiar black Maltese Cross markings of World War I Germany, flashed by the control tower.

In another circumstance the sergeant would have probably dropped to the floor if an airplane buzzed the control tower at no more than five feet. But his amazement at seeing a very real ghost from the dim skies of the Western Front was too much for his senses to grasp, and he stood stock still. As the plane passed, the pilot brazenly waved from his cockpit. He was so close that the sergeant could see the features of his face under the faded leather helmet and goggles. The spectre from the past was grinning and patting the butts of the twin machine guns, mounted on the cowling.

Was this some sort of colossal joke? Is the pilot a nutty Greek with a circus? Where did he come from? The sergeant's brain spun with questions but no answers. Suddenly he became aware of twin, blinking spots of light, emitting behind the propeller of the plane. Then the glass of the control tower windows shattered and disappeared around him.

A moment in time stopped and war came to Brady Field. The pilot of the World War I fighter dipped around the control tower and strafed the sleek modern jets parked lazily on the runway. One by one the F-105 Starfires were raked and slashed by ancient eight millimeter bullets that tore into their thin aluminum skin. Three of them burst into flames as their full tanks of jet fuel ignited. They burned fiercely, melting the soft asphalt into smoking puddles of tar. Again and again, the bright yellow flying antique soared over the field, spitting a leaden stream of destruction. One of the C-133 Cargomasters went next. It erupted in a gigantic roar of flames that rose hundreds of feet into the air.

In the tower the sergeant lay on the floor, looking dazedly at a red trail of blood that oozed from his chest. He gently pulled the black notebook from his breast pocket and stared in fascinated surprise at a small, neat hole in the middle of the cover. A dark veil began to circle his eyes and he shook it off. Then he struggled to his knees and looked around the room.

Glittering fragments of broken glass blanketed the floor, the radio equipment, the furniture. In the center of the room, the air conditioner lay upside down like a dead mechanical animal; its legs thrown stiffly in the air and its coolant trickling onto the floor from several round punctures. The sergeant dully peered up at the radio. Miraculously it was untouched. Painfully, he crawled across the floor, slicing his knees and hands on the crystal slivers. He reached the microphone and grasped it tightly, bloodying the black plastic handle.

Darkness crowded the sergeant's thoughts. What is the proper procedure, he wondered? What does one say at a time like this? Say something, his mind shouted, *say anything!*

"To all who can hear my voice. MAY DAY! MAY DAY! This is Brady Field. We are under attack by an unidentified aircraft. This is not a drill. I repeat, Brady Field is under attack . . ."

1

Major Dirk Pitt adjusted the headset on his thick black hair and slowly turned the channel crank on the radio, trying to fine-tune the reception. He listened intently for a few moments, his dark, sea-green eyes reflecting a trace of bewilderment. A frown cut his forehead in a series of grooves and hung there in the tanned leathery skin.

It wasn't that the words crackling over the receiver weren't understandable. They were. He just didn't believe them. He listened again, and listened hard over the droning roar of the PBY Catalina's twin engines. The voice he heard was fading, when it should have been getting stronger. The volume control was turned to full-on, and Brady Field was only thirty miles away. Under those conditions, the air traffice operator's voice should have blasted Pitt's eardrums out. The operator is either losing power or he's seriously injured, thought Pitt. He pondered a minute and then reached over to his right and shook the sleeping figure in the co-pilot's seat.

"Come out of it, sleeping beauty." He spoke in a tone that was soft and effortless, yet had a way of making itself heard in a throbbing airplane or a crowded room.

Captain Al Giordino wearily raised his head and yawned loudly. The fatigue of sitting in an old vibrating PBY flying boat for thirteen hours straight was evident in his dark, bloodshot eyes. He flung his arms upward, puffed out his barrel chest and stretched. Then he came erect and leaned forward, peering out in the distance beyond the cockpit windows.

"Are we over the *First Attempt* yet?" Giordino mumbled through another yawn.

"Almost," replied Pitt. "There's Thasos dead ahead."

"Oh hell," Giordino grunted; then grinned. "I could have slept another ten minutes. Why'd you wake me?"

"I intercepted a message from Brady Control that said the field was under attack by an unidentified aircraft."

"You can't be serious," Giordino said incredulously. "It must be some kind of a joke."

"No, I don't think so. The control operator's voice didn't sound like it was faking." Pitt hesitated and kept an eye on the water only fifty feet away as it flashed under the PBY's hull. Just for practice he had wave-hopped the last two hundred miles; a means of keeping his reflexes honed and sharp.

"It might be that Brady Control was telling the truth," said Giordino, peering through the cockpit windshield. "Look over there toward the eastern part of the island."

Both men stared at the approaching mound rising out of the sea. The beaches bordering the surf were yellow and barren, but the round sloping hills were green with trees. The colors danced in the heat waves and vividly contrasted against the encircling blue of the Aegean. On the eastern side of Thasos a large pillar of smoke rose into the windless sky and formed a giant, spiral-shaped, black cloud. The PBY's bow soared closer to the island, and soon they could distinguish the orange movement of flames at the base of the smoke.

Pitt grabbed the mike and pressed the button on the side of the handgrip. "Brady Control, Brady Control, this is PBY-086, over." There was no response. Pitt repeated the call twice more.

"No answer?" queried Giordino.

"Nothing," returned Pitt.

"You said an *unidentified aircraft*. I take it, that means one?"

"That's precisely what Brady Control said before they went off the air."

"It doesn't make sense. Why would one plane attack a United States Air Force Base?"

"Who knows," Pitt said, easing the control column back slightly. "Maybe it's an irate Greek farmer who's tired of our jets scaring his goats. Anyway, it can't be a full-scale attack, or Washington would have notified us by now. We'll have to wait and see." He rubbed his eyes and blinked away the drowsiness. "Get ready, I'm going to take her up, circle in over those hills and come down out of the sun for a closer look."

"Take it nice and easy." Giordino's eyebrows came together and he grinned a serious grin. "This old bus is way overmatched if that's a rocket firing jet down there."

"Don't worry," Pitt laughed. "My main goal in life is to stay healthy as long as possible." He pushed the throttles forward, and the two Pratt & Whitney Wasp engines increased their beat. His large, brown hands moved efficiently, pulling back on the control column, and the plane aimed its flat snout at the sun. The big Catalina rose steadily, gaining altitude by the second, and circled above the Thasos mountains in the direction of the growing smoke cloud.

Suddenly, a voice broke in over Pitt's headset. The unexpected sound nearly deafened his ears before he could lower the volume—the same voice he heard before, but stronger this time.

"This is Brady Control calling. We are under attack! I repeat, we are under attack! Come in . . . anybody, please reply!" The voice was near hysteria.

Pitt replied, "Brady Control, this is PBY-086. Over."

"Thank God, someone answered," the voice gasped.

"I tried to raise you before, Brady Control, but you faded and went off the air."

"I was hit in the first attack, I . . . I must have passed out. I'm all right now." The words sounded broken, but coherent.

"We're approximately ten miles west of you at six thousand feet." Pitt spoke slowly and did not repeat his position. "What is your situation?"

"We have no defense. All our aircraft were destroyed on the ground. The nearest interceptor squadron is seven hundred miles away. They'll never get here in time. Can you assist?"

Pitt shook his head from side to side from habit. "Negative, Brady Control. My top speed is under one hundred ninety knots and I only have a couple of rifles on board. We'd be wasting our time engaging a jet."

"Please assist," the voice pleaded. "Our attacker is no a jet bomber but a World War I biplane. I repeat, our attacker is a World War I biplane. Please assist."

Pitt and Giordino merely looked at each other, dumbfounded. It was a full ten seconds before Pitt could pull his senses back into reign.

"Okay, Brady Control, we're coming in. But you'd better know your aircraft identification, or you're going to make a pair of little old silver-haired mothers damn sad if my co-pilot and I buy the farm. Over and out." Pitt turned to Giordino and spoke quickly without facial expression, his tone confident and calculating. "Go aft and throw open the side hatches. Use one of the carbines and make like a sharpshooter."

"I can't believe what I'm hearing," Giordino said stunned.

Pitt shook his head. "I can't quite accept it either, but we've got to give those guys down there on the ground a helping hand. Now hurry it up."

"I'll do it," Giordino muttered. "But I still don't believe it."

"Yours is not to reason why, my friend," Pitt lightly punched Giordino on the arm and smiled briefly. "Good luck."

"Save it for yourself, you bleed just as easily as I do," Giordino said soberly. Then, muttering quietly under his breath, he rose from the co-pilot's seat and made his way to the ship's waist. Once there he pulled the thirty caliber carbine from an upright cabinet and shoved a fifteen shot clip into the receiver. A blast of warm air struck his face, filling the compartment when he opened the waist hatches. He checked the gun once more and sat down to wait; his thoughts drifting to the big man who was piloting the plane.

Giordino had known Pitt for a long time. They'd played together as boys, ran on the same high school track team and dated the same girls. He knew Pitt better than any man alive; any woman too, for that matter. Pitt was, in a sense, two men, neither of them directly related to the other. There was the coldly efficient Dirk Pitt who rarely made a mistake, and yet was humorous, unpretentious and easily made friends with everyone who came in contact with him; a rare combination. Then there was the other Pitt, the moody one, the one who often withdrew to himself for hours at a time and became remote and aloof, as though his mind were constantly churning over some distant dream. There had to be a key that unlocked and opened the door between the two Pitts, but Giordino had never found it. He did know, however, that the transition from one Dirk Pitt to the other took place more frequently in the past year—since Pitt lost a woman in the sea near Hawaii; a woman he had loved deeply.

Giordino remembered noticing Pitt's eyes before coming back to the main cabin; how the deep green had transformed to a glinting brightness at the call of danger. Giordino had never seen eyes quite like them, except once, and he shuddered slightly at the recollection as he glanced at the missing finger on his right hand. He jerked his thoughts back to the reality of the present and slid off the safety catch on the carbine. Then, strangely, he felt secure.

Back in the cockpit, Pitt's tanned face was a study in masculinity. He was not handsome in the movie star sense: far from it. Women rarely, if ever, threw themselves at him. They were usually a little awed and uncomfortable in his presence. They somehow sensed that he was not a man who catered to feminine wiles or silly coquettish games. He loved women's company and the feel of their soft bodies, but he disliked the subterfuge, the lies, and all the other ridiculous little ploys it took to seduce the average female. Not that he lacked cleverness at getting a woman between the sheets; he was an expert. But he had to force himself to play the game. He preferred straightforward and honest women, but there were far too few to be found.

Pitt eased the control column forward, and the PBY nosed over in a shallow dive toward the inferno at Brady Field. The white altimeter needles slowly swung backward around the black dial, registering the descent. He steepened the angle, and the twenty-five year old aircraft began to vibrate. It was not built for high speed. It was designed for low speed reconnaissance, dependability and long range, but that was about all.

Pitt had requested the purchase of the craft after he had transferred from the Air Force to the National Underwater Marine Agency at the request of the Agency Director, Admiral James Sandecker. Pitt still retained his rank of Major and, according to the paperwork, was assigned to an indefinite tour of duty with NUMA. His title was that of Surface Security Officer, which was nothing to him but a fancy term for trouble shooter. Whenever a project ran into unknown difficulties or unscientific problems, it was Pitt's job to unravel the difficulty and get the operation back on the track. That was the purpose behind his request for the PBY Catalina flying boat. Slow as it was, it could comfortably carry passengers and cargo, and what was most important, land and take off in water; a prime factor since nearly ninety percent of NUMA's operations were miles at sea.

Suddenly a glint of color against the black cloud caught Pitt's attention. It was a bright yellow plane. It banked sharply, suggesting high maneuverability, and dived through the smoke. Pitt slipped the throttles backward to reduce the speed of his sharp angle of descent and prevent the PBY from overshooting his strange adversary. The other plane materialized out of the opposite side of the smoke and could clearly be seen strafing Brady Field.

"I'll be damned," Pitt boomed out loud. "It's an old German Albatros."

The Catalina came on straight from the eye of the sun, and the pilot of the Albatros, intent on the business of destruction, did not see it. A sardonic grin spread on Pitt's face as the fight drew near. He cursed the fact that there were no guns waiting for his command to spout from the nose of the PBY. He applied pressure to the rudder pedals and sideslipped to give Giordino a better line of fire. The PBY thundered in, still unnoticed. Then, abruptly, he could hear the crack of Giordino's carbine above the roar of the engines.

They were almost on top of the Albatros before the leather helmeted head in the open cockpit spun around. They were so close Pitt could see the other pilot's mouth drop open in shocked surprise at the sight of the big flying boat, boring down from the sun—the hunter became the quarry. The pilot recovered quickly and the Albatros rolled sharply away, but not before Giordino drilled it with a fifteen shot clip from the carbine.

The grim, incongruous drama in the smoke-ridden sky over Brady Field reached a new stage as the World War II flying boat squared off against the World War I fighter plane. The PBY was faster, but the Albatros had the advantage of two machine guns and a vastly higher degree of maneuverability. The Albatros was lesser known than its famous counterpart, the Fokker, but it was an excellent fighter and the workhorse of the German Imperial Air Service from 1916 to 1918.

The Albatros twisted, turned and zeroed in on the PBY's cockpit. Pitt acted quickly and yanked the controls back into his lap and prayed the wings would stay glued to the fuselage as the lumbering flying boat struggled into a loop. He forgot caution and the accepted rules of flying; the exhilaration of man-to-man combat surged in his blood. He could almost hear the rivets popping as the PBY twisted over on its back. The unorthodox evasive action caught his opponent off guard, and the twin streams of fire from the yellow plane went wide, missing the Catalina completely.

The Albatros then made a steep left hand turn and came straight at the PBY, and they approached head-on. Pitt could see the other plane's tracer bullets streaking about ten feet under his windshield. Lucky for us this guy's a lousy shot, he thought. He had a weird feeling in his stomach as the two planes sped together on a collision course. Pitt waited until the last possible instant before he pushed the nose of the PBY down and swiftly banked around, gaining a brief, but favorable position over the Albatros. Again Giordino opened fire. But the yellow Albatros dived out of the spitting hail from the carbine and shot vertically toward the ground, and Pitt momentarily lost sight of it. He swung to the right in a steep turn and searched the sky. It was too late. He sensed, rather than felt, the thumping from a river of bullets that tore into the flying boat. Pitt threw his plane into a violent falling leaf maneuver and successfully dodged the smaller plane's deadly sting. It was a narrow escape.

The uneven battle continued for a full eight minutes while the military spectators on the ground watched, spellbound. The strange aerial dogfight slowly drifted eastward over the shoreline, and the final round began.

Pitt was sweating now. Small glistening beads of the salty liquid were bursting from the pores on his forehead and trickling in snail-like trails down his face. His opponent was cunning, but Pitt was playing the strategy game too. With infinite patience, dredged up from some hidden reserve in his body, he waited for the right moment, and when it finally arrived he was ready.

The Albatros managed to get behind and slightly above the Catalina. Pitt held his speed steady and the other pilot, sensing victory, closed to within fifty yards of the flying boat's towering tail section. But before the two machine guns could speak, Pitt pulled the throttle back and lowered the flaps, slowing the big craft into a near stall. The phantom pilot, taken by surprise, overshot and passed the PBY, receiving several well placed rounds in the Albatros' engine as the carbine spat at near point-blank range. The vintage plane banked in front of Pitt's bow, and he watched with the respect one brave man has for another when the occupant in the open cockpit pushed up his goggles and threw a curt salute. Then the yellow Albatros and its mysterious pilot turned away and headed west over the island, trailing a black streak of smoke that testified to the accuracy of Giordino's markmanship.

The Catalina was falling out of its stall into a dive now, and Pitt fought the controls for a few unnerving seconds before he regained stable flight. Then he began a sweeping, upward turn in the sky. At five thousand feet he leveled off and searched the island and seascape, but no trace of the bright yellow plane with the maltese cross markings was visible. It had vanished.

A cold, clammy feeling crept over Pitt. The yellow Albatros had somehow seemed familiar. It was as though an unremembered ghost from the past had returned to haunt him. But the eerie sensation passed as quickly as it had arrived, and he gave out a deep sigh as the tension faded away, and the welcome comfort of relief gently soothed his mind.

"Well, when do I get my sharpshooter's medal?" said Giordino from the cabin doorway. He was grinning despite a nasty gash in his scalp. The blood streamed down the right side of his face, staining the collar of a loud, flowered print shirt.

"After we land I'll buy you a drink instead," replied Pitt without turning.

Giordino slipped into the co-pilot's seat. "I feel like I've just ridden the roller coaster at the Long Beach Pike."

Pitt could not help grinning. He relaxed, leaning back against the back rest, saying nothing. Then he turned and looked at Giordino, and his eyes squinted. "What happened to you? Were you hit?"

Giordino gave Pitt a mocking, a sorrowful look. "Who ever told you that you could loop a PBY?"

"It seemed like the thing to do at the time," said Pitt, a twinkle in his eye.

"Next time, warn the passengers. I bounced around the main cabin like a basketball."

"What did you hit your head on?" Pitt asked quizzically.

"Did you have to ask?"

"Well?"

Giordino suddenly became embarrassed. "If you must know, it was the door handle on the john."

Pitt looked startled for an instant. Then he flung back his head and roared with laughter. The mirth was contagious, and Giordino soon followed. The sound rang through the cockpit and replaced the noise of the engines. Nearly thirty seconds passed before their gaiety quieted, and the seriousness of the present situation returned.

Pitt's mind was clear, but exhaustion was slowly seeping in. The long hours of flight and the strain of the recent combat fell on him heavily and soaked his body like a numbing, damp fog. He thought about the sweet smell of soap in a cold shower and the crispness of clean sheets, and somehow they became vitally important to him. He looked out the cockpit window at Brady Field and recalled that his original destination was the *First Attempt*, but a dim hunch, or call it a hindsight, made him change his mind.

"Instead of landing in the water and rendezvousing alongside of the *First Attempt*, I think we'd better set down at Brady Field. I have a foreboding feeling we may have taken a few bullets in our hull."

"Good idea," Giordino replied. "I'm not in the mood for bailing."

The big flying boat made its final approach and lined up on the wreckage strewn runway. It settled on the heat baked asphalt, and the landing gear bumped and emitted an audible screech of rubber that signaled the touch-down.

Pitt angled clear of the flames and taxied to the far side of the apron. When the Catalina stopped rolling he clicked off the ignition switches, and the two silver bladed propellers gradually ceased their revolutions and came to rest, gleaming in the Aegean sun. All was quiet.

He and Giordino sat stone still for a few moments and absorbed the first comfortable silence to penetrate the cockpit after thirteen hours of noise and vibration.

Pitt flipped the latch on his side window and pushed it open, watching with detached interest as the base firemen fought the inferno. Hoses were lying everywhere, like highways on a roadmap, and men scurried about shouting, adding to the stage of confusion. The flames on the F-105 jets were almost contained, but one of the C-133 Cargomasters still burned fiercely.

"Take a look over here," said Giordino pointing.

Pitt leaned over the instrument panel and stared out of Giordino's window at a blue Air Force stationwagon that careened across the runway in the direction of the PBY. The car contained several officers and was followed by thirty or forty wildly cheering enlisted men who chased after it like a pack of braying hounds.

"Now that's what I call one hell of a reception committee," Pitt said amused and broadly smiling.

Giordino mopped his bleeding cut with a handkerchief. When the cloth was soaked through with red ooze he wadded it up and threw it out of the window to the ground. His gaze turned toward the nearby coastline and became lost in the infinity of thought for a moment. Finally he turned to Pitt. "I guess you know we're pretty damn lucky to be sitting here."

"Yes, I know," said Pitt woodenly. "There were a couple of times up there when I thought our ghost had us."

"I wish I knew who the hell he was and what this destruction was all about?"

Pitt's face was a study in speculative curiosity. "The only clue is the yellow Albatros."

Giordino eyed his friend questioningly. "What possible meaning could the color of that old flying derelict have?"

"If you'd studied your aviation history," Pitt said with a touch of goodnatured sarcasm, "You'd remember that German pilots of the First World War painted their planes with personal, but sometimes outlandish, color schemes."

"Save the history lesson for later," Giordino growled. "Right now all I want to do is get out of this sweat box and collect that drink you owe me." He rose from his seat and started for the exit hatch.

The blue stationwagon skidded to a halt beside the big silver flying boat and all four doors burst open. The occupants leaped out shouting and began pounding on the plane's aluminum hatch. The crowd of enlisted men soon engulfed the aircraft, cheering loudly and waving at the cockpit.

Pitt remained seated and waved back at the cheering men below the window. His body was tired and numb but his mind was still active and running at full throttle. A title kept running through his thoughts until finally he muttered it aloud. *"The Hawk of Macedonia."*

Giordino turned from the doorway. "What did you say?"

"Oh nothing, nothing at all," Pitt let his breath escape in a long audible sigh. "Come on—I'll buy you that drink now."

2

When Pitt awoke, it was still dark. He did not know how long he had slept. Perhaps he just dozed off. Perhaps he had been lost under the black cloak of sleep for hours. He did not know, nor did he care. The metal springs of the Air Force cot squeaked as he rolled over, seeking a more comfortable position. But the comfort of deep sleep eluded him. His conscious mind dimly tried to analyze why. Was it the steady humming noise of the air conditioner, he asked himself? He was used to drifting off under the loud din of aircraft engines, so that couldn't be it. Maybe it was the scurrying cockroaches. God knows Thasos was covered with them. No, it was something else. Then he knew. The answer pierced the fog of his drowsy brain. It was his other mind, the *unconscious* one that was keeping him awake. Like a movie projector, it flashed pictures of the strange events from the previous day, over and over again.

One picture stood out above all the rest. It was the photograph in a gallery of the Imperial War Museum. Pitt could recall it vividly. The camera had caught a German aviator posing beside a World War I fighter plane. He was garbed in the flying togs of the day, and his right hand rested upon the head of an immense white German Shepherd. The dog, obviously a mascot, was panting and looking up at his master with a patronizing, doe-like expression. The flyer stared back at the camera with a boyish face that somehow looked naked without the usual Prussian dueling scar and monocle. However, the proud Teutonic military bearing could be easily seen in the hint of an insolent grin and the ramrod straight posture.

Pitt even remembered the caption under the photo:

> *The Hawk of Macedonia*
> *Lieutenant Kurt Heibert, of Jagdstaffel 91,*
> *attained 32 victories over the allies on the*
> *Macedonian Front; one of the outstanding*
> *aces of the great war. Presumed shot down*
> *and lost in the Aegean Sea on July 15, 1918.*

For some time, Pitt lay staring in the darkness. There would be no more sleep tonight, he thought. Sitting up and leaning on one elbow, he reached over a bedside table, groped for his Omega watch and held it in front of his eyes. The luminous dial read 4:09. Then he sat up and dropped the bare soles of his feet on the vinyl tile floor. A package of cigarettes sat next to the watch, and he pulled out one and lit it with a silver Zippo lighter. Inhaling deeply, he stood up and stretched. His face grimaced; the muscles of his back stung from the back slapping he had received from the cheering men of Brady Field right after he and Giordino had climbed from the cockpit of the PBY. Pitt smiled to himself in the dark as he thought about the warm handshakes and congratulations pressed upon them.

The moonlight, beaming in through the window of the Officers' Quarters, and the warm clear air of early morning made Pitt restless. He stripped off his shorts and rummaged through his luggage in the dim light. When his touch recognized the cloth shape of a pair of swim trunks, he slipped them on, snatched a towel from the bathroom and stepped out into the stillness of the night.

Once outside, the brilliant Mediterranean moon enveloped his body and laid bare the landscape with an eerie ghost-like emptiness. The sky was all studded with stars and revealed the milky way in a great white design across a black velvet backdrop.

Pitt strolled down the path from the Officers' Quarters toward the main gate. He paused for a minute, looking at the vacant runway, and he noticed a black area every so often in the rows of multi-colored lights that stitched the edges. Several of the lights in the signal system must have been damaged in the attack, he thought. However, the general pattern was still readable to a pilot making a night landing. Behind the intermediate lights, he could make out a dark outline of the PBY, sitting forlornly on the opposite side of the apron like a nesting duck. The bullet damage to the Catalina's hull turned out to be slight and the Flight Line Maintenance crew promised that they would begin repairs first thing in the morning, the restoration taking three days. Colonel James Lewis, the base commanding officer, had expressed his apologies at the delay, but he needed the bulk of the maintenance crew to work on the damaged jets and the remaining C-133 Cargomaster. In the meantime, Pitt and Giordino elected to accept the Colonel's hospitality and stay at Brady Field, using the *First Attempt*'s whale boat to commute between the ship and shore. The last arrangement worked to everyone's advantage since living quarters aboard the *First Attempt* were cramped and at a premium.

"Kind of early for a swim, isn't it, buddy?"

The voice snapped Pitt from his thoughts, and he found himself standing under the white glare of floodlights that were perched on top of the guard's shack at the main gate. The shack sat on a curb-lined island that divided the incoming and outgoing traffic and was just large enough for one man to sit in. A short, burly looking Air Policeman stepped from the doorway and eyed him closely.

"I couldn't sleep." As soon as he said it, Pitt felt foolish for not being more original. But what the hell, he thought, it's the truth.

"Can't say as I blame you," said the AP. "After all that's happened today, I'd be real surprised if anyone on the base was sound asleep." The mere thought of sleep triggered a reflex, and the AP yawned.

"You must get awfully bored, sitting out here alone all night," said Pitt.

"Yeah, it gets pretty dull," the AP said, hooking one hand in his Sam Browne belt and resting the other on the grip of a .45 Colt automatic, clinging to his hip. "If you're going off base, you'd better let me see your pass."

"Sorry, I don't have one," Pitt had forgotten to ask Colonel Lewis for a pass to get on and off Brady Field.

A swaggering, tough look crossed the AP's face. "Then you'll have to go back to the barracks and get it." He swatted at a moth that flapped by his face, toward a floodlight.

"That would be a waste of time. I don't even own a pass," said Pitt, smiling helplessly.

"Don't play dumb with me, buddy. Nobody gets in or out of the gate without a pass."

"I did."

The AP's eyes became suspicious. "How did you manage that?"

"I flew in."

A surprised look hit the AP. His eyes beamed in the brightness of the floods. Another passing moth lit on his white cap, but he did not notice it. Then it burst from him. "You're the pilot of that Catalina flying boat!"

"Guilty as charged," said Pitt.

"Say, I want to shake your hand." The AP's lips opened in a big tooth displaying smile. "That was the greatest piece of flying I've ever seen." He thrust out a massive hand.

Pitt took the outstretched hand and winced. He had a strong grip of his own, but it seemed puny compared to the AP's. "Thank you, but I'd have felt a lot better about it if my opponent had crashed."

"Oh hell, he couldn't have gone far. That old junk pile was smoking up a storm when it crossed over the hills."

"Maybe it crashed on the other side?"

"No chance. The colonel had the whole Air Police squadron chasing all over the island in jeeps, looking for it. He searched until dark, but didn't spot a thing." He appeared disgusted. "What really pissed me off was getting back to the base too late for the chow line."

Pitt grinned. "It must have gone down in the sea, or else made the mainland before falling."

The AP shrugged his shoulders. "Could be. But one thing's for sure; it ain't on Thasos. You have my personal guarantee on that."

Pitt laughed. "That's good enough for me." He swung the towel over his shoulder and pulled at his swim trunks. "Well it's been nice talking to you . . ."

"Airman Second Class Moody, sir."

"I'm Major Pitt."

The AP's face went blank. "Oh, I'm sorry, sir. I didn't know you were an officer. I thought you were one of those civilians with NUMA. I'll let you out this time, Major, but I'd appreciate it if you got a base pass."

"I'll see to it first thing after breakfast."

"My replacement comes on at 0800. If you're not back by then, I'll leave word so he'll let you in without any trouble."

"Thank you, Moody. Perhaps I'll see you later." Pitt waved and then turned and walked down the road towards the beach.

Pitt kept to the right side of the narrow paved road and in about a mile came to a small cove that was flanked by large craggy rocks. The moonlight showed him a path, and he took it until his feet crunched softly in the sandy beach. He dropped the towel and walked to the tide line. A wave broke, and the white of its crest slid smoothly across the packed sand and licked his feet. The dying wave hesitated for a moment and then fell back, forming the trough for the next crest. There was barely a breath of wind, and the glistening sea was relatively calm. The moon cast its glow on the dark water and left a shaft of silver that traveled over the surface to the horizon where the sea and sky melted together into absolute blackness. Pitt soaked up the warm stillness and moved into the water, swimming along the silver shaft.

An inner feeling always overcame Pitt when he was alone and near the sea. It was as though his soul seeped out of his body, and he became a thing without substance, without form. His mind was purified and cleansed: all mental labor ceased and all thoughts vanished. He was only vaguely aware of hot and cold, smells, touch, and all the other senses, except hearing. He listened to the nothingness of silence; the greatest, but most unknown, treasure of man. Forgotten for the moment were all his failures, all his victories and all his loves, even life itself was buried and lost in the stillness.

He lay dead and floated in the water for nearly an hour. Finally, a small swell slapped at his face and he unwittingly inhaled a few drops of salt water. He snorted, dispelling the discomfort and again became aware of his bodily sensations. Without watching his progress, he effortlessly backstroked toward the shore. When his hands arched and touched the dense sand, he stopped swimming and drifted onto the beach like a piece of flotsam. Then he dragged himself forward until he was only half-out of the water, letting it swirl around his legs and buttocks. The warm Aegean surf rose out of the dim light and flooded up the beach, caressing his skin, and he dozed off.

The stars were beginning to blink out one by one with the pale light of the approaching dawn when an inner alarm sounded in Pitt's brain, and he suddenly became alert to a presence. Instantly he was awake, but he made no movement, other than peering through half-open eyes. He barely could make out a shadowy form standing over him. Focusing and straining his eyes in the faint light, he tried to distinguish a detailed shape. Slowly, an outline materialized. It was a woman.

"Good morning," he said and sat up.

"Oh my God," the woman gasped. She threw a hand to her mouth as if to scream.

It was still too dark to see the wild look in her eyes, but Pitt knew it was there. "I'm sorry," he said gently. "I didn't mean to startle you."

The hand slowly dropped. She just stood there looking down at him. Finally she found her voice. "I . . . I thought you were dead." She stammered the words softly.

"I can hardly blame you. I suppose if I stumbled on someone sleeping in the tide at this time of morning, I would think the same thing."

"You gave me quite a frightful shock, you know, sitting up and talking like that."

"Again, my sincere apologies." It suddenly occurred to Pitt that the woman was speaking English. Her accent was decidedly British, but it had a trace of German. He rose to his feet. "Please allow me to introduce myself; my name is Dirk Pitt."

"I'm Teri," she said, "and I can't tell you how happy I am to see you alive and healthy, Mister Pitt." She didn't offer her last name, and Pitt didn't press for it.

"Believe me, Teri, the pleasure is all mine." He pointed to the sand. "Won't you join me and help raise the sun?"

She laughed. "Thank you, I'd like that. But then again, I can hardly see you. For all I know you might be a monster or something." There was a note of whimsy in her tone. "Can I trust you?"

"To be perfectly honest, no. I think it only fair to warn you that I've assaulted over two hundred innocent virgins right here on this very spot." Pitt's humor was overly forward, but he knew it was a good system for testing a female's personality.

"Oh blimey, I would dearly loved to have been number two hundred and one, but I'm not an innocent virgin." There was enough light now for Pitt to see the white of her teeth arched in a smile. "I certainly hope you won't hold that against me."

"No, I'm very broadminded about that sort of thing. But I must ask you to keep secret the fact that two hundred and one wasn't pure as the driven snow. If it ever leaked out, my reputation as a monster would be ruined."

They both laughed and sat down together on Pitt's towel and talked while the hot sun reluctantly began its climb over the Aegean Sea. As the blazing orange ball threw its first golden rays over the shimmering horizon, Pitt gazed at the woman in the new light and studied her closely.

She was about thirty and wore a red bikini swim suit. The bikini was not the exaggerated brief kind, even though the lower half began a good two inches below the navel. The material had a satin sheen to it and clung tautly to her body like an outer layer of skin. Her figure was a beguiling mixture of grace and firmness; the stomach looked smooth and flat and the breasts were perfect, not too small but not too large and out of scale. Her legs were long, creamy colored and slightly on the thin side. Pitt decided to overlook this faint imperfection and swung his eyes to her face. The profile was exquisite. Her features possessed the beauty and mystery of a Grecian statue and would have rated near perfection except for a round pockmark beside her right temple. Ordinarily the scar would have been covered by her shoulder length black hair, but she had thrown her head back as she watched the sunrise and the ebony strands angled back behind her shoulders, touching the sand and revealing the thin blemish.

Suddenly she turned and caught Pitt's examining stare.

"You're supposed to be watching the sunrise," she said with a bemused smile.

"I've seen sunrises before, but this is the first time I've ever come face to face with a lovely, genuine Grecian Aphrodite." Pitt could see her dark brown eyes flashing with enjoyment at his compliment.

"Thank you for the flattery, but Aphrodite was the Greek goddess of love and beauty, and I'm only half Greek."

"What's the other half?"

"My father was German."

"In that case I must thank the gods that you look after your mother's side."

She gave a pouting glance. "You'd better not let my uncle hear you say that."

"A typical kraut?"

"Yes, indeed. In fact he's why I happen to be on Thasos."

"Then he can't be all bad," Pitt said, admiring her hazel eyes. "Do you live with him?"

"No, actually I was born here, but I was raised in England. I suffered through school there, and when I was eighteen I fell in love with a dashing motorcar salesman and married him."

"I didn't know car salesmen could be dashing."

She ignored his sarcastic remark and continued. "He loved to race cars on his time off, and he was good at it too. He won trials and hill climbs and sporting car events." She shrugged and began drawing circles in the sand with her finger. Her voice became strange and husky. "Then one weekend he was racing a supercharged MG. It was raining, and he skidded off the course and hit a tree. He was dead before I could reach his side."

Pitt sat silent for a minute, staring at her sad face. "How long ago?" he asked simply.

"It's been eight and a half years now," she replied in a whisper.

Pitt felt dazed. Then anger set in. What a waste, he thought. What a rotten waste for a beautiful woman like her to grieve over a dead man for nearly nine years. The more he thought about it the angrier he became. He could see tears welling in her eyes as she lost herself in the remembrance, and the sight sickened him. He reached over and gave her a hard backhand slap across the face.

Her eyes jerked wide, and her whole body tensed from the sharp blow. It was as if she was struck by a bullet. "Why did you strike me?" she gasped.

"Because you needed it, needed it badly," he snapped. "That torch you carry around is as worn out as an overcoat. I'm surprised someone hasn't taken you over a knee and spanked it off. So your husband was dashing. So what? He's dead and buried, and mourning over him for all these years won't resurrect him from the grave. Lock away his memory somewhere and forget him. You're a beautiful woman—you don't belong chained to a coffin full of bones. You belong to every man who turns and admires you as you pass by and who longs to possess you." Pitt could see his words were penetrating her weak defenses. "Now you think about it. It's your life. Don't throw it away and play 'Camille' until you're withered and gray."

Her face was distraught in the morning sun, and her breath came in sobs. Pitt let her cry for a long time. When she finally raised her head and turned it towards him, he could see that her cheeks were streaked with tears, mixed with tiny grains of sand, clinging to the wetness. She looked up at him, and he caught the gleam in her eyes. They were soft and scared-looking, like a little girl's. He lifted her in his arms and kissed her. Her lips were warm and moist.

"When was the last time you had a man?" he whispered.

"Not since . . ." Her voice trailed away.

Pitt took her as the long shadows of the rocks crept upward over the beach, shielding their bodies from the sun. A flight of sandpipers circled overhead and descended upon the damp sand at the water's edge. They scurried back and forth, playing tag with the surf. Every so often one of the birds would cast a beady eye at the two lovers in the shade, staring for a fleeting instant before returning to the chore of stabbing its long, curved beak in the sand for food. The shadows shortened as the sun rose higher in the sky. A fishing boat chugged by a hundred yards from the end of the rocks. The fishermen, dropping their nets in the water, were too busy to notice anything unusual on the shore. At last Pitt drew back and gazed down at Teri's serene and smiling face.

"I don't know whether to ask for your thanks or your forgiveness," he said softly.

"Please accept them both along with my blessing," she murmured.

He kissed her lightly on the eyes. "See what you've been missing all these years," he said grinning.

"I agree. You've certainly shown me a wonderful antidote for my depression."

"I always prescribe seduction. It's guaranteed to cure any and all rare maladies and common ailments."

"And what is your fee, doctor?" she said, accompanied with a feminine giggle.

"Consider it paid in full."

"You're not going to get off that easily. I must insist you come to my uncle's house for dinner tonight."

"I shall consider it an honor," he said. "What time and how do I get there?"

"I'll have my uncle's driver pick you up at the entrance to Brady Field at 6 o'clock."

Pitt's eyebrows raised. "What makes you think I'm stationed at Brady Field?"

"You're obviously an American and that's where all the Americans on the island are." Teri grasped his hand and pressed it to her face. "Tell me about yourself. What type of job do you perform in your Air Force? Do you fly? Are you an officer?"

Pitt did his best to look serious. "I'm the base garbage collector."

Her eyes opened wide in surprise. "Are you really? You're much too intelligent to be a garbage collector." She looked into his strong tan face and his intense green eyes. "Oh well, I won't hold your occupation against you. Have you been promoted to sergeant yet?"

"No. I've never been a sergeant."

Suddenly a bright flash in the rocks about two hundred feet away caught Pitt's attention. A shiny object reflected the sun's rays for a brief instant. He watched the area where the glint had shown but could detect no further flash or movement.

Teri felt him tense. "Is something the matter?" she asked.

"No, nothing," Pitt lied. "I thought I saw something floating in the water, but it's disappeared now. He looked at her upraised face, and his eyes turned devilish. "Well I'd better be getting back to the base, I've got a lot of garbage to collect."

"I should return also. My uncle will probably wonder what happened to me."

"Are you going to tell him?"

"Don't be silly," she laughed. She stood up and brushed the sand from her body and adjusted the bikini.

Pitt smiled, getting to his feet. "Why is it women always seem so shy and demure before they've been laid yet so sparkling and carefree after?"

She shrugged lightheartedly. "I guess it's because sex releases all our frustrations and makes us feel earthy." Her brown eyes flashed with intensity. "You see, we women have animal instincts too."

Pitt playfully slapped her on the buttocks. "Come on, I'll walk you home."

"You've got a long walk. My uncle's villa is in the mountains behind Liminas."

"Where are the mountains and where is Liminas?"

"Liminas is a small village about six miles up the road," she said pointing north. "But I don't understand what you mean by asking about the mountains?" Her pointing hand swung toward the inland slopes a mile behind the road. "What do you call those?"

"In California, where I come from, we call anything under three thousand feet of elevation *hills*."

"You Yanks are always bragging."

"It's a great American pastime."

They leisurely walked up the path from the cove. On the shoulder, off to one side of the blacktop, sat a sporty little open-top Mini-Cooper. The British racing green paint on the tiny car was barely visible beneath an outer coating of Thasos dust.

"How do you like my smashing Grand Prix racing car?" Teri asked proudly.

Pitt laughed; not so much at her exaggerated statement but rather the British use of the word *smashing* in reference to a car. "By jove, that's a bit of all right," he said, mimicking her native terminology. "Is it yours?"

"Yes, I purchased it new in London just last month and drove it all the way from Le Havre."

"How long will you be staying with your uncle?"

"I took a three month holiday so I'll be here at least another six weeks. Then I'm going to return home by boat. The drive across the continent was fun but far too tiring."

Pitt opened the door for her, and she slid behind the steering wheel. She groped under the front seat for a moment and pulled out a set of keys. She inserted one in the ignition and started the engine. The exhaust coughed once and then blasted forth with a nasty little growl.

He leaned on the dusty door and lightly kissed her. "I hope your uncle won't be waiting for me with a shotgun."

"Don't worry, he'll probably talk your arm off. He likes Air Force men. He was a flyer in the First World War."

"Don't tell me," Pitt said sarcastically. "I bet he claims to have flown with Richthofen."

"Oh no, he was never in France. He fought right here in Greece."

Pitt's sarcasm vanished and a cold, eerie feeling came over him. He gripped the doorframe until his knuckles turned white. "Has your uncle ever mentioned . . . Kurt Heibert?"

"Many times. They used to fly patrols together." She shoved the gearshift into first. Then she smiled and waved. "See you tonight. Now don't be late, cheery bye."

Before Pitt could say another word, the midget car leapt up the road. He watched it snarl off into the distance toward the north. The dusty green blur passed over a crest of pavement and the last thing he saw was Teri's black hair whipping in the wind.

Already it was beginning to get uncomfortably hot. Idly, he turned and began walking back to the airfield. He stepped on a sharp object with his bare foot and cursed under his breath while he hopped about on one leg trying to remove a small burr. Jerking it from his heel angrily, he flipped it in a roadside bush. He was carefully watching the ground to avoid another sting when he noticed a set of footprints. Whoever made them had been wearing hobnailed soles.

Pitt knelt and studied the indentations. He could easily distinguish his and Teri's prints since they had both been barefoot. His mouth twisted grimly. In several places, the shoe prints covered the bare ones. Someone had followed Teri toward the beach, he reasoned. He raised one hand, and shielded his eyes, looking at the sun. It was still quite early so he decided to pursue the trail.

The tracks led half-way down the path and then veered off in the direction of the rocks. Here the trail ended so he scrambled over the hard craggy surface and picked up the scent again on the other side. The tracks angled back to the road, only further away from the path this time. A branch scraped a thorny limb across Pitt's arm, drawing thin lines of blood, but he was not aware of it. He was beginning to sweat when he stepped back on the road. At last the hobnailed prints ended and heavy tire tracks began. The tire's tread left a peculiar set of diamond-shaped patterns in the dirt beside the pavement.

There was no traffic visible in either direction so Pitt calmly laid the towel down in the center of the road, sat on it and began to re-enact the scene in his mind.

Whoever shadowed Teri had parked here, walked back to her car and then followed her down the path. But before reaching the beach, the stalker must have heard voices so he turned and made his way in the darkness to the rocks where he hid, spying on the girl and Pitt. After it became light from the dawn, the intruder returned to the road, using the rocks to conceal his movements.

It was an elementary puzzle, and it fit neatly together, except for the fact that three pieces were missing. Why had Teri been followed and by whom? A thought occurred to Pitt and he smiled to himself. The simple answer was very likely a local peeping tom. If that were the case the observer got more than he bargained for.

A knot formed in Pitt's stomach. It was the third missing piece that bothered him the most. Something in his logical mind would not jell. He looked over at the tire tracks again. They were too large for an ordinary car. They could only come from a more massive vehicle, say a truck. His eyes narrowed, and his brain began to churn. He wouldn't have heard Teri drive up because he was asleep. And the truck had probably coasted to a stop, noiselessly.

Pitt's intent gaze turned from the diamond tread tire tracks to the beach. The tide was creeping over the sand and erasing all signs of recent human activity. He gauged the distance from the road to the beach and began to term the problem in the manner of a fifth grade school teacher.

If a truck is at point A, and two people are on the beach 250 feet away at point B, why wouldn't the two people on the beach hear the truck start its engine in the silence of early morning?

The answer eluded him, so Pitt shrugged and gave up. He shook out the towel and wrapping it around his neck, walked back along the deserted road toward the main gate, whistling, "It's a Long Road to Tipperary."

3

The young blond crewman cast off the lines, and the little twenty-six foot double-ended whaleboat surged sluggishly away from the makeshift dock near Brady Field, setting a course over the blue carpet of water toward the *First Attempt*. The throbbing four-cylinder Buda engine pushed the sturdy boat along at eight knots and cast the familiar nautical stink of diesel fumes over the deck. It was a few minutes to nine now, and the sun was hotter and even a slight breeze from the sea offered no relief.

Pitt stood and watched the shore recede until the dock became a dirty speck on the surf line. Then he hoisted his one hundred and ninety pounds onto the high tubular railing that circled the stern and sat with his buttocks hanging precariously over the boat's frothing white wake. From his unusual position he could feel the pulsations from the shaft, and by looking straight down, he could see the propeller drill its way through the water. The whaleboat was only a quarter of a mile from the *First Attempt* when Pitt noticed the young crewman at the helm eyeing him with a mild look of respect.

"Excuse me, sir, but you look like you've spent some time in a double-ender." The blond crewman nodded at Pitt's seat on the railing. The young man had an academic air about him that implied scientific intelligence. Well tanned from the Aegean sun, he wore Bermuda shorts and nothing else except a long, sparse, yellow beard.

Pitt wrapped a hand around the stern light staff for support and groped in a breast pocket with his other hand for a cigarette. "I used to have one when I was in high school," he said casually.

"You must have lived near the water," said the young crewman.

"Newport Beach, California."

"That's a great place. I used to drive up there all the time when I was taking post graduate courses at Scripps in LaJolla." The young crewman cracked a crooked smile, "Man oh man, was that ever a great place for girls. You must have had a ball growing up there."

"I could think of worse places to go through puberty." As long as the young man was talking freely, Pitt switched the subject. "Tell me, what sort of trouble have you been having on the project?"

"Everything went fine for the first couple of weeks, but as soon as we found a promising location to investigate, things turned sour and we've had nothing but rotten luck since."

"For instance?"

"Mostly equipment failure; broken cables, missing and damaged parts, generator break-downs, you know, things like that."

They were nearing the *First Attempt* now and the young crewman turned back to the helm and maneuvered the small boat along side of the boarding ladder.

Pitt stood and looked up at the larger vessel, surveying its outward appearance. By maritime standards she was a small ship; eight hundred twenty tons, one hundred fifty-two feet in length overall. Her keel was originally laid on an ocean-going tug in the Dutch shipyards of Rotterdam before World War II. Immediately after the Germans invaded the lowlands, her crew slipped her away to England where she performed outstanding and meritorious service throughout the war, towing torpedoed and crippled ships into the British port of Liverpool under the noses of Nazi U-boats. After the end of European hostilities, her tired and battered hull was traded by the Dutch Government to the U.S. Navy, who promptly enlisted her in the mothball fleet at Olympia, Washington. There she sat for twenty-five long years, sleeping under a gray plastic cocoon. Then the newly formed National Underwater Marine Agency purchased her remains from the Navy and converted her to a modern oceanographic vessel, rechristening her the *First Attempt*.

Pitt squinted from the bright glare of the white paint, coating the ship from stem to stern staff. He climbed the boarding ladder and was greeted on the deck by an old friend, Commander Rudi Gunn, the skipper and project director of the ship.

"You look healthy," said Gunn unsmilingly, "except for your blood-shot eyes." He reached for a cigarette. Before he lit it, he offered one to Pitt, who shook his head and held up one in his hand.

"I hear you've got problems," said Pitt.

Gunn's face turned grim. "You're damn right I do," he snapped. "I didn't ask Admiral Sandecker to send you all the way from Washington just for fun and games."

Pitt's eyebrows went up in surprise. This sudden harshness did not fit Gunn. Under normal circumstances the little commander was a warm and humorous person. "Take it easy, Rudi," said Pitt softly. "Let's get out of the sun, and you can brief me on what this mess is all about."

Gunn removed his horned rimmed glasses and rubbed a wrinkled handkerchief across his forehead. "I'm sorry, Dirk, it's just that I've never seen so many things go wrong at one time. It's highly frustrating after all the planning that went into this project. I guess it's beginning to make me irritable as hell. Even the crew has noticeably avoided me the last three days."

Pitt placed an arm on the shorter man's shoulders and grinned. "I promise not to avoid you even if you are a nasty little bastard."

Gunn looked blank for a moment, and then a

sense of relief seemed to flood his eyes, and he flung back his head and laughed. "Thank God you're here," he gripped Pitt's arm tightly. "You may not solve any mysteries, but at least I'll feel a hell of a lot better just having you around." He turned and pointed toward the bow. "Come along, my cabin is up forward."

Pitt followed Gunn up a steep ladder to the next deck and into a small cabin that must have been designed by a closet-maker. The only comfort, and it was a large one, was a cool blast of air that emitted from an overhead ventilator.

He stood in front of the opening for a moment and soaked in the cool breeze. Then he straddled a chair and leaned his arms across the top of the backrest, waiting for Gunn to give the briefing.

Gunn closed the porthole and remained standing. "Before I begin, let me ask you what you know about our Aegean expedition?"

"I only heard that the *First Attempt* was researching the Mediterranean for zoological purposes."

Gunn stared at him, shocked. "Didn't the admiral supply you with any detailed data concerning this project before you left Washington?"

Pitt lit another cigarette. "What makes you think that I came straight from the Capital?"

"I don't know," Gunn said hesitantly. "I only assumed that you . . ."

Pitt stopped him with a grin. "I haven't been anywhere near the States in over four months." He exhaled a puff of smoke toward the ventilator and watched the blue haze swirl into nothingness. "Sandecker's message to you simply stated that he was sending me directly to Thasos. He obviously neglected to mention where I was coming from and when I would arrive. Therefore, you expected me to come soaring out of the blue sky four days ago."

"Again, I'm sorry," Gunn said shrugging. "You're right, of course. I figured two days at the most for that old tin duck of yours to fly from the Capital. When you finally flew into that fiasco at Brady Field yesterday you were already four days late by my schedule."

"It couldn't be helped. Giordino and I were ordered to airlift supplies into an ice probe station, camped on an ice floe north of Spitzbergen. Right after we landed, a blizzard hit and grounded us for over seventy-two hours."

Gunn laughed. "You certainly flew from one extreme in temperature to another."

Pitt didn't answer, but merely smiled.

Gunn pulled open the top drawer of a small compact desk and handed Pitt a large manilla envelope that contained several drawings of a strange looking fish. "You ever see anything like this before?"

Pitt looked down at the drawings. Most of them were different artist's conceptions of the same fish, and yet each varied in details. The first was an ancient Greek illustration on the side of a vase. Another had obviously been part of a Roman fresco. He noted that two of them were more modern, stylized drawings, depicting the fish in a series of movements. The last was a photograph of a fossil imbedded in sandstone. Pitt looked up at Gunn questioningly.

Gunn handed him a magnifying glass. "Here, take a closer look through this."

Pitt adjusted the height of the thick glass and scrutinized each picture. At first glance the fish looked similar in size and shape to the Bluefin Tuna, but on closer inspection, the bottom pelvic fins took on the appearance of small jointed webbed feet. There were two more identical limbs located just in front of the dorsal fin.

He whistled softly. "This is a weird specimen, Rudi. What do you call it?"

"I can't pronounce the Latin name, but the scientists aboard the *First Attempt* have affectionately nicknamed it the *Teaser*."

"Why is that?"

"Because, by every law of nature that fish should have become extinct over two hundred million years ago. But as you can see by the drawings, men still claim they have seen it. Every fifty or sixty years there's a rash of sightings, but unfortunately for science, a *Teaser* has yet to be caught." Gunn glanced at Pitt and looked away again. "If there is such a fish, it must bear a charmed life. There are literally hundreds of accounts of fishermen and scientists who look you in the eye with a straight face and say they had a *Teaser* on a hook or in a net, but before the fish could be hauled on board it escaped. Every zoologist in the world would give his left testicle to obtain a live, or even dead *Teaser*."

Pitt mashed out his cigarette in an ashtray. "What makes this particular fish so important?"

Gunn held up the drawings. "Notice that the artists couldn't agree on the outer layer of skin. They illustrate tiny scales, smooth porpoise-like skin, and one even brushed in a kind of furry hide like a sea lion. Now, if you take the possibility of hairy skin, together with the limb extensions, it may be we have the dim beginnings of the first mammal."

"True, but if the skin were smooth you'd have nothing more than an early reptile. The earth was covered with them back in those days."

Gunn's eyes mirrored a confident look. "The next point to consider is that the *Teasers* lived in warm shallow water, and every recorded sighting took place no more than three miles from shore, and they all occurred right here in the eastern Mediterranean where the average surface temperature seldom drops below sixty-two degrees Fahrenheit."

"So what does that prove?" asked Pitt.

"Nothing solid, but since primitive mammal life survives better in milder climates, it lends a little support to the possibility that they might have survived to the present."

Pitt stared at Gunn thoughtfully. "I'm sorry, Rudi. You still haven't sold me."

"I knew you were a hard head," said Gunn. "That's why I left the most interesting part till last." He paused and removed his glasses and rubbed the lenses with a piece of Kleenex. Then he replaced the black rims over his hawkish nose. He continued speaking as if lost in a dream. "During the Triassic Period in geological time, and before the Himalayas and the Alps rose, a great sea swept over what is now Tibet and India. It also extended over Central Europe and ended in the North Sea. Geologists call this once great body of water, the Sea of Tethys. All that remains of it today is the Black, the Caspian and the Mediterranean Seas."

"You'll have to pardon my ignorance of geological time eras," Pitt interrupted, "but when did the Triassic Period take place?"

"Between one hundred eighty and two hundred thirty million years ago," replied Gunn. "During this time an important evolutionary advance occurred in the vertebrate animals as the reptiles demonstrated a great leap over their more primitive ancestors. Some of the marine reptiles attained a length of twenty-three feet and were very tough customers. The most noteworthy event was the introduction of the first true dinosaurs, who even learned to walk on their hind legs and use their tails for a kind of cane."

Pitt leaned back and stretched his legs. "I thought that the era of the dinosaurs occurred much later."

Gunn laughed. "You've seen too many old movies. You're undoubtedly thinking of the behemoths that were always portrayed in the early science fiction films, menacing a tribe of hairy cavemen. They never failed to have a forty ton Brontosaurus or a ferocious Tyrannosaurus or a flying Pteranodon chasing a half-nude, bigtitted heroine through a primeval jungle. Actually these more commonly known dinosaurs roamed the earth and became extinct sixty million years before man appeared."

"Where does your freak fish fit into the picture?"

"Imagine, if you will, a three foot *Teaser* fish who lived, cavorted, made love and finally died somewhere in the Sea of Tethys. Nothing and no one took notice as this obscure creature's body slowly sank to the red mud of the seabed. The unmarked grave was covered over with sediments which hardened into sandstone and left a thin film of carbon. It was this trace of carbon that etched and outlined the *Teaser*'s tissue and bone structure into the surrounding strata." The years passed and turned into millenniums. And the millenniums became eons, until one warm spring day, two hundred million years later, a farmer in the Austrian town of Neunkirchen struck his plow against a hard surface. And presto, our *Teaser* fish, though now a near perfect fossilized version, once again returned to the light." Gunn hesitated and ran his hand through a head of thinning hair. His face looked drawn and tired, but his eyes burned with excitement as he spoke of the *Teaser*. "One vital element you must remember; when the *Teaser* died there were no birds and bees, no hair bearing mammals, no delicate butterflies, even flowers had not yet appeared on the earth."

Pitt studied the photograph of the fossil again. "It doesn't seem possible that any living thing could survive this long without going through drastic evolutionary changes."

"Incredible? Yes; but it has happened before. The shark has been with us for three hundred and fifty million years. The Horseshoe Crab has existed virtually unchanged over two hundred million years. Then, of course, we have the classic example; the Coelacanth."

"Yes, I heard of it," said Pitt. "That was the fish believed extinct for seventy million years until they began to be found off the coast of east Africa."

Gunn nodded. "The Coelacanth was a sensational and important find at the time, but nothing compared to what the scientific world would gain if we could drop a *Teaser* in its lap." Gunn paused for a moment to light another cigarette. His eyes betrayed the gleam of total absorption. "The whole thing boils down to this; the *Teaser* could be an early link in the evolution of mammals, and that includes *man*. What I didn't tell you was that the fossil found in Austria shows definite mammal characteristics in its anatomy. The protruding limbs and other features of its internal organs, place it in a perfect evolutionary line to advance in a general pattern toward the development of humans and animals."

Pitt idly glanced at the pictures again. "If this so called *living fossil* is still floating around in its original form, how could it evolve into an advanced stage?"

"Any plant or animal species is like a related family," Gunn replied. "One branch may produce offspring who are uniform in size and shape, while the cousins over on the other side of the mountain produce a race of giants with two heads and four arms."

Pitt was getting restless. He opened the door and walked out onto the deck. The hot air struck him like a cloud of steam and he winced. All this expense and all these men sweating their asses off to catch a stinking fish, he thought. Who the hell cares if our ancestors were apes or fish—what difference did it make? At the rate mankind was racing toward self-destruction, it would probably be extinct in another thousand years or less anyway. He turned back to the darkened doorway and faced Gunn.

"Ok," Pitt said slowly. "I know what you and your boatload of academic brains are searching for. Now the only question in my mind is where do I come in? If you're having trouble with broken cables, faulty generators or missing tools, you don't need me, you need a good mechanic who knows how to take care of his equipment."

Gunn's face looked puzzled for a moment, then he grinned. "I see that you've been pumping information out of Dr. Knight."

"Dr. Knight?"

"Yes, Ken Knight, the young fellow who picked you up in the whaleboat this morning. He's quite a brilliant marine geophysicist."

"That's an impressive description," said Pitt. "He seemed friendly enough during the boat ride, but he hardly struck me as brilliant."

The heat outside was becoming unbearable and the metal railing gleamed ominously. Pitt, not thinking, put his hand on the metal and instantly cursed as a burning sting etched his palm. Suddenly the pain set off an immense feeling of irritation within him and he returned to the cabin, slamming the door.

"Let's skip all this crap," Pitt snapped sharply. "Just tell me what miracle I'm supposed to perform that puts a *Teaser* over your fireplace and I'll get to work." He stretched out in Gunn's bunk and took a deep breath and relaxed as the coolness of the state-room calmed him once more. He glanced across the room at Gunn. Gunn's face was expressionless, but Pitt knew him well enough to perceive his discomfort. Pitt smiled and reached over and gripped Gunn on the shoulder. "I don't wish to appear mercenary, but if you want me to join your little crew of scientific pirates it's going to cost you a drink. All this talk makes a man pretty damn thirsty."

Gunn laughed with relief and called over his inter-com for some ice from the ship's galley. Then he pro-duced a bottle of Chivas Regal and two glasses from his bottom desk drawer. "While we're waiting for the ice, you might scan this report I wrote concerning our equipment malfunctions." He passed a yellow folder to Pitt. "I've covered every incident in detail and chronol-ogical order. In the beginning I thought it was merely accidents or bad luck, but now it's gone far beyond the realm of mere coincidence."

"Have you any proof of tampering or sabotage?" asked Pitt.

"None whatsoever."

"The broken cable that Knight mentioned, was it cut?"

Gunn shrugged. "No, the ends were frayed, but that's another mystery. I'll explain it to you." Gunn paused and flicked an ash from his cigarette. "We work with a safety margin of five-to-one. For example; if the specifications of a cable state there is a danger of break-age with a stress of twenty-five thousand pounds or above, we will never place a stress on it higher than five thousand pounds. Because of this large safety factor NUMA has yet to have a single fatality on a project. Lives are more important to us than scientific discov-ery. Underwater exploration is a risky business and the list is long with the names of men before us who have died trying to pry new secrets from the seas."

"What was the safety margin when your cable parted?"

"I was getting to that. It was nearly six-to-one. We only had a four thousand pound stress on it at the time.

It was extremely fortunate that no one was injured from the whiplash of the cable when it snapped."

"May I see the cable?"

"Yes, I've had the parted ends cut from the main sections and saved for your arrival."

A loud knock echoed from the door and a young red-haired boy, no more than eighteen or nineteen, entered the cabin, carrying a small bucket of ice. He sat it on the desk and turned and faced Gunn. "Can I get you anything else, sir?"

"Yes, as a matter of fact, you can," said Gunn. "Run down to the maintenance deck and find the cable sections that broke recently and bring them back here to me."

"Yes sir." The boy did an abrupt about-face and hurried from the cabin.

"One of the crew members?" asked Pitt.

Gunn dropped the ice in the glasses and poured in the scotch. He passed a glass to Pitt. "Yes, we have eight crew members and fourteen scientists on board."

Pitt swirled the yellow liquid around the ice cubes. "Could any one of those twenty-two men be responsible for your problems?"

Gunn shook his head. "I've thought about that, I've even dreamed about it, and I've analyzed each man's personnel record at least fifty times, and I can't see what possible motive any of them might have for hindering the project." Gunn paused to sip his drink. "No, I'm certain my opposition comes from another source. Someone unexplicably wants to stop us from catching a fish that might not even exist."

The boy soon returned with the two halves of the broken cable. He handed the braided steel to Gunn and left the cabin, closing the door after him.

Pitt took another drink from his scotch and climbed from the bunk. He set the glass on Gunn's desk and lifted the cable in his hands, examining the ends closely.

It looked like any other greasy steel cable. Each piece was about two feet in length and contained twenty-four hundred strands that were braided into a standard five-eighth-inch diameter. The cable was not broken in a compact area. The breaks were spread over a fifteen inch distance that gave both frayed wires the appearance of a pair of uneven, unwound horse tails.

Something caught Pitt's eye, and he took the magnifying glass and peered through the heavy lens. His eyes glinted with intensity and his lips slowly spread into a grin of smug satisfaction. The old feelings of excitement and intrigue began to course through his veins. This might turn out to be an interesting operation after all, he thought.

"See anything?" asked Gunn.

"Yes, a great deal," replied Pitt. "Somewhere along the line you've found yourself an enemy who doesn't want you fishing around in his territory."

Gunn became flushed and his eyes opened wide. "What did you find?"

"This cable was purposely cut," said Pitt. His voice was very cold.

"What do you mean: cut," cried Gunn. "Where do you see evidence of human tampering?"

Pitt held up the magnifying glass for Gunn. "Notice how the breaks spiral down and bend inward toward the core? And see how the strands have a smashed appearance. If a cable of this diameter is pulled at each end until it snaps, the strands are clean and the ends have a tendency to point out and away from the core. That didn't happen here."

Gunn stared at the shattered cable. "I don't understand. What could have caused this?"

Pitt looked thoughtful for a moment. "My guess is *Primacord*."

Gunn was stunned. His eyes flew wide behind the big glasses. "You can't be serious? Isn't that an explosive?"

"Yes it is," Pitt said calmly. "*Primacord* looks like string or rope and can be made in any thickness. Mainly, it's used for blasting down trees and setting off different groups of distantly spaced explosives at he same time. It reacts like a burning fuse except that it moves and bursts rapidly, almost with the speed of light."

"But how could anyone plant explosives under the ship without being seen. The water is crystal clear in this area. Visibility is over one hundred feet. One of the scientists or crew members would have seen any intruder . . . Not to mention hearing the sound of an explosion."

"Before I attempt to answer that, let me ask you two questions. What equipment was attached to the cable when it parted? And at what time did you discover the break?"

"The cable was connected to the underwater decompression chamber. The divers have been working at one hundred and eighty feet and it has become necessary to begin decompression underwater for long periods of time to prevent the *bends*. We discovered the broken cable at about 0700 in the morning right after breakfast."

"I take it that you left the chamber in the water overnight?"

"No," replied Gunn. "It's our habit to lower the chamber before dawn so it'll be in place and ready to receive the divers in case of an early morning emergency."

"There's your answer!" Pitt exclaimed. "Someone swam under cover of the pre-dawn darkness to the cable and set off the *Primacord*. Visibility may be one hundred feet after the sun comes up but at night it's less than one foot."

"And the noise from the blast?"

"Elementary my dear Gunn," Pitt grinned. "I should guess that a small amount of *Primacord* detonating at approximately eighty feet of depth would sound very similar to a sonic boom from one of Brady Field's F-105 Starfires."

Gunn looked at Pitt with respect. It was basically a sound theory, and obviously there was little he could think of to debate about. His forehead creased, "Where do we go from here?"

Pitt downed the scotch and banged the glass onto Gunn's desk. "You just stay in the briny and fish for your *Teaser*. I'm going back to the island and try my hand at a little hunting. There may be a tie-in with your disruptions and the attack on Brady yesterday, and the next step will be to find who's behind this mess and what their motives are."

Suddenly the door burst open and a man leaped into the cabin. He wore only a pair of abbreviated swim trunks and a wide belt, containing a knife and a nylon net bag. His wet, sun-bleached hair was streaked with whitish yellow and freckles dotted his nose and chest. As he stood there, the water dripped to the carpet around his feet in spreading dark stains. "Commander Gunn," he shouted excitedly. "I've seen one! I've actually seen a *Teaser*, not more than ten feet in front of my mask."

Gunn jumped to his feet. "Are you sure? Did you get a close look at him?"

"Better than that, sir, I took a picture of him."

The freckle-nosed man stood there, grinning with every available tooth. "If only I had a speargun, I might have got him, but I was shooting coral formations with my camera instead."

"Quick," snapped Gunn. "Get that film to the lab and have it developed."

"Yes sir." The fellow turned and dashed out of the door, spraying Pitt with a few drops of saltwater as he passed.

Gunn's face had a happy but determined look. "My God. To think I was about to give up, throw my tail between my legs and set a course for home. Now, dammit, I'm going to stay anchored here until I die of old age or catch a *Teaser*." His eyes twinkled as he glanced at Pitt. "Well, Major, what do you think of that?"

Pitt merely shrugged. "Personally, I perfer angling for girls." With very little effort his mind dropped the business at hand and formed a tantalizing picture of Teri standing on the beach in her red bikini.

4

It was a few minutes past five when Pitt arrived back at his quarters on Brady Field. Within seconds of discarding his sticky clothing, he was firmly entrenched on his back in a narrow shower stall. It was a tight fit; his head was crooked into one corner, his back pressed flat on the wet tile floor, and his hairy legs and feet thrust upward on a ninety degree angle in the opposite corner. To anyone who might have peeked, it looked like a contorted and bone torturing position, but Pitt found it thoroughly comfortable and immensely satisfying. When time allowed, he always relaxed in the shower in this manner. Sometimes he dozed off, but mostly he used the simulated rainy atmosphere and the solitude to think. At this moment his mind simmered with a multitude of perplexing questions.

He mentally juggled the facts and unknowns together, seeking a pattern and trying to concentrate on the most important problems. It was no use. His mind eluded his grasp and stubbornly chewed on the minor and inconsequential riddle of the noiseless truck by the beach.

For some inexplicable reason the riddle irritated him and he endeavored vainly to shake it, but it remained. Finally he gave in to it and closed his eyes and recreated the scene, hoping to visualize a sign or solution.

Suddenly a blurred form appeared on the other side of the shower door.

"Hello in the shower," Giordino's voice rumbled over the running water. "You've been in there nearly half an hour. You must be thoroughly water-logged by now."

Pitt resigned himself to the interruption and reached up and turned the faucet to *off*.

"You better hurry," Giordino shouted. Then it occured to him that the water was no longer running. He lowered his voice. "Colonel Lewis is on his way over—he'll be here any second.

Pitt sighed. Pushing his body to a sitting position, he awkwardly struggled to his feet, nearly slipping on the slick tile floor. A towel sailed over the shower door, falling in folds around his head. The mere thought of being prodded and pushed in order to impress a higher ranking officer made the hairs on his neck bristle. He glared through the fuzzy glass panel.

"Tell Colonel Lewis he can play with himself while he waits." His voice had a nice frost to it. "I'll come out when I damn well feel like it," he said succinctly. "Now get the hell out of my bathroom, you bastard, before I cram a bar of soap up your anal canal." Abruptly, Pitt felt his cheeks heating. He hadn't really meant to be rude to his old friend. Immediately sorry, he felt a wave of guilt. "I'm sorry, Al. My mind was elsewhere."

"Forget it." Without another word Giordino shrugged and left the bathroom, closing the door behind him.

Pitt briskly dried his lean body and then shaved. After he finished, he blew the tiny black hairs out of the cordless electric shaver and patted his face with *British Sterling* after shave lotion. When he stepped into the bedroom, Giordino and Colonel Lewis were waiting.

Lewis sat on the edge of the bed and twisted one end of an immense red handlebar moustache. His large rosy face and twinkling blue eyes, along with the large bush on his upper lip gave him the appearance of a jolly lumberjack. His movements and his speech were rapid, almost jerky, giving Pitt the impression that the Colonel had a pound of ground glass in his crotch.

"Sorry to break in on you like this," boomed Lewis. "But I'm interested in knowing whether or not you've run onto anything substantial concerning the attack yesterday."

Pitt was nude, but he didn't give a damn. "No, nothing positive. I've several hunches and a couple of ideas, but very few absolute facts to build an airtight case with."

"I was hoping you might have stumbled on a lead. My Air Investigation Squadron has struck out."

"Have you found any remains of the Albatros?" asked Pitt.

Lewis rubbed a hand across his sweaty forehead. "If that old crate crashed into the sea, it left no trace; not even a small oil slick. It and its pilot must have vanished into thin air."

"Maybe it reached the mainland," said Giordino.

"Negative," replied Lewis. "We can't find a soul over there who saw it going or coming."

Giordino nodded in agreement. "An old plane painted bright yellow with a top speed of only one hundred and three miles an hour couldn't help but be noticed if it crossed over the strait into Macedonia."

Lewis took out a package of cigarettes. "What really confuses me is the fact that the attack was well planned and executed. Whoever raided the field knew no aircraft were scheduled to land or take off during his strafing runs."

Pitt buttoned his shirt and adjusted the gold oak leaves on his shoulders. "Obtaining information would be easy since everyone on Thasos probably knows that Brady Field becomes a ghost town on Sundays. Actually this whole affair is very similar in strategy to the attack on Pearl Harbor by the Japanese down to the detail of sneaking in through a pass in the island mountain range."

Lewis lit his cigarette, being careful not to singe his moustache. "You're right, of course but there's no doubt that your unexpected arrival in the flying boat caught our attacker, as well as ourselves, off guard. Our own radar failed to track your Catalina because you flew the last two hundred miles on the deck." He exhaled a cloud of smoke. "I can't begin to tell you what a welcome surprise it was to see your old bird come thundering down out of the sun."

"It must have surprised our friend in the Albatros too," Giordino grinned. "You should have seen his jaw drop when he turned and saw us for the first time."

Pitt finished knotting his tie. "No one expected us because my flight plan did not include Brady Field. I originally planned to set down in the sea next to the *First Attempt*. That's why our flying ghost and Brady Control were both unaware of our ETA." He paused, reflecting as he looked down at Lewis. "I strongly suggest, Colonel, that you take extreme defensive measures. I've a feeling we haven't seen the last of the yellow Albatros."

Lewis stared up at Pitt curiously. "What makes you so certain he'll return?"

Pitt's eyes glinted. "He had a definite purpose for attacking the field, and it wasn't to kill men or destroy aircraft belonging to the United States. His plan was simply to throw you into a panic."

"What would he gain by that?" asked Giordino.

"Stop and think about it for a moment." Pitt glanced at his watch, then to Lewis. "If this situation looked truly threatening and perilous, Colonel, you'd have to evacuate all American civilians to the mainland."

"Yes, that's true," admitted Lewis. "But at the moment I see no reason to take such steps. The Greek government has assured me they're offering their complete cooperation in finding the pilot and plane."

"But if you thought you had reason," pressed Pitt. "Wouldn't you also order Commander Gunn to remove the *First Attempt* from the Thasos area?"

Lewis' eyes narrowed. "As a safety precaution, of course. That white ship makes one hell of an inviting target for an aerial sniper."

Pitt flicked his Zippo and lit a cigarette. "Believe it or not, sir, that's your answer."

Giordino and Lewis looked at each other and then at Pitt, puzzled.

Pitt continued. "As you know, Colonel, Admiral Sandecker ordered Giordino and myself to Thasos to investigate the strange mishaps that have occurred during the NUMA's offshore operations. This morning, while conversing with Commander Gunn, I discovered evidence of a sabotage which leads me to believe that there's a definite connection between the raid and the accidents aboard the *First Attempt*. Now, if we take this assumption one step further, we begin to see that Brady Field was not the main objective of our reincarnated adversary. The raid was only an indirect means of removing Commander Gunn and the *First Attempt* from Thasos."

Lewis looked at Pitt thoughtfully. "I suppose the next question is why?"

"I don't have an answer yet," said Pitt. "But I'm certain our mysterious friend and his flair for dramatics has a high powered reason behind his game. He wouldn't go to such devious lengths for penny ante stakes. He's most likely hiding something of great value and the NUMA researchers on the ship are in a position to stumble onto it."

"That *something* you speak of could be sunken treasure," Lewis' lips gleamed wetly.

Pitt pulled an overseas cap out of his suitcase and set it jauntily on his head. "That's one obvious conclusion."

A faraway look came into Lewis' eyes and he said softly, "I wonder what it could be and how much it's worth?"

Pitt turned and faced Giordino. "Al, contact Admiral Sandecker and ask him to research all possible lost or sunken treasure troves in the Aegean Sea within spitting distance of Thasos and send us the data as soon as possible. Tell him it's urgent."

"Consider it done," Giordino said. "It's eleven

o'clock in the morning in Washington so we should have an answer by breakfast."

"Now we're getting somewhere," Lewis boomed. "The sooner I get answers, the sooner I can get the Pentagon off my back. Is there any way I can help?"

Pitt glanced at his watch again. "As the Boy Scouts say—*Be Prepared*. That's all we can do for the present. You can bet Brady Field and the *First Attempt* are being closely observed. When it comes apparent no one is being evacuated and the oceanography ship still floats out there on the Aegean, we can expect another visit from the yellow Albatros. You've had your fun, Colonel. It's my guess Commander Gunn's turn is next."

"Please tell the Commander," said Lewis, "I'll give him whatever assistance I have at my disposal."

"Thank you, sir," said Pitt. "But I don't think it would be wise to warn Commander Gunn just yet."

"For God's sake, why not?" gasped Giordino.

Pitt grinned coldly. "So far, all of this is pure conjecture. Besides, any preparation on board the *First Attempt* would be a dead giveaway of our intentions. No, we've got to bait our unknown World War I ghost and bring him out into the open."

Giordino looked at Pitt evenly. "You can't risk the lives of the scientists and ship's crew without giving them a chance to defend themselves."

"Gunn is in no immediate danger. Our ghost pilot will undoubtedly wait at least one more day to see if the *First Attempt* departs before he attacks again." Pitt smiled until the mirth lines etched into the sides of his eyes. "In the meantime, I'll put my creative talents to work on a plan for a trap."

Lewis got to his feet and faced Pitt. "For the sake of those men on the ship, I hope you come up with a good one."

"No plan is considered foolproof, Colonel," replied Pitt, "until after it's been applied."

Giordino walked toward the door. "I'll run over to Base Operations and send that message to the Admiral."

"When you've finished," said Lewis, "drop by my quarters for supper." Twisting his moustache, he turned to Pitt. "You're invited too. I'll give you men a real treat and whip up my renowned specialty: scallops with mushrooms in white wine sauce."

"It sounds very appetizing," said Pitt. "But I'm afraid I must decline. I have a previous dinner engagement . . . with a very attractive lady."

Giordino and Lewis could only gawk at him in dazed amazement.

Pitt tried to look nonchalant. "She's sending a car to pick me up at the main gate at six. I have just two minutes and thirty seconds to get there, so I'd best be leaving. Good evening, Colonel, and thank you for your invitation. I hope you'll give me a raincheck." He faced Giordino. "Al, let me know the minute the Admiral's reply comes in." Pitt turned and opened the door and left the room.

Lewis slowly shook his head. "Is he bull-shitting or does he really have a date with a girl?"

"I've never known Dirk to bull-shit about women, sir," said Giordino. He was beginning to enjoy Lewis' state of shock.

"But where did he meet her? To my knowledge he hasn't been anywhere except the field and the ship."

Giordino shrugged. "Beats me. But knowing Pitt as I do, it wouldn't surprise me if he picked up a girl on the hundred yards between the main gate and the *First Attempt*'s loading dock."

Lewis' booming laugh cracked across the room. "Well come along, Captain. I'm not a sexy girl but at least I can cook. How about some of my scallops?"

"Why not?" said Giordino. "That's the best offer *I've* had all afternoon."

5

The furnace-like atmosphere cooled slightly as the fading sun fell to the west beyond the Thasos mountains. Long crooked shadows from the mountains' tree-lined summits had moved down the slopes and were touching the seaward edge of Brady Field when Pitt passed through the main gate. He stopped on the outer road and inhaled the pure Mediterranean air, enjoying the inner sensation of having his lungs tingle. The habitual call for a ciagrette tugged at his mind, but he pushed the urge aside and took another deep breath, looking out to sea. Beyond the rolling surf, the setting sun painted the *First Attempt* a colorful golden orange. The visibility was crystal clear, and at a distance of two miles his eyes could pick out an amazing amount of detail on board the ship. He stood quiet and still for almost a full two minutes, lost in the beauty of the scene. Then he glanced about, looking for the car that Teri promised to send for him.

It was there, sitting off to one side of the road like a palatial and sumptuous yacht resting at anchor.

"Well I'll be damned," Pitt muttered, spotting the car. He moved closer and his face betrayed an admiration for fine automobiles.

It was a Maybach-Zepplin town car, complete with a sliding glass partition separating the enclosed passenger compartment from the driver, who sat in the open

exposed to the sun. Behind the large double-M orna-
ment on the radiator, the hood stretched back six feet
and ended at a low split windshield, giving the car an
image of great brutish power. The long flowing fenders
and running boards gleamed black but the coachwork
was painted a deep multi-coated silver. It was a classic
among classics: superb Teutonic craftsmanship evident
in every fitting, every nut and every bolt. If the 1936
Rolls-Royce Phantom III typified the British ideal of
silence and distinguished mechanical efficiency, then its
German counterpart was found in the 1936 Maybach-
Zepplin.

Pitt stepped up beside the car and ran his right
hand over a gargantuan spare tire that sat solidly
mounted in the front fender well. He grinned a grin of
satisfaction and relief as he noted the tire's tread was
deeply grooved in a diamond-shaped pattern. He patted
the big donut-like tire a couple of times and then turned
and looked into the front seat.

The driver sat slouched behind the wheel, idly
drumming his fingers on the door frame. He not only
looked bored, but he yawned to prove it. He was
dressed in a gray-green tunic that strangely resembled
the uniform of a World War II Nazi officer; but the
sleeves and shoulders bore no insignia. A high brimmed
cap covered his head, and the blond color of his hair
was betrayed by the brief hint of his sideburns. Old
fashioned silver-rimmed spectacles covered his eyes and
glinted in the setting sun. A long thin cigarette dangled
conceitedly from one corner of a curled lip, giving the
driver an aura of smugness and arrogance; an image he
made little effort to conceal.

Pitt instantly disliked the driver. Putting a foot on
the running board, he stared penetratingly at the uniformed figure behind the steering wheel. "I think you're
waiting for me. My name is Pitt."

The yellow haired driver did not bother to return
Pitt's stare. He merely flipped his cigarette over Pitt's
shoulder onto the road, sat up straight and turned the
ignition switch. "If you are the American garbage re-

ceiver," he said in a heavy German accent, "you may get in."

Pitt grinned and his eyes hardened. "Up front with the foul smelling rabble or in back with the gentry?"

"Wherever you choose," the driver said. His face turned crimson but he still did not turn or look up.

"Thank you," said Pitt smoothly. "I'll take the back." He pushed down on a huge chrome handle, swung the vault-like door open and climbed into the town car. An old roll style curtain perched over the partition window and Pitt pulled it down, closing off all sight of the driver in front. Then he settled back comfortably into the soft and luxurious morocco leather upholstery, lit a cigarette and prepared to enjoy the early evening ride across Thasos.

The Maybach's engine quietly came to life and the driver shifted through the whisper silent gears, moving the immense car over the road in the direction of Liminas.

Pitt rolled down a door window and studied the fir and chestnut trees dotting the mountain slopes, and the age-old olive trees lining the narrow beaches. Every so often, small fields of tobacco and wheat broke the uneven landscape and reminded him of the small farms he had often seen when flying over the southern United States.

Soon the car cruised through the picturesque village of Panaghia, splashing an occasional puddle that marred the elderly cobbled streets. Most of the houses were painted white to reflect the summer heat. The roofs rose into the fading sky and nearly touched as their eaves leaned toward each other over the narrow streets. In a few minutes Panaghia was left behind the Liminas soon came into view. Then the car abruptly turned, skirting the main section of the little city, and pointed its dinosaurian hood up a dusty cliff road. The incline was gradual at first, but quickly wormed into a series of steep hairpin curves.

Pitt could sense the driver struggling at the wheel of the Maybach; the lumbering town car was designed more for casual rides on the *Unter den Linden* than spring-breaking tours up mule trails. He looked over sheer precipices at the sea and wondered what would happen if another car came from the opposite direction. Then he could see it ahead; a huge white square against the darking gray cliffs. At last the curves ceased and the big diamond treaded tires slid smoothly onto the hard surface of a drive.

Pitt was adequately impressed. In size, the villa nearly matched the splendor of a Roman Forum. The grounds were well kept and there was an atmosphere of wealth and good taste. The entire estate nestled in a valley between two high mountain peaks and overlooked a sweeping panorama of the Aegean Sea. The main gate of a high wall opened mysteriously, apparently pulled by someone unseen, and the chauffeur drove up a neat fir-lined drive without ceremony and braked at a flight of marble steps. In the center of the stairway a large archaic staute of a woman carrying a child stared down mutely, greeting Pitt as he stepped from the Maybach.

He started to climb the steps when he stopped suddenly and returned to the car.

"I'm sorry driver," said Pitt. "But I didn't catch your name."

The driver looked up, puzzled. "My name is Willie. Why do you ask?"

"Willie, my friend," Pitt said seriously, "I must tell you something. Will you step out of the car for a moment?"

Willie's brows wrinkled but he shrugged and stepped from the car, facing Pitt. "Now Herr Pitt, what do you wish to tell me?"

"I see you wear jackboots, Willie."

"Ja, I wear jackboots."

Pitt flashed his best used car salesman's smile "And jackboots have hobnails, don't they?"

"Ja, jackboots have hobnails," said Willie irritably. "Why do you waste my time with such nonsense? I have duties to perform. What is it you wish to say?"

Pitt's eyes grew hard. "My friend, I felt that if you

want to earn your peeping-Tom merit badge, it's my duty to warn you that silver-rimmed spectacles reflect the sun's rays and can easily give your hiding place away."

Willie's face went blank, and he started to say something, but Pitt's fist slammed into his mouth, cutting off the words. The impact jerked Willie's head up and back, throwing his cap in the air. His eyes turned dull and empty, and he slowly swayed like a falling leaf to his knees. He knelt there looking dazed and lost. A stream of bloody mucus dropped from his broken nose and splattered over the lapels of his uniform, creating, what Pitt thought, a rather artistic effect against the gray-green material. Then Willie pitched forward onto the marble steps and folded into an inert heap.

Pitt rubbed the knuckles of his bruised hand, grinning in cold satisfaction. Then he turned and jogged up the steps, taking three at a time. At the top he passed through a stone archway and found himself in a circular courtyard with a glass-like pool in its center. The entire courtyard was encircled by twenty or more majestic lifesized statues of helmeted Roman soldiers. Their sightless stone eyes somberly stared at their white reflections in the pool as if searching for long forgotten memories of victorious battles and wars of glory. The deepening shadows of evening covered each figure with a ghostly cloak, giving Pitt the weird sensation that at any second the stone warriors would come alive and lay siege to the villa.

He hurried around the pool and stopped at a massive double door at the far end of the courtyard. A large bronze knocker in the shape of a lion's head hung grotesquely on the door. Pitt raised the grip, banging it down hard. He turned and glanced at the courtyard again. The entire setting reminded him of a mausoleum. All it lacked, he thought, were a few scattered wreaths and some organ music.

The door swung open silently. Pitt peered across the threshold. Seeing no one, he hesitated a moment. The moment turned into a minute and the minute into

two. Finally, tiring of hide-and-seek, he braced his
shoulders, clenched his fists and stepped through the
portal into an ornately decorated anteroom.

Tapestries depicting ancient battle scenes hung
from every wall, their needlework armies marching in
unison toward battle. A high dome capped the room,
and from its arched apex, came a soft yellowish light.
Pitt glanced around and saw that he was alone so he sat
down in one of two carved marble benches that adorned
the middle of the room, and he lit a ciagarette. Time
passed, and soon he began a futile search for an ashtray.

Then silently, with no warning, a tapestry swung
aside, and an old, heavy-set man entered the room, accompanied by an immense white dog.

6

Pitt, mildly stunned, looked warily at the gigantic German shepherd and then into the face of the dog's elderly master. The evil unsmiling features, so familiar on the late, late movies on television, sat entrenched on a typical round German face, complete with the shaven head, shifty eyes and no neck. Thin lips pressed tightly together as though their owner suffered from constipation. The body fit the villainous image too; heavy set in a rotund frame of solid tissue with no flab. All that was missing was a riding quirt and the polished boots. For an instant Pitt thought, "the man you love to hate, Eric von Stroheim, had returned to life and stood ready to direct a scene from *Greed*."

"Good evening," the old man said in a suspicious guttural tone. "You are, I believe, the gentleman my niece invited to dinner?"

Pitt rose, one eye on the huge panting dog. "Yes sir. Major Dirk Pitt at your service."

An expression of surprise furrowed the brow below the tight skinned head. "My niece led me to believe you were under the rank of sergeant, and your military occupation was garbage collecting."

"You must forgive my American humor," said Pitt, enjoying the other man's confusion. "I hope my little deception has caused you no inconvenience."

"No, a little concern perhaps, but no inconvenience." The old German extended his hand and studied Pitt closely. "It is an honor to meet you, Major. I am Bruno von Till."

Pitt clasped the outstretched hand and returned the stare. "The honor is mine, sir."

Von Till lifted a tapestry, revealing a doorway. "Please come this way, Major. You must join me for a drink while we wait for Teri to finish dressing."

Pitt followed the flat form and the white hound down a dark hallway that led into a large cavernous study. The ceiling arched at least thirty feet high and was supported by several fluted ionic column shafts. The furniture, classic in its simplicity, sparsely dotted the floor and lent an air of grace to the imposing chamber. A cart was already laid with unusual Greek hors d'oeuvres, and a recessed alcove of one wall housed a completely equipped bar. The only item of decor, Pitt noted, that seemed out of place was a model of a German submarine, resting on a shelf above the bar.

Von Till motioned Pitt to sit down. "What will be your pleasure, Major?"

"Scotch rocks would be fine," replied Pitt, leaning back in an armless couch. "Your villa is most impressive. It must have an interesting history."

"Yes, it was originally built by the Romans in 138 B.C. as a temple to Minerva, their goddess of wisdom. I purchased the ruins shortly after the First World War and rebuilt it into what you see today." He handed Pitt a glass. "Shall we drink a toast?"

"To whom or what shall we drink to?"

Von Till smiled. "You may have the honor, Major. Beautiful women . . . riches . . . a long life. Perhaps to the President of your country. The choice is yours."

Pitt took a deep breath. "In that case I propose a toast to the courage and flying skill of Kurt Heibert, *The Hawk of Macedonia.*"

Von Till's face went blank. He slowly eased into a chair and toyed with his drink. "You are a very unusual man, Major. You pass yourself off as a garbage collector. You come to my villa and assault my chauffeur, and then you astound me further by proposing a toast to my old flying comrade, Kurt." He threw a sly grin over his drink at Pitt. "However, your most outstanding performance was in seducing my niece on the beach this morning. For that feat I congratulate and thank you. Today, for the first time in nine years, I saw Teri happily singing and laughing with an intense joy in living. I am afraid you force me to condone your lecherous conduct."

It was Pitt's turn to act surprised, but, instead, he tossed his head back and laughed. "My apologies on every count, except slugging your perverted chauffeur. Willie had it coming."

"You should not blame poor Willie. He was only acting on my orders to follow and guard Teri. She is my only living relative and I wish no harm to come to her."

"What harm could possibly come to her?"

Von Till rose and walked to an open terrace window and looked out over the darkening sea. "Over half a century I have worked hard and paid a great personal price to build a substantial organization. Along the road I also accumulated a few enemies. I never know what one of them might do for revenge."

Pitt's eyes searched von Till. "Is that why you carry a Luger in a shoulder holster?"

Von Till turned from the window and self-consciously adjusted his white dinner jacket over the bulge beneath his left armpit. "May I ask how you know it is a Luger?"

"Just a guess," Pitt said. "You look like the Luger type."

Von Till shrugged. "Ordinarily I do not act quite so mundane, but for the way Teri described you I had every reason to suspect doubtful character."

"I must admit I've performed a few sinful deeds in my day," Pitt said grinning. "But murder and extortion weren't included."

A scowl formed on von Till's face. "I do not think you would be so flippant if you . . . how do you Americans say . . . were in my shoes."

"Your shoes are beginning to sound very mysterious, Herr von Till," said Pitt. "Just what kind of business are you in?"

Suspicion marked von Till's eyes, then his lips faded to a phoney smile. "If I told you, it might upset your appetite. That, my dear Major, would make Teri exceedingly angry since she has spent half the afternoon in the kitchen overseeing tonight's dinner." He shrugged in a typical European gesture. "Some other time, perhaps, when I know you better."

Pitt spun the last swallow of scotch around in the glass and wondered what he had gotten himself into. Von Till, he decided, was either some kind of nut or a very shrewd operator.

"May I get you another drink?" asked von Till.

"Don't bother, I'll get it." Pitt finished the drink and walked over to the bar and poured another. He stared at von Till. "From what I've read about World War I aviation, the circumstances behind the death of Kurt Heibert are nebulous. According to official German records, he was shot down by the British and crashed somewhere in the Aegean Sea. However, the records fail to mention the name of Heibert's victorious opponent. They also fail to state if the body was found."

Von Till idly petted the dog. His eyes seemed lost in the past for a few moments. Finally, he said, "Kurt waged his own private war with the British back in 1918. He seldom flew against them coolly or efficiently. He handled his machine wildly and attacked their formations like a man possessed with a spastic devil. When he was in the air, he cursed and raved and pounded his fists on the edge of the cockpit until they bled. On take-off he always revved his engine to a roaring full throttle so that his Albatros leaped off the ground like a frightened bird. And yet, when he was not on patrol and could forget the war for a few moments, he could be a man of great humor, much unlike your American conception of the German soldier."

Pitt shook his head slowly with a hint of a smile. "You must forgive me, Herr von Till, but most of my comrades-in-arms have yet to meet a German soldier who was a barrel of laughs."

The bald old German ignored Pitt's remark. His face remained serious. "The end for Kurt, when it came, was from a cunning British trick. They studied his tactics closely and soon learned that he had a weakness for attacking and destroying their observation ballons. A battle weary balloon was overhauled and the observer's basket was filled with high explosives and a uniformed dummy stuffed with weeds. A detonating wire ran to the ground and the British then sat and waited for Kurt to make an appearance." Von Till sat down in a deeply pillowed sofa. He looked up at the ceiling, but he didn't see it. His mind looked, instead, into a sky that existed in 1918. "They did not have to wait long. Only one day later, Kurt flew over the allied lines and saw the balloon swinging slowly in the offshore breeze. He no doubt wondered why there was no ground fire. And the observer, leaning on the basket's railing, looked to be asleep, for he made no attempt to leap out and parachute to safety before Kurt's guns turned the hydrogen filled bag into a cloud of fire."

"He had no idea it was a trap?" asked Pitt.

"No," von Till replied. "The balloon was there and it represented the enemy. Almost automatically, Kurt dove to the attack. He closed with the balloon and his Spandau machine guns began raking the thin skinned gas bag. Suddenly the balloon erupted in a thunderous explosion that covered the entire area in fire and smoke. The British had detonated the explosives."

"Heibert crashed over the allied lines?" Pitt queried in thoughtful speculation.

"Kurt did not crash after the explosion," von Till answered, shaking his mind back to the present again. "His Albatros burst through the inferno, but the gallant plane that carried him faithfully through so many air battles was badly shattered, and he was seriously wounded. With its fabric wings torn and tattered, its control surfaces blown off and a bloody pilot in the cockpit, the plane staggered over the Macedonian coastline and disappeared out to sea. The *Hawk of Mace-*

donia and his legendary yellow Albatros were never seen again."

"At least not until yesterday." Pitt took a deep breath and waited for an obvious reaction.

Von Till's eyelids widened on his otherwise expressionless face and he said nothing. He seemed to be weighing Pitt's words.

Pitt immediately came back to the original subject. "Did you and Heibert often fly together?"

"Yes, we flew patrol together many times. We even used to take up a two seater Rumpler bomber and drop incendiary bombs on the British Aerodrome which was located right here on Thasos. Kurt would fly while I acted as observer and bombardier."

"Where was your squadron based?"

"Kurt and I were posted to Jasta 73. We flew out of the Xanthi aerodrome in Macedonia."

Pitt lit a cigarette. Then he looked at von Till's old, but erect figure. "Thank you for a very concise and detailed account of Heibert's death. You omitted nothing."

"Kurt was a very dear friend," von Till said wistfully. "I do not forget such things easily. I can even recall the exact date and time. It happened at 9:00 P.M. on July 15, 1918."

"It seems strange that no one else knew the full story," Pitt murmured, his eyes cold and steady with purpose. "The archives in Berlin and the British Air Museum in London have no information concerning the death of Heibert. All the books I've studied on the subject list him as missing in a mysterious situation similar to the other great aces, such as Albert Ball and Georges Guynemer."

"Good God," snapped von Till, exasperated. "The German archives lack the facts because the Imperial High Command never gave a damn about the war in Macedonia. And the British would never dare publish one word about such an unchivalrous deed. Besides, Kurt's plane was still in the air when they saw it last. The British could only assume their insidious plan was successful.

"No trace of man or plane was ever found?"

"Nothing. Heibert's brother searched for him after the war, but Kurt's final resting place remains a mystery."

"Was the brother also a flyer?"

"No. I met him on several occasions prior to the Second World War. He was a fleet officer in the German navy."

Pitt fell silent. Von Till's story was too damn pat, he thought. He had the strange feeling that he was being used, like a wooden decoy on a flight of geese. A faint ominous tingling stirred inside him. He heard a tapping of high heels on the floor and without turning knew that Teri had entered the room.

"Hello everybody." Her voice was light and cheerful.

Pitt swung around and faced her. She was wearing a mini-dress, designed like a Roman toga, that swirled about her slender legs. He liked the color—a golden orange that complemented her ebony hair. She looked at Pitt, her eyes immediately drawn to his uniform. Her face paled slightly, and she raised a hand to her mouth in the same gesture he had noticed on the beach. Then she smiled thinly and approached, radiating a beautiful and sexy warmth.

"Good evening gorgeous creature," Pitt said lightly, taking her outstretched hand and kissing it.

Teri flushed, then looked up at his grinning face. "I was going to thank you for coming," she said. "But now that I've seen through the naughty little trick you've played on me, I've a good notion to toss you out on your bloody . . ."

"Don't say it," Pitt interrupted. His lips curved devilishly. "I know you won't believe me, but just this afternoon the base commander took me off the garbage truck, made me a pilot, and promoted me to Major."

She laughed. "Shame on you. You told me your rank was under that of a sergeant."

"No. I only said that I've never been a sergeant, and that's the truth."

She slipped her hand through Pitt's arm. "Has Uncle Bruno been boring you with his flying tales of the Great War?"

"Fascinating me maybe, but not boring," Pitt answered. Her eyes looked scared behind her smile. He wondered what she was thinking.

Teri shook her head from side to side. "You men and your war stories." She kept staring at Pitt's uniform and insignia of rank. This didn't seem like the same man she had loved on the beach. This one was much more charming and sophisticated. "You may have Dirk after dinner, Uncle Bruno, but right now he's mine."

Von Till expertly clicked his heels and bowed. "As you wish my dear. For the next hour and a half, you shall be our commanding officer."

She wrinkled her nose at von Till. "That's awfully decent of you, Uncle. In that case my first order is for both of you to march to the dinner table."

Teri pulled Pitt out to the terrace and led him down a sloping stairway that ended on a circular overhanging balcony.

The view was breathtaking. Far below the villa the lights of Liminas were blinking on house by house. And across the sea, the early stars began to poke their tips into a spreading blanket of black. In the middle of the balcony, a table was set with service for three. A large yellow globe containing six candles illuminated the setting and cast an intriguing glow over the table, turning the silver dinnerware to gold.

Pitt eased Teri's chair back for her and whispered in her ear. "You better be careful. You know how stimulated I get in romantic atmosphere."

She looked up at him and her eyes smiled. "Why do you think I planned it this way."

Before Pitt could answer, von Till walked up followed by the giant dog, and snapped his fingers. Instantly, a young girl in native Greek costume materialized and set down an appetizer of mixed cheeses, olives and cucumbers. Next came a chicken soup, flavored with lemon and egg yokes. Then the main course; baked oysters mixed with onions and minced nuts. Von Till uncorked the wine—*Retsina*—a fine old Greek wine.

Its resin flavor reminded Pitt of turpentine. After the serving girl cleared the dishes, she brought a tray of fruit and then poured the coffee made in the Turkish manner; the powdered beans settling like silt on the bottom of the cup.

Pitt forced down the strong unsweetened coffee and rubbed knees with Teri. He expected a girlish grin but instead she looked at him with frightened eyes. It seemed she was trying to tell him something.

"Well, Major," said von Till. "I hope you enjoyed our little repast."

"Yes, thank you," replied Pitt. "It was excellent."

Von Till stared across the table at Teri. His face had set like stone, and his voice turned to ice. "I would like to be alone with the Major for a little while, my dear. Why don't you wait in the study, we will be along shortly."

Teri acted surprised. She shuddered faintly, gripping the edge of the table before she answered him. "Please, Uncle Bruno, it's too early. Can't you wait and have your little talk with Dirk later?"

Von Till shot her a withering look. "Do as your Uncle says. I have a few important matters I would like to discuss with Major Pitt. I am sure he will not leave before seeing you."

Pitt found himself becoming angry. Why the sudden family crisis? he wondered. He took a long breath, sensing something very wrong. An odd prickle crept up his back; that old familiar feeling of danger. Like an old and trusted friend, it always tapped him on the shoulder and warned him when a nasty situation was brewing. Unseen, Pitt slipped a paring knife off the plate of fruits and pushed it under his pant leg and into his sock.

Teri looked at Pitt, her face paling. "Please excuse me, Dirk. I don't mean to be a ninny."

He smiled. "Don't worry. I have a weakness for pretty ninnies."

"You never seem to fail to say the right thing," she murmured.

He squeezed her hand. "I'll join you as soon as I can."

"I'll be waiting." Suddenly her eyes brimmed with tears and she turned away and ran up the stairway.

"I am sorry for speaking so harshly to Teri," the old German apologized. "I had to talk to you privately and she rarely appreciates my desire to converse without feminine interruption. It is often necessary to become firm with women. Do you agree?"

Pitt nodded. He could think of nothing worthwhile to say.

Von Till inserted a cigarette in a long ivory holder and lit it. "I am extremely interested in hearing about the attack yesterday on Brady Field. My information from that section of the island tells me it was a very old and unknown type of airplane that struck your facility."

"Old maybe," said Pitt, "but not unknown."

"Are you saying you have determined the make of airplane?"

Pitt studied von Till's face. Silently he dawdled with a fork, then slowly laid it back on the tablecloth. "The aircraft was positively identified as an Albatros D-3."

"And the pilot?" The words came slowly from Von Till's tight mouth. "Do you know the identity of the pilot?"

"Not yet, but we will shortly."

"You seem confident of an early capture."

Pitt took his time about answering. He slowly and methodically lit a cigarette. "Why not. It shouldn't be difficult to trace a sixty year old yellow antique aircraft to its owner."

A smug grin crossed von Till's face. "Macedonian Greece is an area of rugged terrain and desolate countryside. There are many thousands of square miles of mountains, valleys and eroded plains where even one of your monstrous jet bombers could be hidden and never detected."

Pitt grinned back. "Who said anything about searching mountains or valleys?"

"Where else would you look?"

"In the sea," Pitt said pointing at the black water

far below. "Probably in the same spot where Kurt Heibert crashed back in 1918."

Von Till arched an eyebrow. "Are you asking me to believe in ghosts?"

Pitt grinned. "When we were little boys we believed in Santa Claus. And when we became big boys we believed in virgins. Why not add ghosts to the list also?"

"No thank you, Major. I find cold facts and figures superior to superstition."

Pitt's voice was even and distinct. "That leaves us with another avenue to explore."

Von Till sat erect, his eyes squinting at Pitt.

"What if Kurt Heibert is still alive?"

Von Till's mouth dropped open. Then he caught himself and exhaled a cloud of cigarette smoke. "That's ridiculous. If Kurt were still alive he would be over seventy years old. Look at me, Major. I was born in 1899. Do you think a man of my age could fly an open cockpit plane, not to mention attacking an air field? No, I don't think so."

"The facts are on your side, of course," said Pitt. He paused a moment, running his long fingers through his hair. "Still, I can't help wondering if Heibert isn't connected in some way." His eyes shifted from the old German to the great white dog and he felt a vague tension grip his body. Intrigue hung heavily around them. He came to the villa at Teri's invitation expecting only to enjoy a quiet dinner. Instead, he found himself engaged in a battle of wits with her uncle, a shrewd old Teuton who, Pitt was certain, knew more about the raid on Brady Field than he was telling. It was time to cast a spear and the hell with the consequences. He locked his eyes on von Till. "If the *Hawk of Macedonia* really did vanish sixty years ago and reappeared yesterday, the interesting question is; where did he spend his time between? In heaven, in hell . . . or on Thasos?"

A confused look replaced von Till's arrogant mask. "I don't quite understand what you mean."

"Mean hell," snarled Pitt. "Either you're taking me for a complete fool or else you're acting like one. I don't think I should be telling you about the attack on Brady Field, but rather you should be telling me." He lingered over the words, enjoying the situation.

Von Till was on his feet in an instant, his oval face contorted with anger. "You have probed too far and too deep, Major Pitt, into areas that don't concern you. I shall take no more of your absurd implications. I must ask you to leave my villa."

A look of contempt crossed Pitt's face. "Whatever's fair," he said turning to the stairway.

Von Till glared at him bitterly. "No need to return through the study, Major," he said pointing to a small doorway that clung to the far wall of the balcony. "This corridor will lead you to the front entrance."

"I'd like to see Teri before I leave."

"I see no reason to prolong your presence." Von Till blew a contemptuous cloud of smoke toward Pitt's face, driving home the angered words. "I also demand that you never see or talk to my niece again."

Pitt's hand clenched into fists. "And if I do?"

Von Till smiled menacingly. "I will not threaten you, Major. If you persist in exercising aggressive stupidity, I shall merely punish Teri."

"You rotten shit-eating kraut," Pitt snarled, fighting down a surging urge to kick von Till in the crotch. "I don't know what the hell your little conspiracy amounts to, but I can definitely go on record as stating that I'll take great personal pleasure in screwing it up. And I can begin by telling you that the attack on Brady Field failed to achieve its intention. The National Underwater Marine Agency's ship is staying right where it's anchored until its scientific research activities are completed."

Von Till's hands trembled but his face remained impassive. "Thank you, Major. That is a bit of information I did not expect quite so soon.

At last, the old kraut is dropping his guard, Pitt thought. There could be no doubt about it now, it was von Till who had plotted to get rid of the *First Attempt*. But why? The question still remained unanswered. Pitt tried a shot in the dark. "You're wasting your time, von

Till. The divers on the *First Attempt* have already discovered the sunken treasure. They're in the act of raising
it now."

Von Till broke out in a broad smile, and Pitt knew
immediately the lie was a mistake.

"A very poor attempt, Major. You could not be
more wrong."

He drew the Luger from under his armpit and
pointed the dark blue barrel at Pitt's neck. Then he
opened the corridor door. "If you please?" he said,
beckoning with the gun toward the threshold.

Pitt took a quick glance through the darkened
doorway. The corridor beyond was dimly lighted with
candles and seemed completely deserted. He hesitated.
"Please express my thanks to Teri for the excellent dinner."

"I shall pass on your compliment."

"And thank you, Herr von Till," Pitt said sarcastically, "for your hospitality."

Von Till smirked, clicked his heels and bowed. "It
was my pleasure." He placed a hand on the head of the
dog, whose lip curled, showing a prodigious white fang.

The door's archway was low and Pitt had to stoop
to enter the tunnel-like entrance. He took a few cau-
tious steps.

"Major Pitt!". .

"Yes," Pitt replied, turning and facing the fat
shadow at the entryway.

There was a sadistic anticipation in von Till's
voice. "It is a pity you will not be able to witness the
next flight of the yellow Albatros."

Before Pitt could answer the door slammed shut
and a heavy bolt dropped into its catch like a thunderclap and echoed ominously toward the unseen reaches
of the dim corridor.

7

A spasm of anger swept over Pitt. He was half tempted to slam his fist against the door, but one look at the heavy planking changed his mind. Turning again to the corridor, he found it still empty. He shivered unconsciously. He had no illusions as to what lay ahead. It was certain now that von Till never meant for him to leave the villa alive. He remembered the knife and felt a tinge of assurance as he slipped it out of his sock. The flickering yellow light from the candles, mounted in rusted metal holders high on the walls, glinted dully on the blade and made the tiny pointed knife look woefully inadequate for the job of self-defense. Only one comforting thought ran through Pitt's mind: However small, the knife was better than nothing.

Suddenly a blast of heavy, chilling air blew through the corridor like an invisible hand and snuffed out the candles, leaving Pitt standing in a sea of suffocating blackness.

His senses strained to penetrate the gloom, but could detect no sound, no glimmer of light.

"Now the fun begins," he murmured, bracing his body for the unknown.

Pitt's spirits touched zero and he could feel the first terror striking symptoms of panic edging rapidly into his mind. He remembered reading somewhere that nothing is more horrifying or uncomprehending to the human mind than total darkness. To not know or be able to perceive what lies beyond one's sight or touch, acts on the brain like a short circuit in a computer; it runs amok. What the brain cannot see, it creates, usually some nightmarish event that is grossly exaggerated or embellished like a delusion of being bitten by a shark or run over by a locomotive while locked in a closet. Recalling the semi-amusing phraseology, he grinned in the darkness and the first probes of panic slowly reversed into a sensation of logic calm.

His next thought was to use the Zippo to relight the candles. But if someone or something were awaiting in the ambush further down the corridor, he reasoned, it would be best to remain in pitch darkness and keep them at the same disadvantage. Stooping, he quickly unlaced his shoes, discarding them, and began inching along the cool wall. The corridor led him past several wooden doors, each barred by large bands of iron. He was in the midst of testing one of the doors when he paused, listening intently.

There was a sound somewhere ahead in the blackness. It was indefinable and unexplicable, but quite audible. It could have been a moan or a growl; Pitt didn't know which. Then the sound faded and died into nothingness.

Determined now that a real menace was waiting, some creature of the dark, that was physical, could make noises and probably reason, spurred Pitt's sense of caution. He lay down on the corridor floor and crept ahead without sound, his ears listening and his sensitive fingertips feeling out the way. The floor was smooth and unyielding, and in spots it was damp. He crawled on through an oily slime that soiled his uniform, soaking into the material and causing it to stick to his skin. He mentally cursed his uncomfortable predicament as he crept onward.

After what seemed like hours, Pitt imagined he had dragged his stomach over at least two miles of cement, but his rational mind knew it was close to eighty feet. The musty smell of antiquity lay on the floor and reminded him of the interior of an old steamer trunk that once belonged to his grandfather. He remembered hiding in its dark cubicle and pretending he was a stowaway on a ship bound for the mysterious orient. It's strange, he thought incongruously, how smells can bring back dormant and forgotten memories.

Abruptly, the feel of the floor and walls changed from smooth concrete to rough, jointed masonry. The passageway left the more modern construction behind and became old and and hand hewn.

Pitt's hand felt the wall stop and branch to the right. A gentle touch of air on his cheeks told him he had come to cross-passage. He froze and listened.

There it was again . . . The sound was halting and furtive. This time it was a clicking noise, like the kind long nailed animals make on a hard surfaced floor.

Pitt shivered uncontrollably and broke out in a cold sweat. He pressed his body flat into the damp cobbled ground, knife pointed in the direction of the approaching sound.

The clicking became louder. Then it stopped and a torturous silence set in.

Pitt tried to contain his breathing to hear better; all his ears could detect was his own heartbeat. Something was out there, not ten feet away. He compared himself with a blind man who was being stalked down a backstreet alley. The eerie, spine-chilling atmosphere of the surroundings numbed his thinking with a sense of hopelessness. He shook it off, forcing his mind to concentrate on methods of combating the unseen terror.

The musty stench of the tunnel suddenly became overpowering, nearly making him sick. He also detected a faint animal odor. But from what kind of animal?

Quickly a plan formed in Pitt's mind, and he decided to take a gamble on the unknown quantity. The Zippo came out of his pocket. He flipped the little wheel against the flint and held it a brief instant until the wick burned brightly. He cast it up and into the air ahead. The tiny flame sailed through the darkness and illuminated two glowing fluorescent eyes, backed by a giant shadow that danced hellishly on the walls and floor of the passageway. The lighter clinked to the ground, its flame snuffed out by the fall. A low menacing growl came from the eyes and echoed through the stone labyrinth.

Pitt reacted instantly and coiled on the hard floor. Then he whipped over on his back and thrust the knife up into the dark void, holding the handle tightly in the sweating palms of both hands. He could not see his ghostly attacker, but he knew now what it was.

The beast had noted Pitt's exact location in the brief flickering flame from the lighter. It hesitated for an instant, then it sprang.

The ageless animal instinct of sniffing its prey before attacking spelled the big animal's doom. The delay gave Pitt precious time for his sudden evasive body roll, and the huge white dog overshot his quarry. The action happened with such blinding speed that all Pitt could recall afterwards was the feel of the knife slicing into a soft furry surface and the wetness of heavy liquid splattering in his face.

The growl of the killer turned to the howl of the mortally wounded as the knife laid open the great Shepherd's flank just behind the ribs. The walls of the stone corridors thundered in a chorus of reverberating roars that burst from the thick, hairy throat a split second before the hundred and eighty pounds of animal fury crashed into the vertical stone beyond Pitt and fell heavily to the ground, thrashing in spastic agony for several moments before dying.

At first Pitt thought the dog had missed. Then he felt a sting across his chest, and he knew it hadn't. He lay without moving, listening to the death throes in the blackness. Long minutes after the passageway returned to a ghostly stillness, he remained limp on the uneven floor. The tension finally passed and his muscles started to loosen, and the pain began to arrive in earnest, clearing his mind to a new sharpness.

Pitt slowly rose to his feet and leaned wearily against the unseen blood splattered wall. Another shudder shook his body and he waited until his nerves calmed before stumbling into the darkness ahead where he shuffled his feet back and forth until they came in contact with his lighter. He lighted the little metallic box and surveyed his wounds.

Blood seeped from four evenly spaced furrows that began just above the left nipple and extended up and diagonally over his chest to the right shoulder. The claw marks were deep in the skin but their depth barely penetrated the muscle tissue. Pitt's shirt hung down like a shredded flag of red and khaki. All he could do for the moment was tear off the dangling strips of ragged cloth and pad the gashes. It would have been the easiest thing in the world to collapse to the ground and let a wave of comforting unconsciousness gather him in its trough. The temptation was strong, but he resisted it. Instead he stood on steady legs with a quartz clear mind, planning his next move.

After another minute, Pitt walked over to the dog. Holding the lighter aloft, he stared down at the dead animal. It was laying on its side, the entrails in a gruesome heap outside the body cavity. Trails of blood streaked the floor, running in separate little streams toward an unseen low point somewhere in the direction from which he had crawled. The weariness and the pain dropped from Pitt like a falling coat at the gruesome sight. Rage and anger engulfed his body and soared from the state of fearful, life saving caution to a state of uncaring indifference toward danger and death. One thought held and gripped his mind: murder von Till.

His next step sounded simple, absurdly simply; he must find a way out of the labyrinth. The odds seemed long, and the chances hopeless. Yet the thought of failure never entered his mind. Von Till's words about the next flight of the yellow Albatros settled any doubts for him. The gears in Pitt's head meshed in analytical thought, spitting out facts and possibilities.

Now that the scheming old German knew the *First Attempt* was remaining anchored off Thasos, he would have it attacked by the Albatros. It would be too risky for the old plane to try another afternoon attack, Pitt reasoned. Von Till, no doubt, would send it aloft as soon as possible, probably at dawn. Gunn and his crew must be warned in time. He glanced at the luminous dial on his wrist watch. The needle-like hands registered 9:55. Dawn would break at approximately 4:40, he figured, give or take five minutes. That left six hours and forty-five minutes for him to find an exit from this crypt and alert the ship!

Pitt shoved the knife in his belt, snapped the lighter shut to conserve fuel and started up the left passageway toward the source of a very slight air current. The going was easier now. Pitt was damned if he'd crawl anymore. He hurried without hesitation. The passage narrowed to three feet in width, but the roof stayed out of reach above his head.

Suddenly his outstretched hand struck solid wall. The passage ceased; it was a dead end. He flicked the lighter and saw his mistake. The air current came from a small crack between the rocks. An audible humming noise also issued from the crack. It was the sound of an electric motor, hidden somewhere beyond the wall in the bowels of the mountain. Pitt listened for a moment, but then the sound ceased.

"If at first you don't succeed," he mused aloud, "try another passage." He retraced his steps and quickly reached the intersection, this time taking the tunnel directly opposite the one he had cautiously crawled through.

He lengthened his stride and pounded on into the impenetrable darkness; the cool damp paving numbing his stocking feet. He idly wondered how many other men, or women for that matter, had von Till literally thrown to the dog. In spite of the near chilly air, the sweat ran off his body in streams. The pain across his chest seemed remote, too remote to belong to him. He could feel the blood mingling with the sweat and running down into his pants. He kept going and was determined to keep going until he dropped. A thought tugged at his mind to slow down and rest, but he rejected it and quickened his pace.

Again and again his groping hands and the periodic but welcome flicker of the lighter discovered new passages that branched off into endless nothingness. In some, the rocks had caved in, sealing them off, probably forever.

The lighter was on its last breath, the fluid almost gone. Pitt used it as little as possible, relying more and more on his bruised and scraped fingers. An hour passed, and then another. He continued on, pushing his tired and torn body through the ancient passages.

His foot struck something solid, and he pitched forward onto the bottom steps of a stone stairway. The edge of the fourth step caught him across the nose, gashing the bridge to the bone. Blood spurted down his cheeks and coated his lips. All at once the exhaustion, the emotional drain and the despair flooded over his battered body, and he folded limply on the stairs. Everything began to slow down. He lay and listened to the blood drip on the step beneath his head. A soft white cloud materialized out of the black gloom and gently covered him.

Pitt shook his sore and fuzzy head violently, trying to clear the cobwebs. Slowly, very slowly, like a man lifting a tremendous weight he raised his head and shoulders and began agonizingly to crawl up the stairway. Step by step he struggled, until at last he reached his destination.

A webbing of heavy bars marked the top of the stairway. The grille work was ancient and heavily rusted but still thick and strong enough to hold back an elephant.

Pitt hauled himself painfully onto the landing. A curtain of fresh air greeted his skin, replacing the musty odor of the labyrinth. He gazed through the rectangles between the bars and his spirits soared at the sight of the stars blinking in the sky. Back in the winding passageways he had left like a dead man in a casket. It seemed like an eternity since he saw the outside world. He pulled himself to his feet and shook the bars. There was no movement. The lock on the massive gate had recently been welded closed.

He checked the width between each bar, searching

for the largest opening. The third space from the left, held the greatest spread; about eight and one-half inches. He laboriously stripped off all his clothes and set them on the other side of the barrier. Next he smeared his blood into the sweat and exhaled until his lungs ached in protest. Then, slipping his head between the bars, he strained to push one hundred and ninety pounds into the outside landscape. The rust from the bars flaked off against his slippery skin and stuck to the glue-like blood. A racking moan of pain escaped his mouth as his genitals scraped over the ragged edge of one bar. He desperately clawed at the ground and gave a final heave. His body came free.

Pitt grasped his scraped crotch and sat up, ignoring the stabbing pain and unable to believe his success. He was out, but was he in the clear? His eyes, now acutely used to the dark, darted around the immediate area.

The vaulted bars of the labyrinth faced onto the stage entrance of a great amphitheatre. The ponderous structure reflected a vaguely unearthly glow from the white light of the stars and the moon, whose imperfect circle peeped over a shadowed mountain summit. The architecture was Grecian but the massiveness of the construction signified Roman hands. The edge of the round stage was separated from the theatre's upper rim by almost forty rows of steeply banked seats. Except for the invisible flight of nocturnal insects, the entire amphitheatre was deserted.

Pitt slipped into the remains of his uniform. Knotting the damp sticky cloth of his shirt, he stiffly wrapped his chest with a crude bandage.

Just to be able to walk and breathe in the warm evening air gave him a new surge of strength. He had gambled back there in the labyrinth and without Theseus' string to guide him had beat the immense odds and won. Laughter rang from his lips and traveled in loud echoes to the last row of the amphitheatre and back. The pain and the exhaustion was forgotten as he visualized von Till's face at their next meeting.

"How would you like a ticket to see that?" Pitt shouted at his nonattendant gallery. He waited, caught in the mood of the eerie setting. There was no reply, no applause, only the silence of the warm Thasos night. For a moment he thought he saw a ghostly Roman audience cheering him on, but the toga clad figures faded mutely away into the white marble, leaving Pitt with no answer to his lonely invitation.

He looked up at the maze of stars in the diamond clear air to get his bearings. Polaris blinked its friendly light in return and advertised approximate north. Pitt's eyes scanned a full three hundred and sixty degree circle of sky. Something was wrong. Taurus and the Pleiades should have been overhead. Instead, they were far to the east.

"Goddamn," Pitt cursed aloud, looking at his watch. It was 3:22. Only an hour and eighteen minutes before dawn. Somehow he had lost nearly five hours. What happened, he asked himself, where was the time lost? Then he realized that he must have passed out after colliding with the stairway.

There was no time to lose. He hurriedly walked across the stone paved stage and presently discovered, in the little available light, a small path leading down the mountainside. He took it and set out on a race to beat the sun.

8

A quarter of a mile down the steep slope the pathway turned into a road—no road, really, but two parallel tire-worn indentations in the ground cover. The tracks meandered downward in a tortuous series of hairpin curves. Pitt stumbled along at half trot, his heart pounding viciously under the taxing strain. He was hurt, not badly, but he had lost much blood. Any doctor who might have encountered him would have immediately confined his torn body to a hospital bed.

Over and over, since his escape from the labyrinth, pictures of the defenseless scientists and crew of the *First Attempt* being strafed by the Albatros flashed through Pitt's mind. He could see in perfect detail the bullets tearing into flesh and bone, leaving heavy red blotches on the white paint of the oceanographic research ship. The carnage would all be over before the new interceptor jets at Brady Field could scramble, providing of course the replacement aircraft had arrived from the North Africa depot before dawn. These visions and others drove Pitt on to efforts beyond his normal capacity.

He halted abruptly. Something moved in the shadows ahead. He left the vague trail and circled warily around a thick growth of chestnut trees, creeping closer to the unexpected obstacle. Then he raised up and peered over a fallen, decaying tree-trunk. Even in the

83

dim light there was no mistaking the shape of a well-fed donkey that was tethered to a solitary boulder. The un-attended little animal cocked one ear at Pitt's approach and brayed softly, almost pathetically.

"You're hardly the answer to a jockey's prayer," said Pitt grinning. "But beggars can't be choosy." He untied the lead rope from the rock and quickly made a crude halter. With no little amount of patience he man-aged to push it over the donkey's nose. Then he mounted.

"Okay, mule, giddy up."

The little beast did not move.

Pitt pounded on the stout flanks. Still no move-ment. He kicked, bounced and prodded. Nothing, not even a bray. The long ears laid flat and their obstinate owner refused to budge.

Pitt did not know any Greek words, only a few names. That must be it, he thought. This dumb jackass was probably named after a Greek god or hero.

"Forward Zeus . . . Appollo . . . Poseidon . . . Hercules. How about Atlas?" It seemed as though the donkey had turned to stone. Suddenly an idea occurred to Pitt. He leaned over and inspected his mount's un-derbelly. It was void of exterior plumbing.

"My deepest apologies you gorgeous, ravishing creature," Pitt purred in the pointed ears. "Come my lovely Aphrodite, let us be off."

The donkey twitched and Pitt knew he was getting warm.

"Atlanta?"

Nothing more happened.

"Athena?"

The ears shot up and the donkey turned, looking up at Pitt out of a big confused eyes.

"Come on, Athena, mush!"

Athena, much to Pitt's joy and relief, pawed at the ground a couple of times and then obediently began to amble down the road.

The early morning turned cool, and dew was be-ginning to dampen the forest trimmed meadows when at last Pitt reached the outskirts of Liminas. Liminas was an average Greek coastal village, a unique blend of modern construction built on the site of an ancient city, whose ruins rise here and there among the more recent tile-roofed houses. On the shoreline, jutting into the town with a jagged half-moon curve, a harbor full of flat-beamed fishing boats offered a picturesque travel folder scene with the smells of salt air, fish and diesel oil thrown in. The wooden hulled boats lay dead along the beach like a pack of beached whales, their masts carefully stowed along the gunnels and their anchor ropes stretched loosely to seaward. In rows, behind the white sand beach, high vertical poles stood, supporting long fences of stinking brown fish nets. And, behind those again was the main street of the village, whose shuttered little doors and windows offered no sign of life to the bedraggled Pitt and his plodding four-legged transportation. The white plastered houses with their tiny balconies made a restful real-life painting in the moonlight, a painting that had little bearing on the events which had brought Pitt to the village.

At a narrow intersection Pitt slid off the donkey and tied it to a mailbox. Then he took an American ten dollar bill from his wallet and wrapped it into the halter.

"Thanks for the lift, Athena, and keep the change."

He patted the animal affectionately on the soft rounded nose and, hitching up his disreputable looking pants, walked unsteadily down the street toward the beach.

Pitt looked for the tell-tale lines of a telephone, but could see none. There were no cars or other vehicles parked along the streets either, only a bicycle, but he was too physically drained to consider pedaling the seven miles back to Brady Field. A lot of good it would do, he thought, even if he could find a phone or someone who owned a car, he couldn't speak Greek.

The glowing arms and numbers on the Omega said 3:59. Another hot dawn would hit the island in forty-one minutes. Forty-one minutes to warn Gunn and the men on the *First Attempt*. Pitt looked across the sea, following the inward curve of the Island. If it was seven miles to Brady Field by land, then it was only four miles in a direct line across the water to the ship. There was no time left to loiter, he would simply have to steal a boat. Why not? he reasoned. If he could kidnap a donkey he could pirate a boat.

Within a few minutes he found a well used dory with a high flaring Carvel hull and a rust coated one cylinder gasoline engine. Fumbling in the gloom his fingers found the throttle linkage and the ignition switch. The flywheel was massive and it was all Pitt could do to crank it over. Every aching muscle strained at each silent revolution. Sweat broke from his forehead and dripped on the engine. His head throbbed and blurriness crept into his vision. Time after time he pulled the crank handle rubbing the flesh from his hands. It seemed hopeless; the engine would not fire.

If the need for speed had been vital before; it was desperate now. Precious minutes were running down the drain as he attempted to get the balky engine into action. Pitt reached deep, drawing from the last untapped reservior of his strength. Clenching his teeth he gave a mighty pull. The engine popped briefly and died. He pulled the crank again and slumped exhausted into the oily bilge water. The engine coughed once, then twice, wheezed, coughed again, caught and settled down to a popping thump as the solitary piston began to ram up and down inside its ring-worn sleeve. Too tired to rise, Pitt leaned over and cut the line with the faithful paring knife and kicked the gear lever in reverse. The shabby little boat, its paint peeling down the hull in scaly sheets, chugged backward into the harbor, circled in a hundred and eighty degree arc past the old Roman breakwater and headed out to sea.

Pitt jammed the throttle full against its stop at the dory reeled through the low swells, making perhaps a top speed of seven knots. He hauled himself erect in the stern seat, clutching the tiller tightly between his hands, bleeding from the harsh rasping caused by the rusty crank handle.

A half hour passed, an interminable lapse of time

under a cloudless sky and a brightening east horizon, and still the boat chugged steadily around the island. The progress seemed agonizingly slow to Pitt. But every foot gained was a foot closer to the *First Attempt*. He caught himself dozing off from time to time, head dropping on his chest, then reawakening with a start. He urged his hazy mind on, driving it with a frenzy he didn't know he possessed.

Then his dulled eyes saw it, a low, gray shape, resting beyond the next small point of land, just over a mile away. He recognized the two white, thirty-two point lights on bow and stern that signified a ship at anchor. The probing rays of the sun were rapidly stretching into the sky, clearly silhouetting the *First Attempt* against the eastern horizon; first the superstructure, then the crane and radar mast, then the indiscriminate piles of scientific equipment scattered around the deck.

Pitt talked to the noisy old engine, begging it for more revolutions. The lone cylinder snapped, crackled and popped in reply, turning the warped and bent propeller shaft until it rumbled ominously inside worn and exhausted bearings. The race against the dawn was going to be close.

The hot, orange ball of the sun was barely poking its dome over the watery horizon when Pitt abruptly slowed the little engine, tardily jammed the throttle in reverse and bored clumsily into the side of the *First Attempt*.

"Hello the ship!" Pitt shouted weakly, too fatigued to move.

"You dumb ass," returned an irate voice. "Why don't you watch where you're going?" A shadowed face appeared over the rail and peered down at the dory, bumping against the big ship's hull. "Next time let us know when you're coming so we can paint a target on the side."

In spite of the tension and fiery agony of his wounds, Pitt could not help smiling. "It's too early in the morning for jokes. Can the wisecracks and get down here and give me a hand."

"Why should I?" said the lookout, straining his eyes in the early shadows. "Who the hell are you?"

"I'm Pitt and I'm injured. Now stop screwing around and hurry."

"Is it really you, Major?" the lookout asked hesitantly.

"What the Goddamn hell do you want?" snapped Pitt, "a birth certificate?"

"No, sir." The lookout vanished behind the railing and a moment later reappeared on the boarding ladder with a boathook in one hand. He caught the dory on the aft port gunnel and pulled it to the ladder. Securing a line to the little boat's stern, he leaped on board, caught his foot on a cleat and fell sprawling on top of Pitt.

Pitt clamped his eyes shut, grunting from the impact of the other man's weight. When he opened them again he found himself staring into the yellow beard of Ken Knight.

Knight started to say something, but then he more clearly saw the bloody and ragged body beneath him. The sight of Pitt's condition made the young scientist wince and his face turned ashen. He sat rock-bound in unbelieving shock.

Pitt's lips twisted into a bemused grin. "Don't waste time sitting there like a broken crutch. Help me to Commander Gunn's cabin."

"My God, my God," Knight murmured, shaking his head dazedly and slowly from side to side. "What in the name of God happened?"

"Later," Pitt snapped. "When there's time." He swayed forward onto his hands. "Help me you dumb bastard before it's too late." There was a desperation, a burning fierceness in Pitt's voice that startled Knight into action.

Knight half carried, half dragged Pitt up the ladder and onto the deck. He stopped at Gunn's cabin and kicked at the door. "Open up, Commander Gunn. It's an emergency."

Gunn threw open the door dressed in nothing but a pair of shorts and his horn-rimmed glasses, looking like a confused professor who was just caught in a motel room with the Dean of the University's wife. "What's the meaning . . ." He stopped suddenly, staring at the blood-caked apparition supported by Knight. His brown eyes swelled to immense proportions behind the thick lenses. "My God, Dirk, is that you? What happened?"

Pitt tried to smile again, but it was only a slight curl of his upper lip. "I'm a dropout from hell!" His tone was low, then it came on strongly. "Do you have any meterological equipment on board?"

Gunn didn't answer. Instead, he ordered Knight to get the ship's doctor. Then the bespectacled little skipper led Pitt into the cabin and gently lowered him on the bunk. "Just rest easy, Dirk. We'll have you patched up in no time."

"That's just it, Rudi, there is no time," Pitt said, grasping Gunn's wrists with his ripped hands. "Do you have any meterological equipment on board?" he repeated urgently.

Gunn looked down at Pitt, his eyes reflecting bewilderment. "Yes, we have instruments to record various meteorological data. Why do you ask?"

Pitt's hands released their grip and fell away from Gunn's wrists. A smug cold smile gripped his eyes and spread his lips as he struggled up on his elbows. "This ship is going to be attacked any minute by the same aircraft that raided Brady Field."

"You must be delirious," Gunn said, moving forward to help Pitt sit up.

"My body may look like hell, but my mind at this minute is sharper than yours," Pitt said. "Now listen, and listen closely. Here's what has to be done."

It was the lookout perched on the great A-frame crane, that first spotted the little yellow plane against its vast blue background. Then Pitt and Gunn saw it too, not more than two miles away, flying at eight hundred feet. They should have seen it sooner, but it was coming at the *First Attempt* straight out of the eye of the sun.

"He's ten minutes late," Pitt grunted, holding an arm aloft for a white goateed doctor who worked quickly and skillfully at bandaging his chest.

The elderly physician, oblivious to Pitt's movements on the ship's bridge, cleaned and dressed the raw cuts without bothering to turn and look at the approaching plane. He tied the final knot tightly, making Pitt twinge and display a wry face. "That's the best I can do for you, Major, until you stop running up and down the deck, shouting orders like Captain Bligh."

"Sorry, Doc," Pitt said without taking his eyes from the sky. "But there was no time for a formal office call. You better get below now. If my little battle tactic doesn't work, you're going to do a land office business in about ten minutes."

Without answering, the wiry, deeply tanned doctor closed a large worn leather case, turned and ducked down the bridge ladder.

Pitt drew back from the railing and glanced over at Gunn. "Are you connected?"

"Say when." Gunn was tense, but looked ready and eager. He held a small black box in his hand attached to a wire that led up the radar mast and then into the brilliant morning sky. "Do you think the pilot of the old contraption will take the bait?"

"History never fails to repeat itself." Pitt said confidently, glaring at the nearing plane.

Even in this moment of tense anxiety Gunn found time to marvel at Pitt's complete transformation since dawn: the man who staggered on board the *First Attempt* in such fearful physical condition was not the same man who now stood on the bridge with gleaming eyes and the expectant posture of a war horse inhaling the scent of battle through flaring nostrils. It seemed strange, but Gunn couldn't stop his mind from drifting back many months ago to the bridge of another ship, a tramp steamer called the *Dana Gail*. He remembered as though it was only an hour ago, seeing the same expression on Pitt's face just before the old rusty hulk cast off to find and destroy a mysterious seamount in the Pacific, north of Hawaii. Abruptly he was pulled back to the reality of the present by a strong grip on his arm.

"Get down." Pitt said urgently, "or the shock wave

will blow you overboard. Be ready to join the contacts the instant I give the word."

The bright yellow plane was banking now, circling around the ship, testing it for defenses. The drone of its noisy engine tore across the water, causing a vibration in Pitt's eardrums. He watched it through a pair of borrowed binoculars, smiling with satisfaction as he noted small round patches in the fabric of the wings and fuselage; a record of Giordino's hits with the carbine. Moving the glasses in a near vertical angle he focused on the black wire that led upward, and all at once he felt a hope that began to amount to complete conviction.

"Steady . . . steady," he said quietly. "I think he's going to nibble at the cheese."

The cheese, Gunn thought wonderingly. He calls that damn balloon up there the cheese. Who would have ever thought that Pitt wanted a damn weather balloon when he asked whether the *First Attemp* carried meteorological gear. Now the damn balloon floated up there in the damn sky with a one hundred pound charge of explosives from the damn seismic lab tied to it. Gunn peered above the railing at the big silvery airborne ball and the lethal package dangling beneath it. The cable holding the captive balloon and the electrical wire attached to the explosives both stretched eight hundred feet high and four hundred feet astern; a total distance of four football fields away. He shook his head, it was ironic that the explosive charge, normally utilized for producing underwater shockwaves to analyze the bottom of the sea, would now be used to blow an airplane out of the sky.

The roar of the plane's engine grew louder, and for one brief moment Pitt thought it was going to dive straight-on at the ship, but then he realized that its angle of descent was too low. The pilot was lining the Albatros up for a pass at the balloon. He stood up for a better view, knowing he was a tempting and exposed target. The engine turned into a high pitched snarl and the gun sights aimed for the lazy gas bag, waiting above the sparkling water. There was no delay, no adjusting for range, the yellow wings glistened in the sun, obscuring the flashes from the two guns mounted on the cowling. The sound of the staccato bursts and the whine of the bullets signaled the beginning of the attack.

The rubberized nylon skin of the helium filled bag shuddered under the onslaught of the rapid gunfire. It sagged at first, then wrinkled like a prune and collapsed, flapping in lose folds toward the sea. The yellow Albatros swept over the dropping balloon, making a beeline for the *First Attempt*.

"*Now!*" Pitt yelled, hitting the deck.

Gunn threw the switch.

The next instant seemed to march on to infinity. Then there was a gigantic blast which shook the ship from keel to mast. The early morning silence was shattered with a violent sound like the breaking of a thousand windows by a tornado. And, in the sky, a tower of dense smoke and flame swirled in a huge bursting mass of orange and black. The concussion from the explosion knocked the wind from Pitt and Gunn; squeezing internal organs against spines with the sudden punch of a battering ram.

Slowly, moving with painful stiffness from the tight bandages and struggling for breath, Pitt rose to his feet and peered into the expanding cloud for signs of the Albatros. Shaken for a moment, his eyes darted too high, and he could see nothing but curling smoke; the plane and its pilot were gone. Then he realized what had happened. The brief lag between his shouted signal and the actual explosion saved the plane from instant disintegration. Swinging his gaze down to the horizon he spotted it. The craft was gliding clumsily through the air, its engine dead.

Pitt snatched at the binoculars and quickly sighted them on the Albatros. It was trailing smoke and fiery fragments in a meteoric trail. He watched in morbid fascination as one of the lower wings suddenly folded backward and fell away, causing the plane to tumble in a series of wild gyrations, like a piece of paper thrown from a high office building. Then it seemed to hang suspended for a moment before plunging into the sea, leaving a signature of smoke melting into the warm air.

"It's down," said Pitt excitedly. "We've scored."

Gunn was lying against the far bulkhead corner. He crawled across the deck and lifted his head dazedly. "How far and what heading?"

"About two miles abaft the starboard beam," replied Pitt. He lowered the glasses and looked at Gunn's pale face. "Are you all right?"

Gunn nodded. "Just lost a little wind, that's all."

Pitt smiled, but there was little humor in his eyes. He was smugly satisfied with himself, very pleased with the outcome of his plan. "Send the double-ender and some men out there to dive on the wreck. I'm anxious to find out what our ghost looks like."

"Of course," said Gunn. "I'll personally lead the diving party. But, only on one condition . . . you get your ass down to my cabin immediately. The doc hasn't finished with you yet."

Pitt shrugged, "You're the captain." He turned back to the rail and looked again at the spot that marked the grave of the yellow Albatros.

He was still at the rail ten minutes later when Gunn and four of the *First Attempt's* crew loaded their diving gear on the double-ender whaler and cast off. The little boat made no attempt to circle and search the general surface area but moved straight to the spot where the plane disappeared. Pitt watched until he could see the divers drop into the sparkling blue water at intervals to converge together underwater at the final resting place of the wreck.

"Come along, Major," said a voice at his elbow.

He slowly turned and looked into the face of the bearded doctor. "It's no use chasing me Doc. I won't marry you." Pitt said, a wide grin riding his face.

The blue-eyed old ship's surgeon did not grin back. He merely pointed down the ladder at Gunn's cabin.

Pitt had no choice but to wearily resign himself and turn his battered body over to the doctor's care. In the cabin he fought a half-hearted battle against unconsciousness, but the administered sedatives won a beachhead, and soon he was sheathed in a deep sleep.

9

Pitt stared at the gaunt and repulsive face that echoed his image from a small mirror, hanging in the cabin's head. The black hair dangled down his face and ears, adding an unkempt crown above the deep green eyes that were circled and etched with jagged red blood vessels. He had not slept long; his watch showed a time lapse of only four hours. It was the heat that woke him, the morning blanket of hot air, drifting across the sea from Africa and digging its burning fingers into his skin. He discovered the ventilator that was closed, and he opened it, but the damage was already done. The hot dry air had a head start and the air conditioning would never catch up and cool the cabin, at least not until early evening. He pushed the tap and splashed water over his face, letting the coolness soak into his pores as it dribbled down his back and shoulders.

He briskly dried his damp skin and tried to recall in sequence what had happened the night before. Willie and the Maybach-Zepplin. The villa. Drinking with von Till. Teri's beauty, her paled features. Then the labyrinth, the dog and the escape. Athena; did her owner ever find her? The dory, this morning, the yellow Albatros and the explosion. Now the waiting for Gunn and his crew to salvage the plane and find the body of its mystery pilot. What was the connection with von Till? What was the old kraut's motives. And Teri. Did she know about the trap? Was she trying to warn him? Or, did she bait him into being used and pumped for information by her uncle?

He shook all thoughts and questions from his mind. The bandages itched and he fought the agonizing urge to scratch . . . God, it was hot . . . if only he had a nice cold drink. The only item of clothing the doctor hadn't cut off his body was his shorts. He rinsed them out in the basin and put them on wet. Within minutes they were completely dry.

A light knock came from the door. It slowly swung open and the red-haired cabin boy poked his head around the bulkhead. "Are you awake, Major Pitt?" he queried softly.

"Yes, but just barely." Pitt replied.

"I . . . I didn't mean to bother you," the boy said hesitantly. "The doc asked me to check on you every fifteen minutes to make sure you were resting comfortably."

Pitt threw a withering stare at the cabin boy. "Who the hell can rest comfortably in this furnace with the air conditioning turned off?"

A lost bewildered look crossed the young sunburned face. "Oh my gosh, I'm sorry sir. I thought Commander Gunn left it on."

"What's done is done," Pitt said shrugging. "How about something cold to drink?"

"Would you like a bottle of *FIX*?"

Pitt's eyes narrowed sharply. "A bottle of what?"

"*FIX*. It's a Greek beer."

"All right, if you say so." Pitt couldn't help but grin. "I've heard of taking a fix before, but never drinking one."

"I'll be right back, sir." The boy ducked around the bulkhead and closed the door. Suddenly it jerked open again and the young boy's flaming hair reappeared. "I'm sorry, Major, I almost forgot. Colonel Lewis and Captain Giordino are waiting to see you. The Colonel wanted to bust right in and wake you, but the doc wouldn't hear of it. He even threatened to throw the Colonel off the ship if he tried it."

"All right, send them in," said Pitt with impatience. "Just hurry with the beer before I evaporate."

Pitt lay back on the bunk and let the sweat roll down his body onto the rumpled sheets, sopping the areas that came in contact with his skin. His mind continued to turn, ransacking every detail of the past, assembling for the present, pushing ahead, and plotting future directions.

Lewis and Giordino.

They hadn't wasted any time in coming. If Giordino received an answer from NUMA headquarters, it might help to supply one of the many missing pieces to the puzzle. The four borders were forming, but the middle was a scattered conglomeration of uncertain and unknown quantities. Von Till's evil face leered from the maze, his tight-lipped grin curling in smug disdain. Pitt's mind raced on. The great white dog. He tried to force it into another piece of the puzzle, but it wouldn't fit. That's strange, he thought, the dog doesn't correspond to the piece it's supposed to. For some unfathomable reason he couldn't force the animal between von Till and Kurt Heibert.

Suddenly Lewis burst into the cabin with all the finesse of a sonic boom. His face was red and he was sweating, the tiny beads streamed down his nose and into his moustache where they were absorbed like rain in a forest. "Well now, Major, aren't you sorry you passed up my invitation for dinner?"

Pitt half smiled. "I admit there was a time or two last night when I regretted turning down your scallops." He pointed to the gauze and adhesive tape crisscrossing his chest. "But at least my other dinner engagement gave me a few memories that I can carry for a long, long time."

Giordino stepped from behind Lewis' hulking form and waved a greeting to Pitt. "See what happens every time I let you go out and carouse on your own."

Pitt could see the wide grin on Giordino's face, but he also noticed a fraternal look of concern in his friend's eyes. "Next time, Al, I'll send you in my place."

Giordino laughed. "Don't do me any favors if you're a living example of the morning after."

Lewis parked his bulk heavily in a chair facing the bunk. "God, it's hot in here. Don't these damn floating museums carry air conditioning?"

Pitt enjoyed a tinge of sadistic pleasure at Lewis' steaming discomfort. "Sorry, Colonel, the unit must be overtaxed. I have beer coming that should help make the heat a bit more endurable."

"Right now," Lewis snorted, "I'd even settle for a glass of Ganges River water."

Giordino leaned over the bunk. "For chrissakes, Dirk, what mischief did you get yourself into after you left us last night? Gunn's radio message said something about a mad dog."

"I'll tell you," said Pitt, "But first I need a couple of questions answered myself." He looked at Lewis. "Colonel, do you know Bruno von Till?"

"Do I know von Till?" Lewis repeated. "Only slightly. I was introduced to him once and have seen him occasionally at parties given by the local dignitaries, but that's about all. From what I gather, he's something of a mystery."

"Do you, by chance, know what his business is?" Pitt asked hopefully.

"He owns a small fleet of ships." Lewis paused for a moment, closing his eyes in thought. Then they shot open, transmitting a look of sudden recollection, "Minerva, yes that's it, Minerva Lines: the name of the fleet."

"I've never heard of it," Pitt murmured.

"Small wonder," snorted Lewis. "Judging from the decrepit rust buckets I've seen smoking by Thasos, I doubt whether anyone else knows of its existence either."

Pitt's eyes narrowed. "Von Till's ships cruise along the Thasos coastline?"

Lewis nodded. "Yes, one passes every week or so. They're easy to spot; they all have a big yellow 'M' painted on the smoke funnels."

"Do they anchor off shore or dock at Liminas?"

Lewis shook his head. "Neither. Every ship I've bothered to notice came from the south, circled the island and reversed course south again."

"Without stopping?"

"They lie-to for perhaps half-an-hour, no more, right off the point by the old ruins."

Pitt raised up out of the bunk. He looked questioningly at Giordino, then Lewis. "That's odd."

"Why?" asked Lewis lighting a cigar.

"Thasos is at least five hundred miles north of the main Suez Canal shipping lanes," Pitt said slowly. "Why should von Till send his ships on a thousand mile detour?"

"I don't know," Giordino said impatiently. "And frankly, I could care even less. Why not stop this verbal screwing around and tell us about your nocturnal escapades? What has this von Till character got to do with last night?"

Pitt stood and stretched, wincing from the stiff soreness. His mouth had a sand and gravel taste; he could not recall when his throat had been so dry before. Where was that dumb kid with the beer? Pitt caught sight of Giordino's cigarettes, and he motioned for one. He lit it and inhaled, increasing the rotten taste in his mouth.

He shrugged, smiling wryly. "OK, I'll give it to you from beginning to end, but please feel free to stare at me like I'm crazy; I'll understand."

In the heat tortured cabin, the steel walls almost too hot to touch, Pitt told his story. He held nothing back, not even a thin belief that Teri had somehow betrayed him to von Till. Lewis nodded thoughtfully on occasion but made no comment; his mind seemed to linger elsewhere, returning only when Pitt graphically described an event. Giordino paced the small cubicle unhurriedly, leaning slightly against the slow rolling of the ship.

When Pitt finished, no one spoke. Ten seconds passed, twenty, then thirty. The atmosphere had turned

humid from perspiration and rapidly became stale from
cigar and cigarette smoke.

"I know," Pitt said a little tiredly. "It sounds like a
fairy tale and makes very little sense. But, that's exactly
the way it happened, I left nothing out."

"Daniel in the lion's den," Lewis said flatly, without inflection. "I admit, what you've told us seems far
fetched, but the facts have a strange way of bearing you
out." He pulled a handkerchief from a hip pocket and
dabbed it across his forehead. "You were correct in predicting that the antique plane would attack this ship,
and you even knew when."

"Von Till supplied me with a hint. The rest was
conjecture."

"I can't figure the weird set-up," said Giordino.
"Using an old bi-plane to shoot up the sea and landscape merely to get rid of the *First Attempt* seems
overly complicated."

"Not really," said Pitt. "It soon became obvious to
von Till that his sabotage attempts on the scientific operations of NUMA's expedition were not succeeding
according to plan."

"What crossed him up?" Giordino inquired.

"Gunn was stubborn," Pitt grinned evenly. "In spite
of what he thought were accidents and setbacks due to
natural causes, he refused to weigh anchor and give up."

"Good for him," Lewis grunted, and cleared his
throat to speak, but Pitt went on unruffled.

"Von Till had to find another direction. Using the
old aircraft was a stroke of genius. If he had sent a
modern jet fighter to attack Brady Field, all hell would
have broken out in the form of an international crisis.
The Greek Government, the Russians, the Arabs; all
would have become involved, and this whole island
would have been teeming with military personnel on
emergency alert. No, von Till was smart: the antique
Albatros caused our government some embarrassment
and cost the Air Force a few million dollars, but spared
everyone a diplomatic mess and an armed conflict."

"Very interesting, Major." Lewis' voice was flat,

skeptical. "Very interesting . . . and most instructional. But would you mind answering a question that's been nagging the back of my mind?"

"What is it, sir?" It was the first time Pitt had addressed Lewis as sir, and he found it strangely distasteful.

"Just what are these seagoing eggheads looking for that brought this rotten business down around our heads?"

"A fish," Pitt replied grinning.

Lewis' eyes widened and he almost dropped his cigar on his huge lap. "A what?"

"A fish," Pitt repeated. "It's nick-named *Teaser;* a rare species reported to be a living fossil. Gunn assures me that landing one would be the greatest scientific achievement of the decade." Pitt supposed wryly that he was overdoing it a bit, but he was irritated by Lewis' blustering pompousness.

Lewis' face was not pleasant as he rose trembling from his chair. "You mean to say that I have fifteen million dollars' worth of wrecked aircraft scattered over a base under my personal command, my military career all but ruined, and all because of a goddamned fish?"

Pitt tried his best to look serious. "Yes, Colonel, I guess you might say that."

A saddened look of absolute defeat gripped Lewis' features as he shook his head from side to side. "My God, my God, it's not fair, it's just not . . ."

He was interrupted by a knock on the metal door. The cabin boy entered, carrying a tray containing three brown bottles.

"Keep them coming," Pitt ordered. "And, keep them cold."

"Yes sir," the boy mumbled. He set the tray down on the desk and hurried from the cabin.

Giordino passed Lewis a beer. "Here Colonel, drink up and forget the damage to Brady. The taxpayers will absorb the cost anyway."

"In the meantime I'll probably suffer a coronary," Lewis said gloomily. He sat back down in the chair, collapsing like a leaky inner tube.

Pitt held up the ice frosted bottle and rolled its cold surface across his forehead. The red and silver label was stuck on crooked. He stared idly at the reversed printing that proudly proclaimed: *BY APPOINTMENT TO THE ROYAL GREEK COURT*.

"Where do we go from here?" Giordino said between gulps.

Pitt shrugged, "I'm not sure yet. A lot depends on what Gunn finds in the wreckage of the *Albatros*."

"Any idea?"

"None at the moment."

Giordino mashed his cigarette into an ashtray. "If nothing else, I'd say we're well ahead of the game, especially compared to this time yesterday. Thanks to you our ghost from World War I is kaput, and we have a pretty good lead on the instigator behind the attacks. All we have to do now is have the Greek authorities pick up von Till."

"Not good enough," Pitt said thoughtfully. "That would be the same as a district attorney demanding the indictment of a suspect for murder who had no motive. No, there has to be a reason, not a valid one in our eyes necessarily, but still a reason for all this intrigue and destruction."

"Whatever the cause, it isn't treasure."

Pitt stared at Giordino. "I'd forgotten to ask. Did Admiral Sandecker send a reply to your message?"

Giordino dropped an emptied bottle in a wastebasket. "It came through this morning, just before the Colonel and I left Brady Field for the *First Attempt*." He paused, gazing up at a fly walking across the ceiling. Then he belched.

"Well?" Pitt grunted impatiently.

"The Admiral had a crew of ten men pour through the national Archives on a crash research program. When they were finished they all agreed on the same conclusion: there is no recorded document anywhere that indicates shipwrecked treasure near the Thasos coastline."

"Cargos, could any of the recorded wrecked vessels have carried valuable cargo?"

"Nothing worth mentioning," Giordino pulled a slip of paper from his breast pocket. "The Admiral's secretary dictated over the radio the names of all the ships that were lost on or around Thasos in the last two hundred years. The list isn't impressive."

Pitt wiped the salty sting of sweat from his eyes. "Let's have a sample."

Giordino set the list on his knees and began reading aloud in a rapid monotone. "*Mistral*, French frigate, sunk 1753. *Clara G.*, British coal collier, sunk 1856. *Admiral DeFosse*, French ironclad, sunk 1872. *Scyla*, Italian brig, sunk 1876. *Daphne*, British gunboat . . ."

"Skip to 1915," Pitt interrupted.

"*H.M.S. Forshire*, British cruiser, sunk by German shore batteries on the mainland, 1915. *Von Schroder*, German destroyer, sunk by British warship, 1916. *U-19*, German submarine, sunk by British aircraft, 1918."

"No need to continue," Pitt said yawning. "Most of the lost wrecks on your list were warships. The chances are slim that one of them might have carried a king's ransom in gold."

Giordino nodded. "As the boys in Washington said, 'no recorded documents of sunken treasure'."

The talk over treasure brought an alert gleam in Lewis' eyes. "What about ancient Greek or Roman vessels?" Most records wouldn't go back that far."

"That's true," said Giordino. "But, as Dirk previously pointed out, Thasos is a long way off the beaten shipping paths. The same holds true for the trade routes of antiquity."

"But if there is a fortune under our feet," Lewis persisted, "and von Till found it, he'd most certainly keep it a secret."

"There's no law against finding sunken treasure." Giordino exhaled two streams of smoke through his nose. "Why bother to hide it?"

"Greed," said Pitt. "Insane greed; wanting one hundred percent, refusing to share with others or having to pay the government under which the riches were found any taxes or assessments."

"Considering the huge cut most governments demand," Lewis said angrily, "I can't say as I'd blame von Till for keeping the discovery a secret."

The cabin boy came and went, leaving three more bottles of beer. Giordino downed his with one tilt of the head and then dropped the empty bottle beside its mate in the wastebasket. "This whole game is like a bad deal," he complained. "I don't like it."

"I don't like it either," Pitt said quietly. "Every logical avenue winds up in a cul-de-sac. Even this talk about treasure is meaningless. I tried to bait von Till into admitting he was after treasure, but the wily old bastard offered no indication of interest. He's trying to hide something, but it's not sunken gold bullion or lost diamonds." He broke off and pointed out a porthole across the sea where Thasos slept under the rising heat waves. "The solution lies elsewhere, either near the island, or on it, or maybe, both. We'll soon know more when Gunn raises the Albatros and its occupant."

Giordino, both hands clasped behind his head, leaned his chair back on two legs. "By all rights, we could leave now and be back in Washington this time tomorrow. Since the mysterious renegade plane is destroyed, and we know who instigated the accidents on board the *First Attempt,* things should settle back to normal. I see no reason why we can't pack up and head for home." He threw Lewis an indifferent look. "I'm certain the Colonel can handle any further emergencies that might crop up on Brady Field."

"You can't leave now!" Lewis was sweating heavily, his breath in gasps, barely controlling his temper. "I'll contact Admiral Sandecker and have. . ."

"Don't worry, Colonel," Gunn interrupted from the doorway. He had pushed the cabin door open silently and now stood leaning against the bulkhead. "Major Pitt and Captain Giordino won't be leaving Thasos just yet."

Pitt looked up quickly, expectantly. There was no elated expression on Gunn's face, it merely reflected a mixture of blank nothingness and dejection. It was the face of a man who ceased to care. The small bone structure showed through the shoulders, drooped from exhaustion, and the skin glistened with drops of salt water that clung to the body hair in tiny droplets. He wore nothing but the ever present horn-rimmed glasses and a European style black bikini that did little to enhance the slender frame it covered. Four straight hours of diving had left Gunn exhausted, every bone, every muscle begging for relief.

"Sorry Sir," Gunn mumbled softly. "Bad news I'm afraid."

"For God's sake, Rudi," Pitt asked, "What is it? Weren't you able to raise the plane and recover the pilot's body?"

"Gunn shrugged his thin shoulders. "Neither."

"As bad as that?" Pitt queried, voice and face deadly serious.

"Worse," Gunn replied grimly.

"Let's have it."

For almost thirty seconds, Gunn remained silent. The others in the cabin could hear the faint creaking noises of the ship, rolling in the gentle swells of the Mediterranean, and see the tightening of Gunn's mouth.

"Believe me, we tried," Gunn said wearily. "We used every underwater search trick in the book, but we couldn't locate the wreck." He gestured helplessly with his hands. "It was gone, vanished, God knows where."

10

"The Thasians were great lovers of the theatre, considering it a vital part of their education, and everyone, including the town beggar, was encouraged to come. In the ancient city of Thasos, during the premieres of new dramas from the mainland, all shops were closed, all business ceased and prisoners were released from jail. Even the city's whores, barred from most public events, were allowed to practice their trade in the shrubbery by the theatre gateways without fear of legal harassment."

The swarthy Greek National Tourist Organization guide paused his spiel, curling his lip in a pleased grin at the horrified expressions on the faces of the female tourists. It was always the same, he thought. The women whispering in put-on embarrassment while the men, draped in bermuda shorts and festooned with light meters and cameras, guffawed and poked each other's ribs in unison with know-it-all winks.

The guide twisted the end of his magnificent moustache and studied his group more closely. There was the usual sprinkling of fat retired businessmen and their fat wives, viewing the ruins, not for historical interest but rather to impress their friends and neighbors at home. His eyes wandered over four young school teachers from Alhambra, California. Three were plain looking, wore glasses and giggled constantly. It was the fourth girl who attracted his attention. Excellent possibilities. Large protruding breasts, red hair, long legs—like most Americans—and quite shapely. The kind of eyes that flirt and suggest better things to come. Later tonight he would invite *her* on a private moonlight tour of the ruins.

The guide pulled at the lapels of a tight jacket and tucked the bottom neatly under a bright red cummerbund.

Slowly, with a professional kind of carelessness, he turned his gaze toward the rear of the little crowd, stopping it uneasily on two men who leaned indifferently against a fallen column. A tougher, more battered and villainous pair of hard cases he had never seen. The short one with the puffed out chest, obviously an Italian, looked more like an ape than a man. The taller brute with the piercing green eyes, carried himself with an air of sureness and sophistication, yet there was an aura about him that advertised "Caution: highly dangerous." The guide twisted his moustache again. German most likely. Must love to fight judging from the bandages on the nose and hands. Strange, most strange, the guide mused. Why would those two take a dull tour of old ruins? Probably a pair of sailors who jumped ship. Yes, that must be it, he suggested to himself smugly.

"This theatre was excavated in 1952," the guide went on, flashing a set of bright teeth. "So buried under centuries of silt washed off the mountain that it took two years to reveal it all. Please notice the geometric mosaic of the orchestra floor. It was fashioned from naturally colored pebbles and signed *Coenus Set It*." He hesitated a moment, letting his flock of excursionists study the floral design of the worn and faded tiles. "Now, if you will follow me up the stairway to your left, we will take a short walk over the next mound to the Shrine of Poseidon."

Pitt, playing the part of a tired and worn out sightseer, feigned exhaustion and sat down on the steps, watching the rest of the tour climb the granite stairway until their heads disappeared beyond the top. Four-thirty, his watch read. Four-thirty. Exactly three hours since he and Giordino left the *First Attempt* and casually strolled into Liminas, joining the guided tour of the ancient ruins. Now he and Giordino . . . the little Captain was impatiently pacing the stone floor beside him, clutching a small flight bag . . . waited a few more minutes, making absolutely sure the tour was continuing without them. Satisfied that they weren't missed, he silently motioned to Giordino and pointed toward the stage entrance of the amphitheatre.

For the hundredth time, Pitt tugged at the irritating chest bandage, thought about the ship's doctor and grinned in self amusement. Permission to leave the ship and return to von Till's villa had been firmly denied by the bearded doctor, and by Gunn too. But when Pitt insisted that, if necessary, he was ready to fight the entire ship's crew and swim back to Liminas, the old physician had thrown up his hands in defeat and stormed from the cabin. So far, paying for the wine while killing time in a small *taverna*, waiting for the sightseeing trip to begin, was his only contribution to the backdoor reconnaissance of the villa. It was Giordino who had cursed and sweated over the huge lump of rust attached to the dory's propeller shaft, trying to crank it to life. And it was Giordino who nursed the weather-beaten derelict back to the harbor at Liminas. Fortunately the old boat had not been missed . . . no irate owner or local police officer waited on the beach to punish the yankee pirates for boat theft. To tie the dory up to its original mooring and walk across the beach to the main part of town took only a few minutes. Pitt, certain it was a waste of time, led Giordino a block out of their way to see if Athena was still attached to the corner mailbox. The donkey was gone, but immediately across the narrow street, over a neat little white plastered office building, a sign, lettered in English, advertised the Greek National Tourist Organization. The rest was simple; joining a tour, whose itinerary included the amphitheatre, and mingling with a group of sightseers, offered the perfect cover for reaching the labyrinth and gaining entrance to von Till's retreat without detection.

Giordino rubbed a sleeve across his damp brow.

"Breaking and entering in the middle of the afternoon. Why can't we wait until dark like any other honorable burglars?"

The sooner we nail von Till, the better." Pitt said sharply. "If he's off balance from the destruction of the Albatros this morning, the last thing he would expect is a resurrected Dirk Pitt in broad daylight."

Giordino could easily feel and see the revenge in Pitt's eyes. He remembered watching Pitt move slowly, painfully, as best he could, over the steep trail through the ruins without complaint. He had also watched the bitterness, the hopelessness that took and held Pitt's face after Gunn announced the disappearance of the mystery plane. There was something ominous about Pitt's grim features and unmoving concentration. Giordino wondered dimly whether Pitt was driving himself with a sense of duty or with an insane compulsion for retaliation.

"You're sure this is the right way. It might be simpler to. . ."

"This is the only way," Pitt interrupted. "The Albatros wasn't eaten by a whale, yet it vanished without leaving a stray nut or bolt. Knowing the identity of the pilot could have settled a number of loose ends. We have no choice. The only course that lies open is to search the villa."

"I still think we should take a squad of Air Police," Giordino said morosely, "and crash in through the front door."

Pitt looked at him, then looked once more over his shoulder up the stairway. He knew exactly how Al Giordino felt, for he felt the same way himself . . . frustrated, unsure, grasping at every string that offered a small touch of hope for obtaining an answer, no matter how small, to the strange events of the past few days. Much depended on the next hour; whether they could enter the villa unseen, whether they found evidence against von Till, whether Teri was a willful member of her uncle's, as yet unknown, scheme. Pitt glanced at Giordino again, saw the set brown eyes, the grim mouth, the knotted hands, saw all the signs of an intense mental concentration; concentration on the possible dangers that lay ahead. There was no better man to have on your side when the odds were long.

"I can't seem to pound it through your thick head," he said quietly. "This is Greek soil. We have no legal right to invade a private residence. I couldn't begin to think of the problems it would cause our government if we broke in von Till's door. As it is now, if we're caught by the Greek authorities, we'll play the roles of a couple of crewmen from the *First Attempt* who wandered into the underground passage during a guided tour to sleep off a shore leave drunk. They should buy that, they have no reason not to."

"That's why we're not packing any weapons?"

"You guessed it, we'll have to risk a disadvantage to save a possible predicament." Pitt halted at the crumbling archway. The iron grillwork looked different in the daylight, not nearly so massive and indomitable as he remembered it. "This is the place," he said, his fingers idly flaking a spot of dried blood from one of the rusting bars.

"You squeezed through that?" Giordino asked incredulously.

"It was nothing," Pitt replied broadly grinning. "Just another one of my many accomplishments." The grin quickly faded. "Hurry, we don't have much time. The next tour will be through here in another forty-five minutes."

Giordino stepped up to the heavy bars and within seconds was a man absorbed with a difficult and hazardous job to do. He opened the flight bag and carefully removed the contents, laying them out in order on an old towel. Quickly, he fitted two small charges of T.N.T. around a single bar, spacing them twenty inches apart, inserted the primer and heavily wrapped each charge under several layers of metal plumbers tape. Next he spun strands of heavy wire around the bulbous bands and then covered the wire with more layers of thick adhesive tape. A final look at the charges, imbedded in the thick wrappings like cocoons, and he connected the wires to the detonator. Obviously pleased with his handwork, the entire operation had taken less than six minutes from start to finish, he motioned Pitt toward the safety of a wide block retaining wall. Slowly Giordino followed, walking backward, playing out wires leading from the detonator to the charges. At the wall, Pitt grasped him on the arm to draw his attention.

"How far will the explosion be heard?"

"If I did it right," Giordino replied, "it shouldn't sound any louder than a popgun to someone standing a hundred feet away."

Pitt stood on the lower base of the wall and hurriedly scanned a three hundred and sixty degree circle of landscape. Seeing no sign of human activity, he nodded, grinning at Giordino. "I hope dropping in uninvited through the service entrance isn't beneath your dignity."

"We Giordinos are pretty broadminded," he said, returning Pitt's grin.

"Shall we?"

"If you insist."

They both ducked below the top of the old wall, holding the sun-warmed stones with their hands to absorb any shock. Then Giordino turned the little plastic switch on the detonator.

Even at the short distance of ten or fifteen feet the sound of the explosion was nothing more than a mere thump. No shock wave trembled the ground, no black cloud of smoke or shooting flame belched from the archway, no deafening blast rattled their eardrums, only a small undefinable thump.

Swiftly, in a silence bred of expectancy, they leaped to their feet and rushed back to the iron gate. The two balls of tape were torn and smoldering, smelling like the burned out pungent odor of frizzled firecrackers. A tiny curl of smoke wound in a snake-like trail between the grill and disappeared into the damp darkness of the interior passage. The bar was still in place.

Pitt looked questioningly at Giordino. "Not enough punch?"

"It was ample," Giordino said confidently. "The charges were the right size to do the job. Please observe." He gave the bar a vigorous kick with his heel. It remained solid, unyielding. He kicked it again, this time harder, his mouth tight from a jolting pain in his heel and sole. The top end of the bar broke loose, bending its jagged and torn tip inward until it lay on a horizontal plane. A tense smile creased Giordino's mouth and his teeth slowly spread into view. "And now for my next trick. . ."

"Never mind," Pitt snapped brusquely. "Let's get the hell going. We've got to get to the villa and back in time to join the next tour."

"How long will it take to get there?"

Pitt was already climbing through the opening in the gate. "Last night it took me eight hours to get out, we can get in in eight minutes."

"How, you got a map?"

"Something even better," Pitt said quietly, almost grimly, pointing at the flight bag. "Pass me the light."

Giordino reached into the bag, pulled out a large yellow light, nearly six inches in diameter, and passed it through the opening. "It's big enough. What is it?"

"Allen Dive Bright. Aluminum casing is waterproof to a nine hundred foot depth. We're not going diving, but it's rugged and throws out a long narrow beam, backed by one hundred and eight thousand candlepower. That's why I borrowed it from the ship."

Giordino said no more, merely shrugged and slipped between the bars, following Pitt into the passage. "Hold on a second till I remove the evidence."

Giordino's stubby hands nimbly unwound the shredded wrappings—a pile of old fallen stones covered the smoldering remains—before he turned to face Pitt, squinting his eyes until they became accustomed to the dim light.

Pitt played his light into the darkness. "Look there on the ground. See why I don't need the services of a detailed map?"

The powerful beam spotlighted a broken trail of

dried and caked blood leading down the steep uneven
stairway. In a few places the red stains lay in scattered
clusters, separated by occasional tiny round specks. Pitt
descended the steps shivering, not so much from the
sight of his old and discarded blood, but from the sudden change in temperature from the outside afternoon
heat to the damp chill of the musty labyrinth. At the
bottom he took off at a half trot, the swaying light in his
hand casting a series of bouncing shadows that leaped
from the crack-lined ceiling to the rough hewn rock
floor. The loneliness and the fear that gripped him the
night before was not present. Giordino, that indestruct-
able sawed-off package of muscle, a trusted friend for
many years, was beside him now. Damned if anyone or
any barrier would stop him this time, he thought
doggedly.

Passage after passage, like gaping mouths in the
shadows slipped by. Pitt kept his eyes trained on the
ground, analyzing the dark red spots. At the honeycombed intersections he paused briefly, studying the
trail. If the blood led up a tunnel and then returned it
meant a dead end. Wherever the course indicated a single line he pursued it. His body was aching and his vision was hazy at the outer edges; a bad sign. He was
bone tired and felt it to the deadening tips of every
nerve ending. Pitt stumbled and would have gone down,
but Giordino grabbed his arm in a wrench-like grip,
holding him erect.

"Take it easy, Dirk," Giordino said firmly, his
voice followed by a faint echo. "No sense in overdoing
it. You're not in condition to play All American hero."

"It's not far," Pitt said heavily. "The dog should
lie around the next couple of bends."

But the dog was gone. Only the hardened blood
pools remained where the great white animal had
thrashed out the final moments of life. Pitt stared
mutely at the huge stains. The dank odor of blood permeated the passageway, adding to, but not quite over-
coming, the musty atmosphere. He vividly recreated the
attack in his mind; the dog's gleaming eyes, the leap in

the dark, the knife sinking into warm flesh, and the agonized animal howl.

"Keep going," Pitt said grimly, all weariness forgotten. "The entrance is only another eighty feet."

They plunged on amid the black depths of the mountain. Pitt didn't bother to watch the blood trail, he knew where he was to the inch: he so thoroughly recalled the feel of the walls and floor that he would have been completely confident of finding the door at a dead run without the flashlight and in absolute darkness. The light in his hand swayed in wild arcs as they pounded along into the modern corridor construction.

Suddenly the Dive Brite's beam probed the massive door, holding it in a dazzling circle of light.

"This is it," Pitt said softly between labored gasps for breath.

Giordino pushed his way past and knelt to the ground, examining the inside bolts. He wasted no time; already his fingers were probing the slight crack that separated the door from the frame molding.

"Goddamn," he grunted.

"What is it?"

"Big sliding latch on the outside. I don't have the equipment to jimmy it from this side."

"Try the hinges," Pitt murmured. He aimed the light toward the opposite side of the door. Almost before he said it, Giordino had snatched a short pointed bar from the flight bag and was prying the long pins from their rusty shafts.

Giordino laid the hinge pins lightly on the ground and let Pitt ease the door open. It swung noiselessly, only an inch, at his touch. Pitt peeked through the widening crack, taking a swift look around, but there was no one in sight, no sound, except their own breathing.

Pitt pulled the door aside and dashed across the balcony, blinking in the harsh sunlight, and hurried up the stairway. Giordino, he knew, was right on his heels. The doorway to the study was open, the drapes blowing inward in billowing folds from an offshore westerly breeze. He flattened against the wall, listening for voices. Then seconds passed, ticking off to half a minute. The study was quiet. Nobody home, he thought, or if they are they're an awfully dead group. Pitt took a deep breath, turned quickly, and stepped inside the room.

The study seemed quite empty. It was exactly as Pitt remembered it; the columns, classic furniture, the bar. His eyes sped around the room, stopping at the shelf containing the model submarine. He walked over and closely examined the workmanship on the miniature craft. The carved black mahogany that made up the hull and conning tower gleamed with a satin-like sheen. Every detail from the rivets to a tiny embroidered Imperial German battle flag looked fantastically real, so much so that at any second Pitt half expected to see a diminutive crew leap out of a hatch and man the deck gun. The neatly painted numbers on the side of the conning tower identified it as the U-19, a close sister of the U-boat that torpedoed the *Lusitania*.

Pitt whirled sharply from the model as Giordino's fingers dug deeply in his arm, as Giordino's head leaned closely to his own.

"I thought I heard something," the voice was a mere breath.

"Where?" Pitt asked in a whisper.

"I'm not sure, I couldn't get a good fix on it." Giordino cocked his head, listening. Then he shrugged. "Just imagining things I guess."

Pitt turned back to the model submarine. "Do you recall the number of the World War I sub that was sunk near here?"

Giordino hesitated. "Yeah . . . It was the U-19. Why ask now?"

"I'll explain later. Come on, Al, let's get the hell out of here."

"We just got here," Giordino complained, raising his voice to a murmur.

Pitt tapped the model. "We've found what we came for . . ."

He froze into sudden immobility, listening, his hand motioning a silence signal to Giordino.

"We've got company," he said under his breath. "Split up and circle around the far end of the room to that second column. I'll go along the windows."

Giordino nodded. He hadn't even raised an eyebrow.

A minute later their stealthy paths met, joining behind a long high backed sofa. Both men approached it cautiously and peered over the backrest.

Without moving, without uttering a word, Pitt stood rooted to the carpet. He stood there, it seemed to Giordino, for an eternity, his mind absorbing the shock of seeing Teri peacefully asleep on the sofa. But it was no eternity, it was probably only five seconds before Pitt acted.

Teri lay curled in a ball, her head resting on a huge humped armrest, her black hair falling in piles, nearly touching the floor. She wore a long red negligee that fluffed about her arms and covered her body from neck to toe, teasingly displaying the dark triangle below her belly and the two pink discs of her breasts through its diaphanous material. Pitt whipped out his handkerchief and had it firmly stuffed in her mouth before she fully woke. Then snatching the hem of her negligee he yanked it above her head and knotted it around the arms, making her completely helpless. Teri began to struggle back to full consciousness—it was too late. Before she could fully grasp what was happening, she was roughly thrown over Giordino's shoulder and carted off into the sunlight.

"You've got to be crazy," Giordino mumbled irritably when they reached the stairway. "All this hassle to gawk at a toy and steal a broad."

"Shut up and run," Pitt said without turning. He kicked the passage door aside and let Giordino enter first with his kicking burden. Then Pitt pushed the door back into place, aligning the hinge shafts before inserting the pins.

"Why bother replacing the door?" Giordino asked impatiently.

"We got this far without detection," Pitt replied,

grabbing the flight bag. "I want to keep von Till in the dark as long as possible. I'm betting he saw the obvious evidence of my wounds after the dog's attack, and thinks I wandered off into this honeycombed maze and bled to death."

Quickly, Pitt turned and ran through the corridor, holding the light low so Giordino, grunting under his struggling burden, could see where he was stepping. The thick coat of blackness, pierced by the small island of incandescence, opened briefly at their approach and then closed, returning the labyrinth back to its eternal night. One foot before the other, the endless routine repeated over and over. Their feet pounded across the hard floor, echoing through the darkness with a peculiar hollow sound.

The Dive Brite and flight bag clutched tightly in his hands, only dimly aware of the curious tingling in the pit of his stomach, Pitt rushed forward. Rapidly, with no attempt at stealthy caution, no expectancy of trouble, but with that strange inner sensation, half-belief of a man who has accomplished something he had thought was impossible. I'm on the path of von Till's secret and I've got his niece, Pitt said to himself again and again. But somehow a lingering fear prodded his mind.

Five minutes later they reached the stairway. Pitt stepped aside, holding the light on the steps, letting Giordino climb first. Then he turned, beaming the light back in the passage, taking a last look, and his face became grim. He wondered how few men and women too, had suffered but escaped from that honeycombed hell. One thing, he thought, no one will ever know fully the history of the labyrinth. Only the ghosts lingered, the bodies had long since turned to dust. Then his mouth twisted and he looked away. Without another backward glance, he mounted the steps for the last time, vastly relieved at seeing sunlight again at the top landing. He was half-way through the rusting bars, vaguely aware that Giordino was standing oddly quiet with Teri still slung over a shoulder, when he heard a loud contemptuous laugh roar beside the archway.

"My compliments, gentlemen, on your exquisite taste in souvenirs. However, I feel it is my patriotic duty to inform you that the theft of valuable objects from historical sites is strictly forbidden under Greek law."

11

Pitt froze while his mind raced to absorb the shock. He stood there, one leg outside, the other bent awkwardly inside the passage for what seemed to him a lifetime. He threw the Dive Brite and the flight bag behind him down the stairway and then squinted, waiting for his eyes to adjust to the bright sunlight: he could barely discern a vague, formless shape that detached itself from the low stone wall and moved in front of him.

"I . . . I don't understand," Pitt mumbled dumbly, feigning a peasant kind of stupidity. "We're not thieves."

Again the resounding laugh. And the blurred form transformed into the Greek National Tourist Organization guide who wore a broad, white toothed smile beneath his great moustache; a swarthy hand gripped a nine millimeter Clisenti automatic pistol, the barrel aimed directly at Pitt's heart.

"Not thieves," the guide said sarcastically in faultless English. "Then kidnapers perhaps?"

"No, no," pleaded Pitt, a forced tremor in his voice. "We're only two lonely seamen on shore leave in a strange land having a bit of fun." He winked and grinned a knowing grin. "You understand."

"Yes, I understand perfectly." The gun remained level and steady as a rock. "That is why you are under arrest."

118

Pitt could feel a knot deep down under in his stomach, the dry, sandy taste of defeat in his mouth. God, this was a worse set-back than he had feared: it could be the end of everything, a trial and then expulsion from the country. He kept the stupid, insipid expression on his face. Then he stepped forward from the gate, making an imploring gesture with his hands.

"You must believe me. We haven't kidnapped anybody. Look," he said pointing to Teri's upended and naked bottom. "This woman is nothing but a village whore we found wallowing in a pig sty of a *taverna*. She told us to take the tour of the ruins, promising to meet us at the amphitheatre."

The guide looked amused. He reached out with his free hand and fingered the material of Teri's negligee, than ran his finger tips lightly over her smooth, rounded mounds, triggering a spasm of thrashing legs and feet.

"Tell me," he said slowly. "How much did she charge?"

"At first she asked two drachmas," said Pitt sullenly. "But after the fun and games she tried to hold us up for twenty drachmas. We, of course, refused to pay."

"Of course," the guide replied dully.

"He speaks the truth," burst Giordino, the words rushed as if he couldn't get them out fast enough. "This dirty tramp is the thief, not us."

"A masterly performance," said the guide. "A pity it is wasted on such a small audience. We Greeks may lead simple, mundane lives compared to you of more sophisticated countries, but we do not possess simple minds." He gestured the gun toward Teri. "This girl is no cheap prostitute. Expensive maybe, but not cheap. Her skin also makes you out a liar, it's far too white. Our island girls are famous for their rich, dark texture and full hips. Hers are much too narrow."

Pitt said nothing. He watched the guide carefully, waiting for an opening. Any movement on his part, he knew, would trigger Giordino into instantaneous action. The Greek looked a dangerous man, cunning and alert, but there was no hint of sadistic antagonism that Pitt could see in the dark, sun wrinkled features. The guide beckoned to Giordino.

"Release the girl, let us have a look at her other end."

Giordino, without taking his eyes off Pitt, slowly dropped Teri, letting her slide down his shoulder to the ground. She stood drunkenly for a moment, unsure of her balance, arms upraised in their trapped position, and swaying like a giant tulip in the wind until Giordino untied the knotted negligee above her head. As soon as she was free, Teri tore the gag from her mouth and stared at Giordino with white hot hatred in her eyes.

"You bloody, rotten bastard," she screamed. "What's the meaning of this?"

"It wasn't my idea, sweetheart," said Giordino, his eyebrows arching slyly. "Talk to your friend over there." He jerked his thumb towards Pitt.

Her head spun in Pitt's direction, and she opened her mouth to say something, but choked off the words with a gasp. The big hazel eyes reflected astonishment for an instant, then they changed with blinking speed to icy coldness, then to a glowing twinkle of warmth. She threw her arms about Pitt and kissed him fervently, too fervently, he thought, under the circumstances.

"Dirk, it really is you," she sobbed. "Back there in the darkness, your voice . . . I couldn't be sure. I thought you were . . . I thought I'd never see you again."

"It seems," he said grinning, "Our meetings are a never ending, constant source of surprise."

"Uncle Bruno said you wouldn't call me, ever."

"Don't believe all you hear from an uncle."

Teri discovered the bandage on his nose and gently touched it. "You've been hurt." Her voice held a blend of concern and distress. "Did Uncle Bruno do that? Did he threaten you?"

"No, I was climbing some stairs and tripped and fell," he said, slightly distorting the truth. "That's all there was to it."

"What is this all about?" the guide asked in exasperation. His gun hand was beginning to droop. "Will the young lady please be so kind as to tell her name?"

"I am the niece of Bruno von Till," she said testily. "And I don't see how that concerns you."

There was a sharp exclamation from the Greek and he took a couple of steps forward, studying Teri's face closely. For almost half a minute he stared at her, then slowly, with deliberate ease, raised the gun level again, still pointing at Pitt. Once, twice he tugged at his moustache, nodding in thoughtful perplexity.

"You may speak the truth," he said quietly. "Then again you may be lying to protect these two unpleasant looking scum."

"Your ridiculous insinuations are of no importance to me," Teri thrust out her chin, matching its protruding uplift with her breasts. "I demand you put down that hideous gun and leave us alone. My uncle has great influence with the island authorities. One word from him and you'll find yourself rotting your miserable life away in a mainland prison."

"I am well aware of Bruno von Till's influence," the guide said indifferently. "Unfortunately it makes little impression on me. The final decision concerning your arrest or release rests entirely with my superior in Panaghia, Inspector Zacynthus. He will wish to see you. Any lies to him and your immediate futures shall be very lamentable indeed. If you will all please step behind the wall, you will find a pathway leading approximately two hundred yards to a waiting car." He swung the gun from Pitt to Teri. "A warning, gentlemen. Do not enterain any thoughts of a foolish move. If I detect even a slight facial tic on either of you, I shall place a bullet in the brain of this delicate and lovely creature. Now, shall we proceed?"

Five minutes later they all reached the car, a black Mercedes parked inconspicuously under a copse of fir trees. The driver's door was open and a man dressed in a spotless ice cream suit sat casually behind the wheel with one foot solidly planted on the ground outside. At their approach he rose and opened the rear door.

Pitt looked at the man for a long moment. The contrast between the neatly pressed white suit and the dark ugly face presented an impressive picture. About two inches above Pitt's own height, the man looked like a chiseled stone colossus, and just as solid. He had the largest set of shoulders Pitt had ever seen, and must have weighted at least 260 pounds. The face was misproportioned and strikingly repulsive, and yet there was a strange sort of beauty about it; the kind that artists sought to capture on canvas. Pitt wasn't fooled. He could read a man who had an indifferent attitude toward killing. His paths had crossed many times with lovable looking brutes who murdered as if it were a run-of-the-mill, everyday routine.

The guide stepped back and walked around to the front of the car. He nodded at the other man.

"We have guests, Darius. Three little goats who have lost their way. We will take them to Inspector Zacynthus. They can stage their little act for him." He turned to Pitt. "You will enjoy the Inspector's company; he is an excellent listener."

Darius soberly gestured at the back seat. "You two in here, the girl rides in front." His voice was what one would have expected, deep and rasping.

Pitt relaxed against the seat and ran through a dozen different plans for escape, each with less chance of success than the previous one. The guide had them by the testicles as long as Teri was present. Without her, he thought, he and Giordino stood tossup odds of overpowering the guide and grabbing the gun. There was also the possibility that if they made an attempt the guide wouldn't have the courage to shoot a woman, but Pitt wasn't about to risk Teri's life to find out. The guide bowed with obviously forced courtesy.

"Be a gentleman, Darius, and offer the lovely young lady your coat. Her . . . ah . . . prominent attractions might prove embarrassing and somewhat distracting as we drive."

"Don't bother," Teri said contemptuously. "I'll not wear that bloody ape's coat. I have nothing I want to hide. Besides, it'll give me great pleasure to see a greasy worm like you squirm."

The guide's eyes grew cold, then he smiled thinly and shrugged. "As you wish."

Teri lifted her negligee tightly around her thighs and climbed into the car. The guide followed, sandwiching her between him and the hulking Darius who hunched over the steering wheel. Then the Mercedes' diesel engine knocked into life and the car started rolling over the narrow, twisting road; on many stretches edged by deep and marsh covered ditches. The guide's flickering eyes bounced from Pitt to Giordino and back again, never once twitching the automatic glued to Teri's right ear. His determined vigilance and unflagging concentration was, it seemed to Pitt, unduly fanatical.

Pitt, warily watching for any negative sign from the guide, very slowly extracted a cigarette from his breast pocket and just as slowly lit it.

"Tell me, whatever your name is . . ."

"Polyclitus Anaxamander Zeno," the guide offered. "At your service."

"Tell me," Pitt repeated without an attempt at pronouncing Zeno's full name. "How did you happen to be coiled back there at the passage when we came out?"

"I have an inquisitive nature," Zeno said through a twisted smile. "When I perceived that you and your friend had mysteriously disappeared from my tour, I asked myself: What would those two surly looking characters find in the ruins that would interest them? The answer eluded my humble mind so I turned my gawking entourage over to a fellow guide and returned to the amphitheatre. You were nowhere to be found. Then I spied the broken bar in the gate . . . no great feat I assure you; I know ever stone and crack on the site. Certain you would reappear, I sat and waited."

"You'd have felt like an idiot if we hadn't."

"It was only a question of time. There is no other way out of the Pit of Hades."

"The Pit of Hades?" Pitt's curiosity was aroused. "Why do you call it that?"

"I find your sudden interest in archaeology quite unexpected. However, since you ask . . ." There was puzzlement in Zeno's eyes, yet a mixture of attention and amusement. "During the golden age of Greece, our ancestors held their criminal trials in the amphitheatre. This location was chosen because their juries consisted of one hundred elected townspeople. It was their contention, and a very wise one, that the more people who rendered a judgment, the more just the verdict. In a matter of circumstantial evidence, the defendant, if decided guilty, was given a choice of instant death or the Pit of Hades."

"What was so bad about the pit?" Giordino asked, his eyes trained on the reflection of Darius' face in the rearview mirror, sizing him up.

"The pit was in reality not a pit," Zeno continued. "But rather a vast underground labyrinth with a hundred different passages and only two openings, an entrance and a hidden exit, which was a closely guarded secret."

"At least the condemned were given an opportunity to reach freedom." Pitt flicked an ash into the tray on the armrest.

"The choice was not as opportune as it might appear. You see, the labyrinth contained a very hungry lion who had little to eat, except, of course, an occasional passing felon."

Pitt's studied calm folded and his face turned grim, but he quickly gained control again. The picture of von Till's smirking features entered his mind again. Why did the old kraut, he wondered, use historical events to cloak his mysterious schemes? Perhaps this obssession for dramatics might prove to be the chink in von Till's armor. Pitt sat back and drew deeply on his cigarette.

"A fascinating myth."

"I assure you it is no myth," Zeno said seriously. "The number of condemned Greeks who died in the Pit of Hades, their screams echoing through the dark tunnels, is endless. Even in recent years, before the entrance was barred, several people wandered into the pit and vanished, swallowed up by the unknown. There is no record of a successful escape."

Pitt flipped his cigarette through an open window into the passing countryside. He looked at Giordino, then more slowly at Zeno. A smug grin spread across his face and widened into a broad smile.

Zeno stared at Pitt speculatively. Then he gave an uncomprehending shrug and motioned to Darius. Darius nodded and a few seconds later the Mercedes turned onto the mainroad. The wheels sped over the worn two lane pavement. The trees, lining the shoulders like forgotten sentinels, flashed past in a blur of dust and green leaves. The air was cooler now, and, twisting around in the seat, Pitt could see the setting sun's rays strike the bald, tree-bare peak of Hypsarion, the highest point on the island. He remembered reading somewhere that a Greek poet had described Thasos as "a wild ass's back, covered with wild wood." Though the description was twenty seven hundred years old, he thought, it was still true today.

And then, Darius back-shifted and the Mercedes was slowing down. It turned again, this time leaving the highway, its tires crunching on a rough, gravel-strewn country lane that led upward into a wooded ravine.

Why Darius had left the main road before reaching Panaghia Pitt could not guess, any more than he could guess why Zeno acted the part of an armed undercover agent instead of a friendly tourist guide. That old feeling of danger tapped Pitt on the shoulder again, and he felt a tinge of uncontrolled anxiety.

The Mercedes bumped heavily over a dip, rose steeply up a long ramp and entered a large barnlike building through a doorway that had been designed to accommodate heavy trucks requiring high roof clearances. The weather beaten walls of the wooden structure were covered with the remnants of gray-green paint, long since peeled and blistered from the fierce Aegean sun. An instant before the inside gloom enveloped the car, Pitt caught a glimpse of an overhead sign whose faded black letters were printed in German. Then, as Darius turned off the ignition, he heard the sound of rusty rollers creaking the door shut behind them.

"The Greek International Tourist Organization must work under a damn paltry budget if this is the best they can scrape up for an office," Pitt said caustically, his eyes darting about the vast, deserted floor.

Zeno merely smiled. It was a smile that left Pitt's heart pounding against an enormous pressure, as if something was holding it, constricting its action. An inner coldness crept over him, bringing with it the acknowledgment of failure, the acknowledgment that he had somehow played into von Till's hands.

Pitt had been aware all along that G.N.T.O. guides do not carry guns or have the authority to make an armed arrest. He also knew that the guides drove around the island in boldly advertised and gaily colored Volkswagen buses, not black, unmarked Mercedes-Benz sedans. Time was getting expensive. He and Giordino must make a move, and make it soon.

Zeno opened the rear door and stepped back. He made a slight bow and gestured with the gun.

"Please remember," he said, his tone rock hard. "No foolishness."

Pitt climbed from the car and turned, offering his hand to Teri through the open front door. She looked up at him seductively for a moment and, squeezing his hand gently, slowly uncoiled from her sitting position. Then quickly, before Pitt could react, she threw her arms around his neck and pulled his head down to her level. Both pair of eyes were open, Pitt's mostly from surprise, as she brazenly covered his sweating face with kisses.

It never fails, Pitt thought in detached fascination, no matter how cool or sophisticated they act toward the world, show a woman danger and adventure and they'll always turn on. It's really a pity, she's ready but it's the wrong time and the wrong place. He forced her back.

"Later," he murmured, "when our audience has gone home."

"A most stimulating little scene," said Zeno impatiently. "Come along, Inspector Zacynthus rapidly loses all compassion when he is kept waiting."

Zeno dropped about five paces behind the group, holding the automatic at hip level. Darius then escorted them across the football field length of the building, up a rickety flight of wooden stairs that led to a hallway, lined on both sides by several doors. Darius paused at the second door on the left and pushed it open, motioning Pitt and Giordino inside. Teri started to follow but was suddenly halted by a huge barrel of an arm.

"Not you," Darius grunted.

Pitt whirled around, anger clouding his face. "She stays with us," he said coldly.

"No need to play rescuing hero," Zeno said lightly, reinforced with an expression of seriousness. "I promise you, no harm will come to her."

Pitt studied Zeno's face carefully, finding no sign of treachery. For some strange reason Pitt experienced a marked degree of trust in his captor.

"I'll take you at your word," he growled.

"Don't worry, Dirk," Teri threw an icy look at Zeno. "As soon as this stupid inspector, whoever he is, finds out who I am, we'll all be free of these wretched people."

Zeno ignored her and nodded at Darius. "Guard our friends here, guard them closely. I suspect they're very cunning."

"I'll be alert," Darius promised confidently. He waited until Zeno and Teri, padding the dusty floor in her bare feet, were gone. Then he closed the door and leaned lazily against it, arms folded across his massive chest.

"Personally speaking," Giordino muttered, for the first time since the ride from the ruins, "I prefer the accommodations at the Hotel San Quentin." His gaze focused on Darius. "At least the roaches weren't king size."

Pitt grinned at Giordino's insulting comment to Darius and scanned the room, taking in every detail of its construction. It was small, no larger than nine by ten feet. The walls consisted of warped boards nailed crudely to warped support posts that stood facing in-

ward at irregular intervals, in rotted and barren stark-
ness. The room was void of any furniture and window-
less; the only available light came through large
horizontal cracks in the walls and a jagged hole in the
roof.

"If I was to guess," said Pitt. "I'd say this place was
a deserted warehouse."

"You're close," Darius volunteered. "The Germans used this building for an ordnance depot when
they occupied the island in forty-two."

Pitt pulled out a cigarette and casually lit it. To
offer Darius a cigarette would have immediately put the
brute on his guard. Instead, Pitt took a step backward
and began tossing the lighter in the air, each time tossing it a little higher till he noticed Darius following it
out of the corner of one eye. Once, twice, four times the
lighter sailed into the air. On the fifth toss it fell
through Pitt's fingers and clattered on the floor. He
shrugged stupidly and bent down, picking it up.

Pitt charged Darius harder than he had ever
charged any halfback, any quarterback, in his Air Force
academy days. Lunging forward from a football crouch,
his feet dug firmly into the coarse grained wood of the
floor, he thrust his head and shoulders like a battering
ram, backed with every driving ounce of power his mus-
cular legs and one hundred and ninety pounds could
muster. At the instant before impact, he drove upward, catching Darius in the unprotected stomach
just above the beltline. It was like running at full speed
into a brick wall, and Pitt gasped at the shock: it felt as
if his neck was broken.

In football terminology it was called a running
block, a vicious, maiming block, and it would have put
most unprepared men in a hospital bed: all others it
would have left on the ground in momentary stunned
helplessness—all others, that is, except Darius. The
giant merely grunted, doubled over slightly from the
force of the blow, and grabbed Pitt by the biceps, lifting
him off the floor.

Pitt went numb. The shock and the pain that

erupted from his arms and neck gave way to utter surprise that any man could not only take such a charge and remain standing but shake it off like a love tap. Darius pushed him against the wall, slowly bending Pitt's body, like a vertical pretzel, around an upright support post. The pain really began to come now. Pitt clenched his teeth and stared into Darius's expressionless face, only a few inches away. His spine felt as if it would snap at any second. His vision began to fade. Darius just stood there, eyes gleaming, and increased the pressure.

Suddenly the pressure stopped and Pitt dimly perceived Darius staring back, his lips working, fighting for breath. Mutely Darius mouthed an agonized groan and sank to his knees, weaving silently from side to side.

Giordino, blocked by Pitt's frontal assault, was forced to stand by helplessly till Darius swung sideways, pinning Pitt to the wall. Then, without hesitation, he hurled himself across the room, his legs jackknifing open, his feet imbedded in Darius' kidneys. He braced himself, half expecting the giant's body to absorb most of the force from the violent blow. It didn't work out that way. It was if a handball had struck a backstop: Giordino rebounded off Darius with a tooth loosening jolt and crashed jarringly to the floor, badly stunned. For a moment he lay quite still, then dazedly he began struggling to his hands and knees, shaking his head back and forth to clear the waves of blackness that threatened to engulf his conscious mind.

It was too late. Darius was the first to recover, triumph etched in every scar of his ugly face. He lunged at Giordino, the great mass of his weight crushing the smaller man beneath him. There was an evil grin on Darius' face now, a sadistic sign of the violence yet to come. Iron hands clasped together, fingers interlocking, around Giordino's head and squeezed—squeezed with the unrelenting pressure of a closing vise.

For what seemed like unending seconds Giordino lay inert, fighting off the shooting pain that burst in his skull from the crushing palms. Then he stirred, slowly raised his hands and grabbed Darius around the thumbs and pulled downward. For his size Giordino was strong as an ox, but he was no match for the man who towered above him. Darius, seemingly oblivious to the bone twisting pull, hunched his shoulders and exerted an even greater effort.

Pitt was still on his feet, but just barely. His back was a spreading sea of pain that flowed to every part of his body. Numbly he stared at the murderous scene on the floor. Move you stupid bastard, he screamed to himself, move fast. He clutched the wall with both hands, preparing to launch himself at Darius. Something gave behind him, and he swung around, new hope ablaze in his eyes.

A wall plank had torn loose from the support post and was dangling at a crazy angle, one end still held by rusty nails. Frantically he jerked at it, first one way then the other, until metal fatigue broke the nails and the board, about four feet long and an inch in thickness, tore free from the post. God, if only it wasn't too late. Pitt raised the board above his head and, drawing on the last of his ebbing strength, brought it down on the back of Darius' neck.

Pitt would never again forget the shock of hopelessness and despair that flooded through his mind at that moment as the rotted plank shattered with all the harmless force of a piece of peanut brittle around the giant's shoulders. Without turning, Darius let loose of Giordino's temples, giving his victim a brief respite, and struck Pitt with a sweeping backhand blow that caught him in the stomach and sent him reeling across the room to fall limply against the doorway and melt slowly down to the floor.

Somehow, clutching the door knob, Pitt pulled himself to his feet and stood there swaying drunkenly, conscious of nothing, not even the pain, the blood that began to seep through the bandages onto his shirt, and Giordino's face, now turning blue under the tremendous hands. One more try, he told himself, knowing it would be his last. Pitt's mind slowed down. The forgotten words of a marine drill sergeant, he once met in a Honolulu bar, returned and pounded into his brain. "The biggest, toughest, meanest sonovabitch in the world will always go down, and go down fast, from a good swift kick in the balls."

Weakly, he staggered behind the crouching Darius, who was too intent on killing Giordino to notice him. Pitt aimed and kicked Darius between the legs. His toe collided with bone and something that was rubbery and soft. Darius released Giordini's head and threw his monstrous hands upward, fingers clawing at the air. Then he rolled over on his side, twisting about the floor in silent agony.

"Welcome to the land of the walking dead," Pitt said, lifting Giordino to a sitting position.

"Did we win?" Giordino asked in a whisper.

"Just barely. How's your head?"

"I won't know till I look for it."

"Don't worry," Pitt grinned. "It's still attached to your neck."

Giordino gently probed his hairline between his fingers. "Christ, my skull feels like it has more cracks than a broken windshield."

Pitt cast a wary look at Darius. The giant, ashen faced and breathing heavily, was stretched out full length on the dusty floor, both hands clutched over his crotch.

"The party's over," Pitt said, helping Giordino to his feet. "Let's disappear before Frankenstein recovers."

Suddenly, the ominous click, the hollow thud of the door flung open against its stop, froze Pitt and Giordino in their tracks. They had no warning, not even a moment to brace themselves, nothing except the knowledge that time had run out and they could fight no more.

Then a tall, thin man with large sad eyes sauntered easily into the room, one hand shoved casually into the pants pocket of an expensive ivy-league suit. He stared at Pitt pensively for a long moment over the bowl of a long-stemmed pipe, gripped tenaciously between uncommonly even teeth. Like an account executive who just stepped out of an advertising agency, he looked suave, neat and citified. His free hand, in a practiced gesture, reached up and removed the pipe.

"Sorry to invade your privacy, gentlemen. I'm Inspector Zacynthus."

12

Zacynthus was hardly what Pitt had expected. There could be no doubt about it, the slurred accent, the neatly styled hair, the casual introduction: Zacynthus was an American.

Ten seconds, each spent scrutinizing every detail of Pitt and Giordino, elapsed before Zachynthus slowly turned and looked down at the moaning Darius. Zacynthus' face seemed glacial with elaborate indifference, but the tone of his voice betrayed bewilderment.

"Remarkable, truly remarkable. I didn't think it was possible." He looked at Pitt and Giordino again, this time with mixed doubt and admiration written in his eyes. "For a highly trained professional to even lay a hand on Darius is considered a great accomplishment, but for a pair of sad looking underdogs like you to wipe the floor with him is nothing short of miraculous. Your names, my friends?"

A devilish glint flashed in Pitt's green eyes. "My little companion is David, and I'm Jack the Giant Killer."

Zacynthus smiled a tired smile. "The day is long and hot, and you've incapacitated one of my best men. Please don't compound my misery with sick humor."

"In that case, Dirk," Giordino murmured slyly. "Tell him the one about the nymphomaniac and the guitar player."

"Come now," Zacynthus said, as if talking to children. "I have no time to waste on such drivel. Information if you please! We'll begin with your correct names."

"Screw you," Pitt snapped angrily. "We didn't beg to be dragged here by that ape who calls himself Zeno, and we didn't ask to be pushed around by Earthquake MaGoon there on the floor. We've done nothing illegal. immoral perhaps, but not illegal. If you hope to get any answers from us, I suggest you supply a few yourself."

Zacynthus stared at Pitt, his lips pressed tightly together. "Your arrogance arouses my professional curiosity, he said tartly. During the years since I chose investigation as my life's work I've confronted scores of shrewd and dangerous felons. A few have spit in my face and threatened revenge, some stood immovable and silent, still others begged on their knees for mercy. But you, my bedraggled friend, have to be different." He waved his pipe accusingly at Pitt. "By God, it's classic, truly classic. I look forward to matching my wits against yours at the interrogation."

He broke off as Zeno stepped into the room. The Greek started to say something, but his mouth hung open and his great moustache appeared to droop in astonishment when he spied Darius, now sitting up in a tight ball. "Great thunderbolts of Zeus, my inspector, what has happened?"

"You should have warned Darius to be more careful."

"But I did warn him," Zeno explained apologetically. "Even then, for Darius to be overpowered; I did not think it possible."

"My words exactly." Zacynthus knocked the ashes from his pipe. "See what you can do for our poor friend. I'm going to take these men to my office and determine if they're as cunning with words as they are with their hands and feet."

"After what they did here, do you think it wise, my inspector, to be alone with them?"

"I think they realize they have nothing to gain by further physical activity." Zacynthus threw Pitt and

Giordino a bantering smile. "Just to be on the safe side, Zeno, handcuff the little one's right wrist to this clever devil's left ankle. Not a foolproof restraint method, by any means, but at least it will make resistance somewhat inconvenient."

Quickly Zeno pulled a pair of chromium plated handcuffs from a clip on his belt, unsnapped the ratchets and secured them into place, leaving Giordino in an awkward stooped position.

Pitt glanced up through the hole in the roof at the evening sky. It was darkening by the moment as the sunlight began to retreat. His back still ached, but he felt grateful that it was Giordino, and not he, who was bent double. He flexed his shoulders, wincing at the pain that erupted from every square inch of his torso, then he looked back at Zacynthus.

"What have you done with Teri?" he asked quietly.

"She's quite safe," Zacynthus replied. "As soon as I can verify her claim of being von Till's niece, I shall release her."

"What about us?" Giordino's voice reached up.

"In due time," Zacynthus said curtly, motioning to the doorway. "After you, gentlemen."

Two minutes later, with Giordino clumsily shuffling beside Pitt, they entered Zacynthus' office. It was a small room but efficiently furnished; complete with detailed aerial photographs of Thasos tacked to the walls, three telephones, and a shortwave radio, conveniently placed on a table directly behind an old scratched and battered desk. Pitt looked around surprised. The whole set-up was too neat, too professional. Quickly he decided that his best hope still lay in a crude show of hostility.

"This looks more like the command headquarters of a general than the office of a two-bit police inspector."

"You and your friend are brave men," Zacynthus said wearily. "Your acts have proved it. But it's stupid of you to continue the role of an oaf. Though, I admit, you do it very well." He walked around the desk and sat down in an obviously unoiled swivel chair. "This time the truth. Your names please?"

Pitt paused before replying. He was puzzled and angry at the same time. The strange, off-beat operation of his captors puzzled him.

There was a curious feeling, almost a cold certainty in his subconscious mind that he had nothing to fear. These people did not fit his conception of run-of-the-mill Greek policemen. And if they were on von Till's payroll, why were they so dead-set on merely obtaining his and Giordino's names; unless, perhaps, the cats were toying with the mice.

"Well?" Zacynthus' voice hardened to a sharp edge.

Pitt pulled himself erect, and took a gamble.

"Pitt, Dirk Pitt, Director of Special Projects, United States National Underwater Marine Agency. And the gentleman on my left is Albert Giordino, my Assistant Director."

"Most certainly, and I'm the Prime Minister of—" Zacynthus broke off in midsentence: his eyebrows rose sharply, and he leaned across the desk, gazing directly into Pitt's eyes.

"Let's have that again. What did you say your name was?" His voice this time was soft and patronizing.

"Dirk Pitt."

Zacynthus did not move or speak for a full ten seconds. Then he slowly settled back, visibly off balance.

"You're lying, you must be lying."

"Am I?"

"Your father's name?" Zacynthus still stared unblinkingly at Pitt.

"Senator George Pitt of California."

"Describe him; appearance, history, family— everything."

Pitt sat down on the edge of the desk and pulled out a cigarette. He fumbled for his lighter, then remembered it was still lying on the floor of the room where it had fallen when he charged Darius.

Zacynthus struck a wooden match against a drawer and held it for him.

Pitt nodded a grateful thank you.

Pitt spoke for ten minutes without stopping. Zacynthus listened thoughtfully, moving only once to switch on a dim overhead lamp as the daylight outside the window faded slowly away. Finally he raised his hand.

"That will do. You must be his son, the person you claim to be. But what are you doing on Thasos?"

"NUMA's Chief Director, Admiral James Sandecker, assigned Giordino and myself to investigate a series of strange accidents that have recently plagued one of our oceanographic research vessels."

"Ah yes, the white ship anchored beyond Brady Field. Now I'm beginning to understand."

"That's nice," Giordino said sarcastically from his uncomfortable stance. "I'm sorry to interrupt, but if my bladder isn't relieved soon, you're going to have an accident right here on the office floor."

Pitt grinned at Zacynthus. "He'd do it too."

A speculative look crossed Zacynthus' eyes, then he shrugged and pressed a hidden button under the desk top. Instantly the door flew open, revealing Zeno with the Glisenti firmly gripped in one hand.

"Trouble, my Inspector?"

Zacynthus ignored the question. "Put away your gun, remove the handcuffs and show—ah—Mister Giordino to our sanitation facilities."

Zeno's eyebrows lifted. "Are you certain—"

"It's all right, old friend. These men are no longer our prisoners, they are our guests."

Without another word or any outward sign of surprise, Zeno holstered the automatic and released Giordino, escorting him down the hall.

"Now it's my turn for answers," Pitt said, exhaling a transparent cloud of bluish smoke. "What's your connection with my father?"

"Senator Pitt is well known and respected in Washington. He serves honorably and efficiently on several senate committees. One of which is the Narcotic Drugs Committee."

"That still doesn't explain where you come in."

Zacynthus pulled a well-worn tobacco pouch from a coat pocket and idly filled his pipe, carefully tamping it with a small coin.

"Because of my lengthy experience and my investigations in the field of narcotics I have often served as liaison between your father's committee and my employer."

Pitt looked up puzzled. "Employer?"

"Yes, Uncle Sam pays my salary just as he does yours, my dear Pitt." Zacynthus grinned. "My apologies for the late formal introduction. I'm Inspector Hercules Zacynthus, Federal Bureau of Narcotics. My friends just call me Zac, I'd be honored if you do the same."

All doubts flew from Pitt's mind and the relief of certainty covered him like a comforting cool wave from the sea. His muscles relaxed, and he became aware of how tense he had been, how keyed-up his thoughts and nerves were against the unknown dangers of the situation. Carefully, holding back an urge to tremble, he crushed his cigarette in an ashtray.

"Aren't you a little out of your territory?"

"Geographically yes, professionally no." Zac paused to puff his pipe into life. "About a month ago the Bureau received a report through INTERPOL that a massive shipment of heroin was loaded aboard a freighter in Shanghai . . ."

"One of Bruno von Till's ships?"

"How did you know?" Zac's voice was quizzical.

A wry smile crossed Pitt's lips. "Just a guess. I'm sorry for interrupting, please continue."

"The ship, a Minerva Lines freighter called the *Queen Artemisia,* left the Shanghai harbor three weeks ago with a seemingly innocent cargo manifest of soybeans, frozen pork, tea, paper and carpets." Zac could not help grinning. "Quite a variety, I admit."

"And the destination?"

"The first port of call was Colombo in Ceylon. Here the ship unloaded the Communist Chinese trade goods and took on a new cargo of graphite and cocoa. After a fuel stop at Marseille, the *Queen Artemisia*'s next and final port is Chicago via the Saint Lawrence Seaway."

Pitt thought a moment. "Why Chicago? Surely New York, Boston or the other eastern seaboard ports are better equipped by the underworld to handle foreign drug shipments."

"Why not Chicago?" Zac retorted. "The Windy City is the greatest distribution and transportation center in the good old United States. What better place to dump one hundred and thirty tons of uncut heroin."

Pitt looked up, disbelief etched on his face. "That's impossible. No one on this earth could get that kind of an amount through a custom's inspection."

"No one, that is, except Bruno von Till." The voice was a low murmur, and Pitt suddenly felt cold. "It's not his real name of course. That was lost somewhere in his past, long before he became an elusive smuggler, the most diabolic and crafty purveyor of human misery of all time." Zac swung around and gazed unseeing out the window. "Captain Kidd, the blockade runners of the Confederacy and all the slave traders rolled into one couldn't hold a candle to von Till's setup."

"You make him sound like the arch villain of the century." Pitt ventured. "What did he do to deserve the honor?"

Zac flickered a glance at him, then looked again through the window.

"The numerous revolutionary bloodbaths suffered by Central and South America in the last twenty years would never have occurred without secret arms shipments from Europe. Do you recall the great Spanish gold theft of nineteen fifty-four? Spain's already shaky economy nearly toppled after a large government gold reserve vanished from the secret vaults of the Ministry of Treasury. Shortly after, India's black market was glutted with gold bars bearing the crest of Spain. How was a cargo that size smuggled seven thousand miles? It's still a mystery. But we do know a Minerva Lines freighter left Barcelona the night of the theft and arrived in Bombay a day before the gold appeared."

The swivel chair squeaked, and Zac refaced Pitt. The inspector's melancholy eyes looked vague and lost in contemplation.

"Immediately prior to Germany's surrender in World War II," he continued, "eighty-five high ranking Nazis suddenly materialized in Buenos Aires on the same day. How did they get there? Again, the only ship arrival that morning was a Minerva Lines freighter. Again in the summer of nineteen fifty-four an entire bus load of teenage school girls disappeared on an outing in Naples. Four years later an Italian embassy aid discovered one of the missing girls wandering aimlessly through one of the back alleys of Casablanca." Zac paused for nearly a minute, then went on very quietly. "She was completely insane. I saw photographs of her body. It was enough to make a grown man cry."

"And her story?" Pitt prompted gently.

"She remembered being carried aboard a ship with a large 'M' painted on the funnel. That was the only thing she said that made any sense. The rest was insane babble."

Pitt waited for more, but Zac had fallen silent, relighting his pipe and filling the room with a sweet aromatic odor.

"White slavery is a rotten business," Pitt said tersely.

Zac nodded. "Those are only four cases of hundreds that are indirectly connected to von Till. If I could quote word for word from the INTERPOL files we would be sitting here for a month, and then some."

"Do you think von Till masterminds the crimes?"

"No, the old devil is much too smart to become involved in the actual deed. He merely supplies the transportation. Smuggling is his game, and on a grand scale at that."

"Why in hell hasn't the filthy bastard been stopped?" Pitt asked half angry, half confused.

"I wish I could answer that without a feeling of shame," Zac shook his head sadly. "But I can't. Nearly every law enforcement agency in the world has tried to catch von Till with the goods, so to speak, but he has eluded every trap, murdered every agent sent to infiltrate Minerva Lines. His ships have been searched and researched a thousand times, yet nothing illegal is ever found."

Pitt idly watched the smoke curl from Zac's pipe. "No one is that clever. If he's human, he can be caught."

"God knows we've tried. Our combined law enforcement agencies have studied every inch of the Minerva ships, shadowed them day and night at sea, guarded them like hawks at the docks, and searched every bulkhead with electronic detection gear.

"I can rattle off the names of at least twenty investigators—damn good ones too—who have made von Till's arrest their life's work."

Pitt lit a second cigarette and stared at Zac steadily. "Why are you telling me all this?"

"Because I think you might help us."

Pitt sat silent, scratching the irritating chest bandage. Might as well nibble at the bait he thought.

"How?"

For the first time a flicker of devilishness showed in Zac's eyes, then disappeared as quickly as it had come.

"I understand you're quite friendly with von Till's niece."

"I've laid her if that's what you mean."

"How long have you known her?"

"We met for the first time on the beach yesterday."

The surprise on Zac's face slowly turned to a sly grin. "You're either a very fast worker or a very adept liar."

"Suit yourself," Pitt said offhandedly. He stood up, stretching to loosen his sore muscles. "I know what you're thinking, and you can forget it."

"It would be interesting to learn just what you see in my thoughts."

"The oldest tactic in the world," Pitt smiled knowingly. "Your intention would have me continue my intimate friendship with Teri in the hope that von Till would accept me as one of the family. This arrangement would in turn give me the run of the villa and a chance to observe the old kraut's actions at first hand."

Zac met his eyes evenly. "You have excellent perception, my dear Pitt. What do you say, are you game?"

"No chance!"

"May I ask why?"

"I met von Till over dinner last night, and we didn't part the best of friends. In fact, he even sicced his dog on me."

Pitt knew Zac would not appreciate the humor. But what the hell, he thought, why go through the whole maddening story again. He began to wish longingly for a drink.

"From sex with the niece to dinner with the uncle, and all in the same day." Zac shook his head incredulously. "You are indeed a fast worker."

Pitt merely shrugged.

"It's a pity," Zac continued. "You could have been a great help to us on the inside." He puffed on his pipe until the embers in the bowl glowed a vivid orange-red. "We've had the villa under constant surveillance from a distance, but could detect nothing out of the ordinary. Two hundred yards; that was as near as we could get without arousing von Till's suspicions. We thought our little masquerade as tourist guides had finally paid off when you and his niece were apprehended by Colonel Zeno."

"*Colonel* Zeno?"

Zac nodded, then paused deliberately for effect.

"Yes. He and Captain Darius are members of the Greek Gendarmerie. Technically, Zeno outranks me a few steps, you might say."

"A rank of Colonel in the police?" Pitt asked. "Isn't that a bit unusual"

"Not if you understood their law enforcement system. You see, with the exception of Athens and a few other larger cities which have their own metropolitan bureaus, the Greek rural and suburban areas are policed by the Gendarmerie; a branch of the national army, and a very elite and efficient outfit."

In spite of his hatred for Zeno and Darius, Pitt was impressed.

"That explains their presence, but what about you, Inspector? A narcotics agent after illegal drugs in Greece is the same as an FBI agent after a spy in Spain; it's just not done."

"In an ordinary case, you're quite correct." Zac's face turned grim and his voice hard. "But von Till is not an ordinary case. When we get him behind bars and put an end to his filthy smuggling operation we will automatically cut international crime by twenty percent. And that, I assure you, is no small margin." An inner anger had taken control of Zac and he stopped for a moment, taking several deep breaths until it subsided. "In the past, each country worked separately, using INTERPOL channels to relay vital information across national borders. For instance, if I learned through the Narcotics Bureau's undercover sources that an illegal shipment of drugs was bound for England, I would simply send my information to INTERPOL London, who in turn would alert Scotland Yard. Time willing, they'd set a trap and apprehend the smugglers."

"Sounds like a neat and workable arrangement."

"Unfortunately it has yet to work with von Till," Zac said quietly. "No matter how many warnings, how many traps, he always manages to evade the nets and come up like the proverbial sweet smelling rose, fresh out of the excretion barrel. But this time it's going to be different." He pounded the desk for effect. "Our governments have allowed us to form an international investigation team that can cross any border, use any police facilities, and have at their command, men and equipment of the military." Zac sighed heavily, then went on apologetically.

"I'm sorry, Pitt, I didn't mean to be long winded. But I hope I've answered your question as to why I'm on Thasos."

Pitt studied Zac carefully. The Inspector looked like a man who was not used to failure. Every movement, every gesture was thoughtfully planned in advance; even his words carried an air of confident forethought. Yet, Pitt could not help detecting a glimmer of fear behind Zac's eyes; a fear of losing the game to von Till. Pitt began to wish more than ever for a drink.

"Where are the other members of your team?" Pitt asked. "So far I've only seen three of you."

"At this moment a British Inspector is on board a Royal Navy destroyer, trailing *Queen Artemisia,* while a representative from the Turkish Police Bureau is observing her from the air in an antiquated, unmarked DC-3." Zac spoke woodenly, as if quoting from a legal document. "Two detectives of the French Sureté Nationale are also on hand, posing as Marseille dockworkers, awaiting the *Queen's* arrival for refueling."

A feeling of detached unreality began to creep up on Pitt. Zac's words were becoming dull and unmeaning. Indifferently, almost, with a kind of hazy academic interest, he wondered how much longer ,he could stay awake. He had had only a few hours sleep in the last two days and it was catching up. Pitt rubbed his eyes and shook his head vigorously, then forced his mind back to alertness.

"Zac, old buddy," It was the first time Pitt had called him by name. "I wonder if you would do me a personal favor."

"If I can," Zac grinned hesitantly, *"old buddy."*

"I want Teri released in my custody."

"Released in *your* custody?" Zac arched his eyebrows in accompaniment to wide innocent eyes. Steve McQueen couldn't have done it any better. "What lecherous scheme do you have up your sleeve?"

"No lechery," Pitt said seriously. "You have no choice but to release her. Once free, it will take Teri all of twenty minutes to storm back to the villa—hell hath no fury like the wrath of a woman humiliated—demanding that Uncle Bruno do something about her shameful captivity. The old boy will put his shrewd mind into gear and, within the hour, your little underground spy network will be blown from Thasos back to the States."

"You underestimate us," Zac said urbanely. "I'm well aware of the consequences. Plans have been made for just such an emergency. We can be out of these quarters and working under a different cover by morning."

"Too late," Pitt countered sharply. "The damage is done. Von Till will be wise to your presence. He's sure to double every precaution."

"You have a very convincing argument."

"You're damn right I have."

"And if I turned her over to you?" Zac asked speculatively.

"As soon as Teri is missed, if she hasn't been already, von Till will turn Thasos upside down in an exhaustive search. The safest place to hide her now is on board the *First Attempt*. He won't think to look for her there, at least not until he's sure she isn't on the island."

Zac stared a long moment at Pitt, examining every inch of the man as if he were seeing him for the first time, wondering why someone with an excellent position and influential family would take such difficult and dangerous risks, never knowing when a miscalculation might spell the end of his career or even his death. Zac idly tapped his pipe against an ashtray, knocking the loose ashes from the round briar bowl.

"It will be as you say," Zac murmured. "Providing, of course, the young lady will cause no trouble."

"I don't think so," Pitt grinned. "She has other things on her mind besides international drug smuggling. I'd say that sneaking off to the boat with me holds more interest than another dull evening with Uncle Bruno. Besides, show me a woman who doesn't crave a little taste of adventure, now and then, and I'll show you a—"

He broke off as the door opened and Giordino walked in, followed by Zeno. Giordino had a wide grin stretched across his cherub face and he clutched a bottle of Metaxa Five Star brandy in one hand.

"Look what Zeno found," Giordino flicked off the bottle lid and sniffed the contents, screwing up his face into a mock look of ecstasy. "I've decided they're not such bad guys after all."

Pitt laughed and turned to Zeno. "You'll have to excuse Giordino. He always comes unglued at the mere sight of booze."

"If so," Zeno grinned beneath his moustache, "We have much in common." He stepped around Giordino and set a tray with four glasses on the desk.

"How's Darius?" Pitt asked.

"He is on his feet," Zeno replied. "But he will be limping for a few days."

"Tell him I'm sorry," Pitt said sincerely. "I regret—"

"No regrets are necessary," Zeno interrupted. "In our line of work these things happen." He passed a glass to Pitt, noticing for the first time the blood stained shirt. "You seem to have your injuries also."

"Courtesy of von Till's dog," Pitt said, holding the glass to the light.

Zac nodded silently. He now grasped more fully Pitt's hatred for von Till. He relaxed, hands hanging limply over the arms of the swivel chair, secure in the knowledge that Pitt had revenge on his mind, not sex.

"After you get back to your ship, we'll keep you posted by radio on von Till's activities."

"Good," Pitt said simply. He sipped the brandy, enjoying the fiery lava-like liquid that trickled down his throat into the stomach. "One more favor, Zac. I'd like you to use your official status and send a couple of messages to Germany."

"Of course. What do you wish to say?"

Pitt had already picked up a pad and pencil off the desk. "I'll write everything down including names and addresses, but will have to fake my German spelling." When Pitt finished he passed the pad to Zac. "Ask them to forward their reply to the *First Attempt*. I've added NUMA's radio frequency."

Zac scanned the pad. "I don't understand your motives."

"Just a wild hunch." Pitt poured another shot of

Metaxa in his glass. "By the way, when will the *Queen Artemisia* make her detour by Thasos?"

"How . . . but how do you know that?"

"I'm psychic," Pitt said briefly. "When?"

"Tomorrow morning." Zac looked at Pitt long and consideringly. "Sometime between four and five A.M. Why do you ask?"

"No reason, just curiosity." Pitt braced himself for the burn and downed the drink. The jolt was almost too much. He shook his head from side to side, blinking away the tears that burst from his eyes.

"My God," he whispered hoarsely. "That stuff goes down like battery acid."

13

The eerie, phosphorescent froth gradually diminished and fell away from the old straight up and down bow of *Queen Artemisia* as the aging ship slowly lost way and came to a stop. Then the anchor clattered down into ten fathoms of water, and the navigation lights blinked out, leaving a black silhouette resting on an even blacker sea. It was as though the *Queen Artemisia* had never been.

Two hundred feet away, a small wooden packing crate bobbed lazily on the swells. It was a common type of crate, one of empty thousands that float in cast off neglect on every sea and waterway of the world. To the casual eye, at least, it looked like ordinary flotsam; even the stenciled letters that advertised "THIS END UP" pointed incongruously downward toward the seabed. There was, however, one thing that made this particular crate quite different; it wasn't empty.

There must be a better way, Pitt thought wryly from inside the box as a wave bumped it against the top of his head, but at least this was a damn sight better than swimming in plain view when the morning light appeared. He took a mouthful of saltwater and coughed it out. Then he puffed lightly into the mouthpiece of his flotation vest, increasing his buoyancy, and returned his gaze to the ship through a jaggedly cut peephole.

The *Queen Artemisia* lay silent, only the faint hum

of her generators and the slap of the waves of her hull betrayed her presence. Gradually the sounds faded away and the ship became a part of the silence. For a long time Pitt listened, but no other sounds traveled across the water to his bobbing outpost. No footsteps on a steel deck, no masculine voices shouting commands, no clank of human operated machinery, nothing. The silence was total and very puzzling. It was like a phantom ship with a phantom crew.

The starboard anchor was down, and Pitt made his way toward it, slowly pushing the box from within. The light breeze and the incoming tide worked in his favor, and soon the box gently nudged the anchor chain. He swiftly removed the U.S. Divers airtank and attached its backpack webbing through one of the big steel chain links. Then using the regulator's single air hose as a line, he slipped his fins, mask and snorkel over the second stage mouthpiece and let the whole package dangle just beneath the surface.

Pitt grabbed the chain, looking up at the seemingly endless links that vanished into the darkness, and felt like Jack climbing the beanstalk. He thought of Teri, lying asleep in a cozy bunk back on the *First Attempt*. He thought of her soft and fluid body and he began to wonder what in hell he was doing *here*.

Teri had wondered too, but over a different question. "Why take me to a ship? I can't go out there and meet all those brainy scientists looking like this." She lifted the hem of her transparent negligee, displaying her legs to the thighs.

"Oh what the hell," Pitt laughed. "It'll probably be the sexiest thing that's happened to them in years."

"What about Uncle Bruno?"

"Tell him you went shopping on the mainland. Tell him anything, you're over twenty-one."

"I guess it would be fun to be naughty," she giggled. "It's just like a romantic adventure story in the cinema."

"That's one way to look at it," Pitt had said. He'd figured she would think that, and he'd been right.

Pitt went up the anchor chain, copying the style of

a Polynesian native climbing a palm tree after coconuts. He soon reached the hawserhole and peered over the rail. He hesitated, listening and watching for any movement in the shadows. Not a soul was visible. The foredeck was deserted.

He swung over the side, crouched low and moved silently across the deck to the foremast. The blacked-out ship was a blessing. If the cargo loading lamps had been on, the midships and foredeck would have been bathed in a flood of white light; not the best circumstances for sneaking around unnoticed. Pitt was also thankful that the darkness blotted out his dripping water trail across the foredeck. He paused, waiting for the expected sounds and movements that never came. It was quiet, far too quiet. There was something else about the ship that didn't jell in Pitt's subconscious mind, but he couldn't pin it down. It eluded him for the present.

Pitt reached down, unsheathing the diver's knife strapped to his calf, and moved aft, holding the seven inch stainless blade well out in front of him.

It seemed incredible, but Pitt had a clear view of the bridge and, as far as he could see, it was abandoned. He melted into the shadows and climbed the ladder to the bridge, his feet padding noiselessly on the steel steps. The wheelhouse was dark and empty. The spokes of the wheel reached out in dark loneliness, and the binnacle stood like a mute, brass-plated sentinel. Pitt couldn't make out the wording, but he knew from the angle of the pointers that the telegraph stood at All Stop. In the dim light from the stars he was able to make out a rack attached to the ledge below the port window. His fingers played over the contents; Aldis lamp, flare gun, flares. Then he got lucky. His hand touched the familiar cylindrical shape of a flashlight. He slipped out of his swimtrunks and wrapped them around the lens till the light offered nothing but a faint glow. Then he checked every foot of the wheelhouse; deck, bulkheads, equipment. The tiny indicator lights of the control console showed the only glimmer of life.

The curtains were drawn in the chartroom at the back of the wheelhouse. It was inconceivable that any chartroom could be so clean. The charts lay in orderly stacks, their fields of squares and numbers crossed by precisely drawn pencil lines. Pitt slipped the knife back in its sheath, propped the flashlight against a copy of *Brown's Nautical Almanac* and scanned the chart markings. The lines coincided exactly with the *Queen Artemisia's* known course from Shanghai. He noted the fact that there were no mistakes or erasures by whoever figured the compass corrections. It was neat, too much so.

The log book was open at the last entry: *03.52 hours - Brady Field Beacon bearing 312°, approximately eight miles. Wind southwest, 2 knots. The God's protect Minerva.* The time showed that this entry had been made less than an hour before Pitt swam out from the beach. But where was the crew? There was no sign of the deck watch and the lifeboats were secure in their davits. The abandoned helm didn't make sense. None of it made sense.

Pitt's mouth was dry—a dusty cavern in which his tongue lay like a rubber sponge. A hammer pounded in his head, blurring his thinking. He left the wheelhouse, softly closing the door behind him, and found an alleyway leading to the captain's cabin. The door was ajar. He gently eased it full open and stepped soundlessly and sideways into the steel cubicle.

A movie set, it looked like a movie set. That was the only way Pitt could describe it. Everything was neat and tidy, and exactly where it should have been. Across the far bulkhead, the *Queen Artemisia* loomed in tranquil splendor from an amateurish oil painting. Pitt shuddered at the choice of colors; the ship sailed on a purple sea. The signature in the lower right corner was signed by a Sophia Remick. There was the usual photograph on the desk with a matronly, round-faced woman staring out of a cheap metal frame. The inscription read: *To the Captain of my heart from his loving wife.* It was unsigned, but obviously written by the same hand that had autographed the painting. And next to the photograph, on an otherwise barren desk top, a carefully laid pipe reposed in an empty ashtray. Pitt picked it up and smelled the blackened bowl; it hadn't been smoked in months. Nothing looked used or handled. It was a museum without dust, a house without odor. And, like the ship herself, quiet as a graveyard.

He returned to the alleyway, closing the door behind him, almost wishing some strange voice, any voice, would shout, "Who goes there?" or "What are you doing here?" The stillness made his sweat run cold. Pitt began to imagine vague shapes in shadowy corners. His heartbeat thumped at an accelerating pace. It couldn't have been more than ten seconds that he stood there not moving a muscle, forcing his mind back into rational control.

It'll be dawn soon, he thought. Hurry, must hurry. He ran down the port alleyway, ignoring any attempt at stealth and secrecy, and threw open the other cabin doors. Each small compartment was like the black Hole of Calcutta. One quick sweep of the hooded light told the same story as the captain's cabin. He also searched the radio cabin. The transmitter was warm and pre-set on a VHF frequency, but the radio operator was conspicuous by his absence. Pitt slipped the door shut and headed aft.

Companionways, port and starboard alleyways, they all seemed to merge into one long, black, underground tunnel. It was an effort not to lose his sense of direction in the maze. A naked man, except for the flotation vest, in a dark nightmare of gray paint and steel walls. He tripped over a bulkhead step and fell, banging a shin and dropping the flashlight; all in harmony with an uttered, "Goddamn!"

The flashlight had fallen on the hard deck, shattering the lens and blinking out. He knelt on his hands and knees, muttering additional curses and searching frantically. After agonizing seconds his hands grasped the aluminum-plated case. The glass of the lens tinkled with grim foreboding inside the cloth cover. He picked it up and pushed the switch forward. The bulb blinked on as dull as ever. Pitt uttered a gasp of relief and shined the subdued beam down the passage. It dimly illuminated a door that was titled *Fire Passage - Number Three Hold*.

The great chambers of Carlsbad Caverns couldn't have looked much less formidable than Number Three Hold. All that Pitt's light showed was a vast steel cave crammed with countless sacks and stacked from deck to hatch cover on wooden tiers. The air was permeated with a sweet incense kind of odor. The cocoa from Ceylon, Pitt surmised. He took the diver's knife and cut a small half inch hole in the coarse cloth of one of the sacks. A flow of stony hard beans fell to the deck, bouncing and rattling like a hail on a quonset hut. A quick examination under the flashlight proved the parchment skinned beans to be the genuine article.

Suddenly he heard a noise. It was faint and indistinct, but it was there. He froze, listening. Then it stopped as abruptly as it had come, and silence once more gripped the haunted ship; a deserted ship with all its dark and hidden secrets. Maybe it's a ghost ship after all, Pitt mused. Another *Mary Celeste* or *Flying Dutchman*. All that was missing was a stormy sea with rain lashing the top decks and lightning flashing in the night and a gale shrieking through the derricks.

There was nothing more to see in the hold. Pitt left and headed for the engine room. He lost a precious eight minutes finding the right companionway. The heart of the ship was warm from the heat of the engines and smelled of hot oil. He stood on the catwalk above the huge and lifeless machinery and searched for a sign that would indicate bona fide human activity. The flashlight caught the gleam of burnished pipes that snaked across the bulkheads in geometric parallel lines, ending in a mass fusion of valves and gauges. Then the faint beam fell on a carelessly wadded oily rag. Above the rag was a shelf containing several coffee-stained cups, and to the left of those, a tray of scattered tools with greasy finger marks. At least someone was working this part of the ship, he thought, quite relieved. He knew that most engine rooms were kept as clean as a hospital ward, but this one was messy. But where was the chief engineer and his oilmen? They couldn't have evaporated into the Aegean atmosphere.

Pitt started to leave, then he stopped. There it was

again; the same mysterious sound, echoing through the ship's hull. He stood stock-still, holding his breath for what seemed a lifetime. It was an odd, uncanny sound, like the scraping of a ship's keel over a submerged rock or coral reef. Pitt involuntarily shivered. It also reminded him of the way chalk squeaked across a blackboard. The sound lasted for perhaps ten seconds, then it was punctuated with the dull clank of metal against metal.

Pitt had never sat bathed with cold sweat in a cell on San Quentin's death row, waiting for the warden and the prison guards to escort him to the gas chamber. Nor did he have to be there to describe the experience for he knew exactly what it felt like. To be alone in a claustorophobic atmosphere, expecting the footsteps of death to come treading from the black unknown, was a blood chilling business. When in doubt, he thought, run like a son of a bitch. And run like a son of a bitch he did. Back through the alleyways, back up the companionstairs, until at last his lungs were greeted by the pure, wholesome air on deck.

The early morning was still dark and the derricks reached toward the velvet ceiling of a sky that was alive with a dazzling array of stars. There was scarcely a stir of wind. Over the bridge, the radio mast swayed back and forth across the milky way, and below Pitt's feet, the hull creaked from the rolls of the gentle swells. He hesitated a moment, gazing at the dark line of the Thasos coast, yet a bare mile away. Then he looked down at the smooth black surface of the water. It looked so inviting, so peaceful.

The flashlight still glowed. Pitt cursed his stupidity for not switching it off when he reached the open deck. Might as well have advertised my presence with a neon sign, he thought. He quickly doused the light. Then carefully, so as not to cut himself on the broken glass, he unwrapped his swimtrunks and removed the remains of the lens. He hurled the tiny slivers over the railing and listened till the faint splash, like rain on a pond, reached his ears. He was tempted to deep six the flashlight too, but his mind shifted into gear and rejected the impulse. Leaving the rack in the wheelhouse void of the flashlight would be about as clever as sending the captain, if there was a captain, a telegram and saying, "Just before dawn, there was a prowler on board your ship who ransacked it from stem to stern." It very definitely wasn't a smart move, not with people like these who had outfoxed nearly every law enforcement agency in the world. The fact that the lens was missing would be a gamble that Pitt would have to take.

He glanced at his watch as he hurried back to the wheelhouse. The luminous hands showed 4:13. The sun would be blossoming soon. He scrambled onto the bridge and replaced the flashlight in the rack. His haste was almost frantic. He had to be off the ship, into his diving gear and a good two hundred yards distant before daylight gave him away.

The forward deck was still deserted, or at least it seemed to be. A fluttering noise came from behind Pitt. Instantly he spun around in a sudden renewed fear and unsheathed the knife in one deft movement. His nerves were stretched taut to the border of panic, his head pounded like a drum roll. God, he thought, I can't be caught now, not this close to safety.

It was nothing but a gull that had flown out of the night and landed on a ventilator, the bird pointed a tiny eye at Pitt and cocked its head questioningly. No doubt wondering what sort of crazy human would run around a ship in the early morning, clothed in nothing but a flotation vest while holding a knife in one hand and a bathing suit in the other. The relief made Pitt feel weak at the knees. It had been quite a scare and he was badly shaken. When he boarded the ship he didn't know what he expected to find: what he found was silence tinged with unknown terror. Limply he leaned against the railing, getting a grip on himself. At this rate he'd have heart failure or a mental breakdown before sunrise. He took several deep breaths, exhaling slowly until the fear subsided.

Without a backward glance, he swung over the rail and shinnied down the anchor chain, vastly relieved at departing the ghostly ship. It was a welcome comfort to be in the soothing water again. The sea opened its arms and gave him a sense of remoteness from danger.

It took only a minute for Pitt to slip on his swimtrunks and retrieve his diving gear. Fitting an aqualung tank on your back in the darkness with the swells pushing you against the sides of a steel hull isn't an easy operation. But the Ditch and Recovery experience he had obtained during his early diving days came in handy now, and he accomplished the task with little effort. He looked around for the wooden crate, but it had drifted into the black curtain of night and disappeared; the wave action and incoming tide, by this time, carrying it halfway to the beach.

He lay there dead in the water and considered the possibility of diving under the *Queen Artemisia* and examining her hull. The weird scraping noise he had heard in the engine room seemed to have come from somewhere outside the plates and below the keel. Then it occurred to him the plan was hopeless. Without an underwater light he could see nothing. And he wasn't in the mood to grope like a blind man along a fourhundred foot hull that was encrusted with razor sharp barnacles. He'd heard old tales that described in detail the ancient and brutal practice of keelhauling insubordinate British sailors. He remembered one particularly bloodcurdling account of a gunner's mate who was dragged under the keel of the *H.M.S. Confident* off the coast of Timor in 1786. Punished for stealing a cup of brandy from the captain's locker, the poor fellow was dragged under the keel of the ship until his body was sliced to ribbons and the white of his ribs and backbone were visible. The unfortunate man might have survived, but before the crew could hoist him back on board, a pair of Mako sharks, attracted by the scent of blood, attacked and chewed the man to pieces before the horrified eyes of the men on deck. Pitt knew what a shark could do. He had once pulled a boy from the surf in Key West who had taken a nasty bite by a shark. The boy had lived, but a massive piece of tissue would always be missing from his left thigh.

Pitt cursed out loud. He must stop thinking about

things like that. His ears began to ring from a humming sound. At first he thought it was a trick of his imagination. He shook his head violently: it was still there, only louder; it seemed to be gaining momentum. Then Pitt knew where the humming was coming from.

The ship's generators had started again. The navigation lights blinked on, and the *Queen Artemisia* suddenly came alive with sound. If there was ever a time when the better part of valor was discretion, it was now. Pitt clamped the mouthpiece of the regulator between his teeth and dove clear of the ship. He kicked his fins with every ounce of power in his legs, seeing nothing under the ink black water, hearing only the strange gurgling sound of his exhaust bubbles. It was times like this that he wished he didn't smoke. After covering nearly fifty-five yards, he surfaced and looked back at the ship.

The *Queen Artemisia* rode at anchor in tombstone solitude, her silhouette outlined against the graying eastern sky like an old fashioned shadowgram. Dim shafts of white light came to life here and there about the ship, interrupted only by the green glow of the starboard navigation light. For several minutes nothing more happened. Then without any signal or shouted command, the anchor clattered up from the seafloor and clanged into the hull. The wheelhouse was lit and Pitt could see it clearly; it was still vacant. It just can't be, he repeated to himself over and over again: it just can't be. But the old ship hadn't yet finished the last act of her ghostly performance. As if on cue, the *Queen Artemisia's* telegraph jangled faintly across the calm pre-dawn sea. The engines responded with their gentle throb, and the ship continued on her voyage: the secret of her evil cargo still locked somewhere within her steel plates.

Pitt didn't have to see the ship move to know it was underway; he could feel the beat of her propellers through the water. Fifty-five yards was more than enough. At that distance he was invisible to any lookout and had little to fear from being sucked through the huge propellers and mangled into fish bait.

A seething flood of frustration swept over Pitt as the great hull slowly slid past his bobbing head. It was as though he was watching a ballistic missile lift from a launching pad and hurtle on its pre-set path toward devastation and death. He was helpless, he could do nothing to stop it. Hidden somewhere on the *Queen Artemisia* was enough heroin to drown half the population of the Northern Hemisphere in delirium. God alone knew what chaos would erupt in every city and town if it was distributed to all the peddling scum who preyed on its malignant addiction. How many people would become listless dregs and eventually die from the drug's deadly narcosis? One hundred and thirty tons of heroin on the ship. What was that song again, the little ditty that he'd sung all those long years ago in school. "A hundred bottles of beer on the wall." It had nearly the same ring, but it was for light hearts and souls, not drugged minds and lost hopes.

Then Pitt thought of himself. Not with self pride for destroying the yellow Albatros or searching the *Queen Artemisia* and getting away with it undetected. He thought of himself only as an idiot for risking his life on a job he had no business performing, a job he wasn't paid to do. His orders were to expedite oceanographic expeditions. No one said anything about chasing after drug smugglers. What could *he* accomplish? He wasn't a guardian angel of humanity. Let Zacynthus, Zeno, INTERPOL and every other damn cop in the world play cat and mouse with von Till. It was their game, they were trained for it. And they were paid for it too.

Again Pitt swore loudly to himself. He had already spent too much time daydreaming. It was time to head for shore. Mechanically, his eyes watched the ship's lights diminish bit by bit into the fading darkness of the early morning. He was just wading onto the beach when the sun lifted itself from the horizon and threw its rays on the rock strewn summits of the Thasos mountains.

Pitt stripped off the tank and let it fall to the soft wet sand along with the breathing regulator and his mask and snorkel. Exhaustion curled its numbing tentacles around him and he succumbed to it, dropping to his hands and knees. His body felt sore and beat, but his mind hardly noticed these things; it was busy with something else.

Pitt could find no indication of the heroin on board the ship, nor would the Bureau of Narcotics or the Customs Inspectors. That much was certain. Below the waterline, that was a possibility. But surely the wary investigators would have divers examine every inch of the hull when the ship docked. Besides, there was no way a cargo of that size could be removed, unless it was dropped in the water and recovered later. That wouldn't work either, he thought, it was too obvious; retrieving a watertight container filled with a hundred and thirty tons of solid material would require a full scale salvage operation. No, there had to be a more ingenious method, one that had successfully defied detection for so long.

He took the diver's knife and idly began sketching the *Queen Artemisia's* outline in the wet sand. Then, quite suddenly, the idea of a diagram intrigued him. He stood up and traced a hull that stretched for approximately thirty feet. The bridge, the holds and engine room, every detail he could recall was etched into the yielding white sand. Minutes passed and the ship started to take shape. Pitt had become so totally absorbed in his work that he didn't notice an old man and a donkey, trudging wearily along the beach.

The old man stopped in his tracks and stared at Pitt from a ripened old face that had seen too many decades of strife to show an expression of bewilderment. After a few moments he shrugged uncomprehendingly and ambled off after his donkey.

Finally the diagram was nearly complete, down to the last companionway. The knife flashed in the new sun as Pitt added a final humorous touch; a tiny bird on a tiny ventilator. Then he stepped back to admire his handiwork. He stared at it for a moment, then laughed aloud. "One thing's certain, I'll never be acclaimed for my artwork. It looks more like a pregnant whale than a ship."

Pitt continued to absentmindedly gaze at the sand

drawing. Suddenly his eyes took on a trance-like glaze and his rugged face lost all expression. The spark of a novel and fanciful idea lit dimly in his conscious mind. At first the idea seemed too outlandish for him to consider, but the more he dwelt on its possibilities, the more feasible it became. Quickly he traced additional lines in the sand. Completely absorbed again, he raced to match up the diagram with the picture in his mind. When the last change was finished, his mouth slowly twisted into a grim smile of satisfaction. Damned clever of von Till, he thought, damned clever.

He wasn't tired anymore, his mind was no longer burdened with unsolvable questions. It was a new approach, a new kind of answer. It should have been discovered long before. Quickly, he gathered up the diving equipment and started to hike over the incline that separated the beach from the coastal road. There was no thought of quitting the game now. The next inning would prove to be the most interesting. At the top he turned and looked back at the sketch of the *Queen Artemisia* in the sand.

The rising tide was just washing over and erasing the ship's funnel, the funnel marked with the big Minerva "*M*."

14

Giordino lay stretched out beside a blue Air Force pickup truck, dead asleep, his head resting on a binocular case and both feet propped carelessly on a large rock. A trail of ants tramped across his outflung forearm and, ignoring the obstacle in their path, continued their uninterrupted journey toward a small mound of loose dirt. Pitt looked down smiling. If there was one thing Giordino could do, and do well, he thought, it was sleeping anywhere at anytime and under any condition.

Pitt shook his fins, letting the salty dampness dribble on Giordino's composed face. No drowsy babble, no sudden reaction greeted the rude sprinkling. The only response came from one big brown eye that popped open, gazing straight at Pitt in obvious annoyance.

"Aha! Behold! Our intrepid guardian with the watchful eye!" There was no mistaking Pitt's sarcastic tone. "I shudder to think of the death toll if you should ever decide to become a lifeguard."

The opposite lid slowly raised like a window shade, revealing the matching eye. "Just to set the record straight," Giordino said wearily. "These tired old eyes were glued to the night glasses from the time you got into your packing crate to the time you came ashore and started playing in the sand."

"My apologies old friend." Pitt laughed. "I suppose that doubting your unflagging vigilance will cost me another drink?"

"Two drinks," Giordino murmured slyly.

"Consider it done."

Giordino sat up, blinking in the sun. He noticed the ants and casually brushed them off his arm. "How'd your swim go?"

"Robert Southey must have had the *Queen Artemisia* in mind when he wrote 'No stir in the air, no stir in the sea, the ship was still as she could be.' You might say that I found something by finding nothing."

"I don't get it."

"I'll explain later." Pitt lifted the diving gear and loaded it in the truck bed. "Any word from Zac?"

"Not yet." Giordino trained the binoculars on von Till's villa. "He and Zeno took a platoon of the local gendarmerie and staked out von Till's baronial estate. Darius stayed on the radio at the warehouse, traversing wave lengths in case there was any transmission between the shore and ship."

"Sounds like a thorough effort, but unfortunately a waste of time." Pitt toweled his black hair, then ran a comb through it. "Where can a man find a drink and a cigarette around here?"

Giordino nodded toward the truck cab. "I can't help you on the drink, but there's a pack of Greek cancer sticks on the front seat."

Pitt leaned in the truck cab and removed an oval shaped cigarette from a black and gold box of Hellas Specials. He'd never tried one before and was surprised at the mildness. After his ordeal of the past two hours, rolled seaweed would have tasted good.

"Someone kick you in the shins?" Giordino asked matter-of-factly.

Pitt exhaled a cloud of smoke and peered down at his leg. There was a deep red gash below the right knee and blood was oozing slowly along its entire length. For two inches in every direction the skin was a colorful combination of green, blue and purple.

"I had a bit of bad luck, a run in with a bulkhead door."

"I'd better fix that for you." Giordino turned and pulled an Air Force issue first aid kit from the glove compartment. "A minor operation like this is mere child's play for Doctor Giordino, the world renowned brain surgeon. I don't mean to brag, but I'm rather good at heart transplants too."

Pitt tried to suppress a laugh, but failed. "Just make sure you put the gauze on before, not after the tape."

Giordino feigned a pained expression. "Such a terrible thing to say." The sly look returned. "You'll change your tune when you get my bill."

There was no choice left for Pitt except to shrug in resignation and place his bruised leg in Giordino's hands. Nothing more was said for the next few minutes. Pitt sat and absorbed the silence, gazing at the sky-dyed blue water and the shoreline that rested under the white sands of antiquity. The narrow beach below the road stretched southward for six miles before it faded into a thin line and disappeared behind the western tip of the island. There wasn't a soul to be seen anywhere along the surf's edge; the emptiness possessed all the mystic allure and romantic charm so often pictured on South Seas travel posters. It was indeed a fragment of paradise.

Pitt noted that the surf was running at two feet with eight second intervals between crests. The waves broke low and at least one hundred yards out. Then in a final burst of fury, they surged forward in majestic spray plumed rows, only to slowly dissolve and die in small eddys at the tideline. To a swimmer, the conditions were perfect; to a surfer, they were fair; but to a diver, the shallow sandy bottom and the dark blue water spelled barren waste. For sheer underwater adventure it is the greener, reef strewn waters that attract the diver, for it is there that the beauty of sea life abounds.

Pitt panned his eyes a hundred and eighty degrees and looked to the north. Here it was a different story.

High craggy cliffs, barren of all vegetation, rose out of the sea, their faces worn and etched by the endless onslaught of the breakers. Great fallen rocks and yawning fissures bore mute testimony to what old mother nature could do when given the tools of her trade to work with. There was one particular stretch of rugged cliffline that intrigued Pitt.

Strangely enough, this one sector was not pounded like the others. The waters below the sheer, straight up and down rock mass were calm and flat, a garden pond bordered on three sides by foaming swirling waters. For a hundred square yards the sea was green and still, the boiling white ceased to exist. It seemed unreal.

Pitt speculated on what wonders a diver might find there. Only God alone could have observed the ageless formation of the island, the coming and going of the great ice ages, the changing levels of the ancient sea. Maybe, he thought, just maybe the mountainous breakers carved their fury into the sides of these cliffs, creating an underwater pockmarked surface of sea caves.

"There you are," Giordino said in a humorous tone. "Another triumph for medical science by the great Giordino." Pitt wasn't fooled for a second by the outward display of exaggerated vanity. Giordino's comic dialogue was forever used to camouflage his genuine concern for Pitt. Giordino stood up, running his eyes over Pitt's body, and shook his head in mild wonder. "With all those bandages on your nose, chest and leg, you're beginning to look like a spare tire out of a nineteen thirties, depression era comic strip."

"You're right." Pitt took a few steps to relieve the increasing stiffness in his leg. "I feel more like a bumper tire on a tugboat."

"Here comes Zac," Giordino said pointing. Pitt twisted and looked in the direction of Giordino's extended finger.

The black Mercedes was approaching down a dirt trail from the mountains, pulling a cloud of brown dust behind its rear bumper. A quarter of a mile away it swung onto the paved coastal road, dropping the dust cloud, and soon Pitt could hear the steady purr of the diesel engine above the beat from the surf below. The car rolled to a stop beside the truck and Zacynthus and Zeno unreeled from the front seat. They were followed by Darius, who made no attempt to disguise a painful limp. Zacynthus was dressed in old faded army fatigues, and his eyes were tired and bloodshot. He gave the impression of a man who had spent a dismal and sleepless night. Pitt grinned sympathetically at him.

"Well Zac, how did it go? See anything interesting?"

Zacynthus didn't seem to hear him. He wearily pulled his pipe from a pocket, filled the bowl and lit it. Then he sank slowly to the ground, stretching out and leaning on one elbow.

"The bastards, the dirty cunning bastards," he swore bitterly. "We spent the whole night straining our eyes and sneaking around trees and boulders, with mosquitos attacking us at every turn. And what did we find?" He took a deep breath to answer his own question, but Pitt beat him to it.

"You found nothing, you saw nothing and you heard nothing."

Zacynthus managed a faint smile. "Does it show that much?"

"It shows," Pitt replied briefly.

"This whole business is exceedingly exasperating." Zacynthus accented his words by pounding his fist into the soft earth.

"Exceedingly exasperating?" Pitt echoed. "Is that the best you can do?"

Zacynthus sat up and shrugged his shoulders helplessly. "I've just about reached the end of my rope. I feel as though I've just clawed my way up a steep mountain, only to find the peak enshrouded in fog. Possibly you understand, I don't know, but I've dedicated my life to tracking down scum like von Till." He paused for a moment, then went on very quietly. "I've never failed to crack a case. I can't give up now. That ship must be stopped, and yet, thanks to our lily white code of justice, it can't be stopped. God, can you imagine what will happen if that cargo of heroin reaches the States?"

"I've given it some thought."

"Screw your code of justice." Giordino seemed vexed. "Let me stick a limpet mine on that old tub's hull and *bang*," he formed a blast cloud with his hands. "The fish inherit the drugs."

Zacynthus nodded slowly. "You have a direct approach, but a——"

"Simple mind," Pitt interrupted again. He grinned at Giordino's scornful glance.

"Believe me, I would much prefer to see a hundred schools of doped-up fish than one drug crazed school boy." Zacynthus' voice was grim. "Destroying that ship would only solve the immediate problem; it's like cutting off one tentacle of an octopus. We'd still be left with von Till and his able gang of sea-going smugglers, not to mention the unanswered riddle of his—I am forced to admit—ingenious operation. No, we must be patient. The *Queen Artemisia* hasn't docked at Chicago yet. We'll get another chance at her in Marseille."

"I don't think you'll have any better luck in Marseille," Pitt said doubtfully. "Even if one of your phony French dockworkers slips on board, you have the gilt-edged Pitt guarantee that he won't find anything worth writing home about."

"How would you know that for certain?" Zacynthus suddenly looked up, surprised. "Unless . . . unless you somehow searched the ship yourself."

"With him, anything's possible," Giordino murmured. "He was seaward of the ship when it anchored. I lost him through the night glasses for almost half an hour."

Now all four men looked at Pitt questioningly.

Pitt laughed and flipped his cigarette over the embankment. "The time has come, the walrus said, to speak of many things. Gather round gentlemen and listen to the cloak and dagger adventures of Dirk Pitt, the naked cat burglar."

Pitt finally leaned back against the truck and became silent. For a long moment he stared at the thoughtful faces in front of him.

"There you have it. As neat a little set-up as you can find." He smiled wryly. "The *Queen Artemisia* is in reality nothing but a false front. Oh sure, it sails the briny blue, picking up and delivering cargo. That's where any similarity between a bona fide cargo freighter and *Queen* ends. She's an old ship, true, but beneath her steel skin beats a complete up-to-date centralized control system. I saw the same equipment on an old ship in the Pacific just last year. No large crew is required. Six or seven men can handle her easily."

"No fuss, no muss," Giordino said admiringly.

"Precisely," Pitt nodded. "Each compartment, each cabin is set up as a stage prop. When the ship reaches port the crew materializes from the wings and turns into a cast of actors."

"Pardon this humble man's blind perception, Major." The peasant choice of words failed to mask the Oxford accent of Zeno's voice. "I do not understand how the *Queen Artemisia* can engage in commercial shipping without the necessary maintenance during long voyages."

"It's like a historical landmark," Pitt explained. "Let's say a famous castle where the fires in the fireplaces still burn, the plumbing still works, and the grounds are always trimmed and neat. Five days out of the week the castle is closed, but on the weekends it opens for the tourists, or, in this case, the Customs Inspectors."

"And the caretakers?" Zeno asked quizzically.

"The caretakers," Pitt murmured, "live in the cellar."

"Only rats live in cellars," Darius ventured dryly.

"A very appropriate observation, Darius," Pitt said approvingly. "Particularly when you consider the two-legged variety we're dealing with."

"Cellars, stage props, castles. A crew buried somewhere in the hull. What are you driving at?" Zacynthus demanded. "Please get to the point."

"I'm coming to it. To begin with, the crew isn't quartered in the hull. They're quartered under it."

Zacynthus' eyes narrowed. "That's not possible."

"On the contrary," Pitt grinned. "It would be entirely possible if the good *Queen Artemisia* was pregnant."

There was a brief incredulous silence. All four stared at Pitt in blank skepticism. Giordino broke the silence first.

"You're trying to tell us something, but I'll be damned if you're getting through."

"Zac admitted that von Till's method of smuggling is ingenious," Pitt said. "And he's right. The ingenuity lies in the simplicity. The *Queen Artemisia* and the other Minerva ships can operate independently or they can be controlled by a satellite vessel attached to their hulls. Think about it for a minute. It's not as ridiculous as it sounds." Pitt spoke with a calm surety about him that began to crack any doubts. "The *Queen* didn't cruise two days off her course just to blow kisses at von Till. Contact must have been made somehow." He turned to Zacynthus and Zeno. "You and your men watched the villa and saw no sign of a signal."

"Nor did anyone enter or leave," Zeno added.

"Same goes for the ship," said Giordino eyeing Pitt curiously. "No one set foot on the beach except you."

"Darius and I make it unanimous," said Pitt. "He heard no radio transmissions and I found the radio cabin deserted."

"I'm beginning to see your point," Zac said thoughtfully. "Any communication between the ship and von Till could only have taken place underwater. But I'm still not sure I buy your satellite vessel theory."

"Try this one." Pitt paused. "What travels long distances under water, carries a crew, has the capacity to hold a hundred and thirty tons of heroin, and would never be searched by Customs or the Bureau of Narcotic Inspectors? The only logical answer is a full scale submarine."

"Nice try, but it won't pass." Zac shook his head. "We've had divers search beneath the waterline of every Minerva ship at least a hundred times. They have yet to discover a submarine."

"They most likely never will." Pitt's mouth felt dry and his cigarette tasted like burnt cardboard. He flipped the butt out into the middle of the road and watched it smoke until the tar beneath the glowing ember melted into a tiny black pool. "It's not the method that's at fault. Your divers are missing the boat—if you'll forgive the pun—because of timing."

"Are you suggesting the sub is released before the ships dock?" Zacynthus asked.

"That's the general idea," Pitt agreed.

"What then? Where does it go?"

"For the answers let's begin with the *Queen Artemisia* in Shanghai." Pitt paused a moment, collecting his thoughts. "If you had been standing on the wharves of the Whangpoo River, watching the ship take on cargo you'd have seen an ordinary loading operation. Cranes lifting sacks—they would be easiest to handle the heroin into the ship's holds. The heroin came first, but it didn't remain in the holds. It was transferred to the sub, probably through a hidden hatch that wouldn't show up on any Customs detection gear. The legitimate cargo was then loaded on board and the *Queen* shoved off for Ceylon. There, the soybeans and tea were exchanged for the cocoa and graphite—another legitimate cargo. The detour to Thasos came next. For orders from von Till most likely. Then on to Marseille for fuel and the final drop in Chicago."

"There's something bugging me," Giordino murmured.

"Such as?"

"I'm no expert on pigboats so I can't figure how one could play baby kangaroo with a freighter or where it could accommodate two hundred and sixty thousand pounds of drugs."

"Modifications had to be made," Pitt acknowledged. "But it wouldn't take any great engineering feat to remove the conning tower and other projections until the top deck fitted flush against the mother ship's keel. The average fleet-type sub of World War II had a displacement of fifteen hundred tons, a length of over three hundred feet, a hull height of ten feet, and a beam of twenty-seven feet—roughly twice the size of a suburban house. Once the torpedo rooms, the eighty man crew quarters and the unnecessary paraphernalia were cleared out there would be more than ample space to store the heroin."

Pitt saw that Zacynthus was regarding him in a very peculiar manner: there was a deep look of contemplation on his face. Then his features showed the first traces of genuine understanding.

"Tell me, Major," he asked. "What speed could the *Queen Artemisia* make with a sub fastened to her hull?"

Pitt thought a moment. "I'd say about twelve knots. Unencumbered, however, the ship's normal cruising speed would be closer to fifteen or sixteen."

Zacynthus turned to Zeno. "It's quite possible the Major's on the right track."

"I know what you are thinking, my Inspector." Zeno's teeth parted beneath the great moustache. "We have often concerned our thoughts with the puzzling variance of the cruising speeds among Minerva ships."

Zacynthus' eyes came back to Pitt. "The heroin drop, when and how is it made?"

"At night during high tide. Too risky during the day. The sub could be spotted from the air—"

"That checks." Zacynthus interrupted. "Von Till's freighters are always scheduled to reach port after sunset."

"As to the drop," Pitt hadn't even taken notice of the interruption. "The sub is released immediately after entering port. Without a conning tower or periscope it must be guided from the surface by a small craft. Here, the only real chance of failure comes in, being rammed in the dark by an unsuspecting vessel."

"No doubt they'd have a pilot on board who was familiar with every inch of the harbor," Zacynthus said thoughtfully.

"A first rate harbor pilot is an absolute necessity for an operation like von Till's," Pitt agreed. "Dodging underwater obstacles over a shallow bottom in the dark is no exercise for an amateur yachtsman."

"The next problem on the agenda," Zacynthus said slowly, "is to determine the location where the sub can unload and distribute the heroin without fear of detection."

"How about a deserted warehouse?" Giordino volunteered. His eyes were closed and he looked like he was dozing, but Pitt knew from long experience that he hadn't missed a word.

Pitt laughed. "The evil villain who slinks around deserted warehouses went out with Sherlock Holmes. Waterfront property is at a premium. An idle building would only arouse instant suspicion. Besides, as Zac here can tell you, a warehouse would be the first place an investigator would look."

A faint smile crossed Zacynthus' lips. "Major Pitt is right. All docks and warehouses are closely watched by our Bureau and Customs, not to mention the County Harbor Patrols. No, whatever the method, it must be extremely clever. Clever enough to have worked smoothly and successfully all these years."

There was a long pause, then he went on quietly.

"Now at long last we have a definite lead. It's only a thread, but if it's attached to a rope and the rope is attached to a chain, then with a bit of good fortune von Till will be found at the other end."

"If you wish to pursue the Major's supposition, it is vital that Darius inform our agents in Marseille." Zeno's tone was that of a man trying to convince himself of something that was not a positive fact.

"No, the less they know, the better," Zacynthus shook his head. "I want no action taken that might put a bug in von Till's ear. The *Queen Artemisia* and the heroin must reach Chicago without interference."

"Very sly," Pitt grinned. "Using von Till's cargo to attract the sharks."

"It's not difficult to guess," Zacynthus nodded. "Every big time hood and every underworld organization engaged in illegal drug traffic will be on hand to greet that sub." He paused to take a puff on his pipe. "The Bureau of Narcotics will be more than happy to host the reception."

"Providing you can find the drop location," Pitt added.

"We'll find it," Zacynthus said confidently. "The *Queen* won't enter the Great Lakes for at least three weeks. That will give us time enough to search every pier, boat yard and yacht club that even touches the shoreline. Discreetly of course, no sense in blowing the whistle and losing all the players."

"That won't be easy."

"You underestimate the Bureau," Zacynthus acted hurt. "We happen to be experts at this sort of thing. To put your mind at ease, we won't attempt to pinpoint the exact location, only the general area. Radar will track the sub to its final destination. At the opportune moment we move in."

Pitt looked at him somberly. "You're taking a great deal for granted."

Zacynthus stared back. "I'm surprised at you, Major. It was you who gave us a direction. The first feasible direction, I might add, that INTERPOL and the Bureau have had in twenty years. Can it be you're beginning to doubt your own deductions?"

Pitt shook his head. "No, I'm certain I've guessed right about the submarine."

"Then what is your problem?"

"I think you're putting all your eggs in one basket by concentrating your main effort in Chicago."

"What better place to set a trap?"

Pitt spoke slowly and precisely. "A hundred and one things could happen between now and when the

Queen Artemisia is boarded by Customs. You yourself said three weeks was enough time to search the city's waterfront. Why rush things? I strongly suggest that you want and do a little more fact digging before you fully commit yourself."

Zacynthus looked at Pitt quizzically. "What do you have in mind?"

Pitt leaned against the truck; already the blue-coated metal was hot to the touch. He looked out toward the sea again, the rugged face beneath the wavy black hair intense with concentration. He breathed deeply, drawing in the salt scented air of the Aegean, and he was lost for long seconds at the wonder of the intoxicating sensation. With effort he shook his mind back to the cold reality of the moment, and when he spoke he knew there was something he had to do.

"Zac, I need ten good men and an old sea dog who is familiar with the waters around Thasos."

"Why?" Zacynthus asked simply.

"It stands to reason that if von Till carries out his smuggling activities from the villa and communicates with his ships under water he must have a hidden base of operations somewhere along this coastline."

"And it is your intention to find it."

"That's the general idea," Pitt stated flatly. He looked Zacynthus straight in the face. "Well?"

Zacynthus thoughtfully toyed with his pipe before answering. "Impossible." The voice was firm. "I cannot allow it. You're a talented man, Major. Up to now your judgment rang with practical logic. And nobody appreciates more than me the great help you have been to us. However, I cannot take any chances of alarming von Till. I repeat, the ship and the heroin must reach Chicago without interference."

"Von Till is already alarmed." Pitt was very definite. "He can't help but be wise to you. The British destroyer and the Turkish aircraft that shadowed the *Queen Artemisia* from Ceylon to the Aegean were a dead give away that INTERPOL was on to the heroin.

I say stop him now, before any more of his ships load or unload illegal cargo!"

"Until that ship deviates from its set course, and not before, I insist on a hands off policy regarding von Till." Zacynthus broke off for a few seconds, then he went on quietly. "You must understand: Colonel Zeno, Captain Darius and myself are narcotics men. If we are to do our job efficiently we cannot concern ourselves with white slavery, stolen gold or illegal transportation of known criminals. It sounds cruel and heartless, I admit, but INTERPOL has other good men and departments who specialize in these crimes. And they would say the same thing if this particular ship carried a cargo that was under their jurisdiction. No, I'm sorry, we may lose von Till in the end, but at that we'll lock up the biggest illegal drug distributors in North America, not to mention, drastically cut the outside flow of heroin."

There was a short period of silence, then Pitt exploded angrily.

"Bull-shit! If you round up the heroin, the submarine and its crew, and every dope peddler in the States, you still won't stop von Till. The minute he finds new buyers he'll be back with another boatload of drugs."

Pitt waited for a reaction. There was none.

"You have no authority over Giordino and me," Pitt continued. "Whatever we have to do from here on in, we'll do it without any cooperation from you."

Zacynthus' lips were pressed tightly together. His eyes stared fiercely at Pitt, then he glanced at his watch. "We're wasting time. I have only one hour to get to the Kavalla Airport and catch the morning flight for Athens." He pointed his pipe at Pitt like a gun. "I dislike losing arguments but you leave me no alternative. My regrets, Major. Though I am deeply in your debt, I must once again place you and Captain Giordino in custody."

"The hell you will," Pitt said coldly. "We're not going to oblige."

"You will suffer the indignity of forcible arrest if

you don't." Zacynthus patted a holstered forty-five automatic that clung to his hip.

Giordino lazily rose from the ground and grabbed Pitt by the arm. He was grinning. "Don't you think this would be a pretty good time for Giordino the Kid to practice his quick draw?"

Giordino was wearing a tee shirt and khaki pants; there was no sign of a tell-tale bulge. Pitt was mystified, but his confidence in his old friend was firm. He looked at Giordino with a mixture of hope and suspicion in his eyes.

"I doubt if you'd ever find a more opportune moment."

Zacynthus unsnapped the holster flap over the forty-five. "What the devil have you got up your sleeve this time? I must warn you—"

"Wait." The rasping voice came from Darius. "If you please, Inspector." The murderous intent. "I have an account to settle with these two."

Giordino was not to be hurried. He ignored the threat from Darius and spoke as calmly as if he were asking Pitt to pass the potatoes. "My cross draw is sheer art, but actually I'm faster from the hip. Which would you like to see first?"

"About now," Pitt said more curious than amused, "I'd settle for a fast draw from the crotch."

"Stop! Enough!" Zacynthus gestured his pipe irritably. "I suggest you be sensible and cooperate."

"How do you intend to keep us on ice for three weeks?" Pitt asked.

Zacynthus shrugged. "The jail on the mainland has excellent accommodations for political prisoners. Colonel Zeno here might be persuaded to use his influence and get you a cell overlooking the—" Zacynthus' mouth abruptly dropped open in midsentence; his brown eyes narrowed in helpless rage and he froze as immobile as a city park statue.

A tiny gun, no larger than an ordinary cap pistol, had suddenly materialized in Giordino's hand, the pencil thin muzzle pointed directly at the spot between Zacynthus' eyebrows. Even Pitt was caught off guard. Pure logic told him that Giordino had been bluffing; the last thing he or anyone else expected was for Giordino to produce an honest-to-god firearm.

15

A gun, no matter if it looks small and insignificant or massive and downright mean, is always a perfect attention getter. To say that Giordino was the center of attraction would be a classic understatement. He played the role to the hilt; the automatic held at full arm's length, a grim smile on the face. If academy awards were given for sheer bravado, he'd have won at least three.

For a long moment no one spoke. Then finally Zeno rammed a fist into one hand. A wane smile etched his swarthy face. "It was I who said you two men were cunning and dangerous, and yet, I am foolish enough to keep offering you new opportunities to prove it."

"We don't relish these embarrassing little scenes any more than you do," Pitt said equably. "Now if you gentlemen will excuse us, we'll close up shop and go home."

"No sense getting shot in the back." Giordino waved the baby automatic negligently at the three narcotics officers. "We'd better borrow their guns before we exit stage right."

"That won't be necessary," Pitt said. "No one is going to pull any triggers." He looked into Zacythus' eyes, then into Zeno's—and found them thoughtful and speculative. "It's really a stand off. You're tempted, but you won't shoot us from behind because you're all honorable men. Besides, it wouldn't be practical, the investigation of our deaths would only prove to be a messy affair. Von Till would love that. On the other hand, you know damn well we won't shoot back because we don't have nearly enough at stake to kill any one of you.

"Patience, I ask nothing but patience on your parts for the next ten hours. I promise you Zac, we will meet again before sunset, and on much friendlier terms." Pitt's voice seemed strangely prophetic, and the speculative look in Zacynthus' eyes changed to blank puzzlement.

Pitt was briefly tempted to prolong the game of cat and mouse, then he thought better of it. Zacynthus and Zeno appeared resigned to defeat, but not Darius. The huge brute moved two steps forward, his face was flushed with anger and his fists opened and closed like the shells of two giant South Pacific clams. It was clearly the time to beat a quick and orderly retreat.

Pitt moved slowly around the front of the truck, using the hood and fenders as a barrier between him and Darius. He climbed behind the steering wheel, wincing slightly as the sun splashed seat burned his naked thighs and back, and started the engine. Giordino followed him into the cab, never taking his eyes off the men beside the Mercedes, the gun very level in his hand. Then calmly, without any sign of desperate speed, Pitt smoothly shifted gears and aimed the truck toward Brady Field and the *First Attempt*'s whaleboat dock. He glanced in the rearview mirror, then to the road and back to the mirror again several times until the three figures in the road disappeared when the truck rounded a curve through an ancient grove of olive trees.

"Nothing like a gun to even the odds," Giordino sighed, leaning back comfortably against the seat.

"Let's see that popgun."

Giordino passed it butt first. "You'll have to admit, it came in damn handy."

Pitt studied the lilliputian gun, looking up from time to time to dodge potholes in the road. He recognized it as a vest pocket Mauser, twenty-five caliber, the type European women favored for protection; it could easily be concealed in a purse or garter. It was only good for close-in work; past ten feet the accuracy, even in the hands of an expert, was hopeless.

"We must consider ourselves extremely lucky."

"Lucky hell," Giordino grunted flatly. "That little baby evened the odds. Why do you think the old time gangsters called a gun an equalizer."

"Would you have pulled the trigger if Zac and his boys had decided not to cooperate?" Pitt asked.

"Without hesitation," Giordino replied confidently. "I'd have only winged them in the arms or legs. No sense in killing someone who keeps you supplied with Metaxa brandy."

"I can see you have a lot to learn about German automatics."

Giordino's eyes narrowed. "What do you mean by that?"

Pitt slowed to pass a small boy who was leading a heavily laden donkey. "Two things. First, a twenty-five caliber gun is hardly a man stopper. You could have emptied the clip into Darius, but without a killing shot to the heart or head you'd never have even slowed him down. And second, the expression on your face when you squeezed off the first shot would have been a sight to behold." Pitt casually tossed the gun onto Giordino's lap. "The safety catch is still on."

Pitt glanced briefly across the truck cab at Giordino. Giordino's eyes fell blankly to the gun in his lap. He made no attempt to pick it up. His face was expressionless, but Pitt knew him well enough to recognize an acute case of bafflement.

Giordino shrugged and gave Pitt a thin smile. "Kind of looks like Giordino the Kid just won the idiot award of the year. I just plumb forgot about the safety."

"You've never owned a Mauser. Where did you get it?"

"It belonged to your little playmate of the month. I discovered it when I was lugging her through the tunnel. She had it taped to her leg."

"You little bastard," Pitt said evenly. "You mean you had it all the time we were having our brains beat out by Darius?"

"Sure," Giordino nodded. "I concealed it inside one of my socks. I never had a chance to use it. You jumped Frankenstein before I was ready. After that, the brawl happened too fast. The next thing I knew I was flat on my back getting my head crushed. Then it was too late, I couldn't reach the peashooter."

Pitt became silent, already his mind was on another subject. It was still early in the morning and the trees edging the road threw their long misproportioned shadows toward the west. He drove mechanically, a hundred questions, a hundred doubts circulating through his mind. He didn't know where to start, and there was the plan that had taken form back there overlooking those surf pounded cliffs. The plan at best was a gamble, a long shot backed by nothing but an overpowering urge to carry it out. And then he was automatically depressing the brake pedal, slowing the truck down and stopping at the Brady Field main gate.

Forty minutes later they were climbing the boarding ladder of the *First Attempt*. The deck was deserted, but a chorus of hearty male laughter accompanied by the high-pitched giggle of a woman echoed from the messroom. Pitt and Giordino entered and found Teri surrounded by the entire crew and scientific staff of the ship. She was dressed, or undressed, in a knotted makeshift bikini that looked as if it would come unfurled at the first sign of a passing offshore breeze. She perched prettily on the mess table, the center of attraction, a queen holding court, and it was obvious that she enjoyed every male eyeball. Pitt bemusedly studied the men's faces for a moment. It was an elementary task to separate the scientists from the professional crewmen. The latter stood quietly and gazed lecherously at the generous display of feminine skin, their minds throwing pornographic scenes on the inside walls of their skulls like movie projectors. Most of the vocal activity came from the scientists. The marine biologists, the meteorologists, the geologists, each vying with frantic zeal for Teri's attention and behaving like schoolboys whose dormitory had just been invaded by a box office sex queen.

Commander Gunn saw Pitt and came over to him. "I'm glad you're back. Our radio man is about to go psycho. Since dawn this morning he's been receiving signals faster than he can write. Most of them are marked for your attention."

Pitt nodded. "Ok, let's go and read my fan mail." He turned to Giordino. "See if you can tear our queen bee away from her ardent admirers for a few minutes and escort her to Gunn's cabin. I want to ask her one or two very personal questions."

Giordino grinned. "From the looks of that crowd I'll probably get lynched if I try."

"If things get too tough just flash your gun," Pitt said sarcastically. "But don't forget to remove the safety."

Giordino's mouth dropped open like a landed fish. Before he could recover, Pitt and Gunn had left.

The radio man, a young black in his early twenties, looked up when they entered. "This one just came in for you, sir." He handed the message to Gunn.

Gunn studied it for a moment, then his lips slowly arched into a wide smile. "Listen to this. 'To Commander Gunn, officer commanding NUMA ship *First Attempt*. What in the goddamn hell kind of hornet's nest have you people stirred up in the Aegean. I sent you out there to study sea life, not play cops and robbers. You are hereby ordered to render every assistance, repeat, every assistance at your command to the local INTERPOL authorities. And don't return home without a goddamn Teaser. Admiral James Sandecker, NUMA, Washington.'"

"I'd say the Admiral is a bit off his usual form," murmured Pitt. "He used 'goddamn' only twice."

"Please lead me out of the dark," Gunn asked mildly. "What possible assistance could we be to INTERPOL?"

Pitt pondered a moment. Gunn would have to be led up to a crucial decision; it was decidedly too early to bare all the facts. Pitt dodged the question.

"We may be the only hope left to destroy von Till and his empire. It may mean taking a few risks, but the stakes are high."

Gunn removed his glasses and stared sharply at Pitt. "How high?"

"Enough heroin to hop-up the entire population of the United States and Canada," Pitt said slowly. "A hundred and thirty tons worth to be exact."

Gunn betrayed no sign of surprise. He calmly held up his glasses to the light, examining the lenses for smudges. Satisfied there were none, he replaced the horned-rims over his low set ears.

"Off hand I'd say that's a pretty fair amount. Why didn't you tell me about this last night when you brought the girl on board?"

"I needed more time and more answers, and right now I'm still short on both. But I think I've run on to something that will put this whole insane puzzle into a transparent pattern."

"I still don't know what you expect from me."

"We've got to hit von Till below the belt, way below the belt. This is an underwater show. I need every able-bodied man you can spare with scuba gear and weapons that can be carried in water; diving knifes, spear guns, anything."

"What guarantee can you give me that no one will get hurt?"

"Absolutely none," Pitt said quietly.

Gunn stared at Pitt for a full ten seconds, his face expressionless. "You realize the seriousness of what you're asking me? Most of the men aboard this ship are scientists, not commandos. They're tigers with a salino-meter, a nansen bottle or a microscope, but their skill at knifing another man in the guts or shooting a barbed spear into a navel leaves much to be desired."

"What about the crew?"

"All good men to have on your side in a barroom brawl, but like most professional seamen, they have an unhealthy dislike for any activity below the surface. They can't, or rather won't, put on a face mask and dive." Gunn shook his head. "I'm sorry Dirk, you're asking too much——"

"Come off it," Pitt snapped rudely. "This isn't the Little Big Horn and I'm not asking you to send the Seventh Cavalry against Sitting Bull and the Sioux nation. Look, not fifty miles from here a Minerva Lines freighter is churning across the Aegean with a cargo that is as lethal as any nuclear bomb. If that amount of heroin were dumped on the market in the States, our grandchildren would still be suffering from the cultural shockwaves. It's a nightmarish thought."

Pitt paused, letting his words sink in. He lit a cigarette and then continued.

"The Bureau of Narcotics and the Customs Department will be waiting. They've set a trap. If, and that's a big if, all goes well, the heroin and the smugglers, plus half the illegal drug sellers in the States, will be neatly scooped up and salted away behind bars."

"Then what's the problem?" Gunn pressed. "Where do the divers fit into the picture?"

"Let's just say I have a nagging doubt. Von Till hasn't come within a nautical mile of being caught with the goods, so to speak, for decades. Legally, our government agents can't board the cargo ship until it touches the United States' continental shelf, three weeks away. By then von Till might sense that INTERPOL is behaving overly cagey. Rather than cooperate with the good guys and sail into the trap, he'd have to reroute the ship at the last minute or else dump the heroin in the Atlantic. That leaves the narcotic agents and the customs inspectors standing around with nothing to do but play with themselves. The only sure way, the safe way, is to stop the ship now, before it leaves the Mediterranean."

"You're the man who said it—legally it can't be done."

"There is one way," Pitt drew on the cigarette, then slowly let the smoke trickle through his nose.

"Prove a solid case against von Till and Minerva Lines before morning."

Gunn shook his head again. "Even then, boarding a ship in international waters, particularly a ship that is registered to a friendly nation, can lead to political repercussions. I doubt if any country would want to touch it."

"There is one opportunity," Pitt said. "The ship stops at Marseilles for fuel. INTERPOL would have to work fast. If they received the necessary evidence and rushed through the legal paperwork they could seize the ship in port."

Gunn leaned against the doorway and gave Pitt a penetrating stare. "The catch is that you want to risk the lives of the people under my command."

"It has to be," Pitt said quietly."

"I think you're hedging," Gunn said slowly. "You're up to your ears in stormy waters. I don't like any of it. I'm responsible to NUMA for this ship and its personnel. All that interests me is the safe completion of this expedition. Why us? I don't see why INTERPOL or the local police can't conduct their own search operation. Finding divers on the mainland is no problem."

This was getting too damn awkward, Pitt thought. At this stage of the game he couldn't let on that Zacynthus was very much against even the slightest harrassment of von Till. Pitt had known Gunn for a little over a year, and in that time they had become good friends. The commander was a smart customer. The next scene would have to be played cool, very cool indeed. Pitt gazed suspiciously at the busy radio operator for a moment, then turned back to Gunn.

"Call it fate, coincidence or any other term you wish to choose, that put the *First Attempt* at Thasos at the exact moment to expose a beautifully planned criminal conspiracy. Von Till's entire smuggling operation depends upon the use of a submarine, maybe more than one, we don't know yet. The heroin is the biggest job he's ever undertaken. It's damn hard for the mind to conceive, but he could easily net over two hundred million dollars on this one shipment. He planned well,

nothing could stand in his way. Then one day he looks
out of his window and there sits an oceanographic research ship, not over two miles away. Learning that you
were scouting the water for a legendary fish he began to
run scared. There was a good chance that one of your
divers might discover his base of operation, and what's
most important, his method of smuggling. He was desperate. He couldn't blow you out of the water. The last
thing he wanted was a full scale investigation into the
loss of this ship. There was no hope of instigating anti-
American riots or violence. The people who live on the island are fun loving farmers and fishermen. They couldn't
care less about staging a demonstration against a scientific expedition. If anything, they welcomed you. The
local merchants aren't about to turn down free spending
researchers. Von Till gambled on a long shot. He staged
that attack on Brady Field, hoping Colonel Lewis would
order you out of the area as a safety precaution. When
this failed he threw caution to the winds and came directly at the *First Attempt*."

"I don't know," Gunn said hesitantly. "You make
it sound logical. Except for the submarines. No civilian
can go to his nearest yacht broker and buy a submarine."

"The only way von Till could lay his hands on a
sub without attracting attention would be to raise one
that was sunk in shallow water during time of war."

"You're beginning to sound interesting," Gunn
said quietly. He was tuned in on Pitt's channel now. He
had the shrewd look of an old prospector who just discovered a map to a hidden gold mine.

Pitt went on. "This is a job for professional underwater divers. By the time INTERPOL could put together a team of their own it would be too late." The
last was only a half truth, but it served Pitt admirably to
drive home the next point. "The time is now. And other
than Cousteau you've got the finest divers and equipment in the Mediterranean. I'm not going to give you
any crap about being the 'last hope of mankind' or that
'it's better to sacrifice a few to save millions.' All I'm
asking you for is a few volunteers to help me explore

the cliffs below von Till's villa. We may strike out and find nothing. On the other hand we may uncover enough evidence to impound the ship and the heroin and put von Till away for good. Hit or miss, we've got to try."

Gunn said nothing. His expression indicated deep thought and concentration. Pitt looked at him, considering, and then threw in the hook.

"It would be interesting if we could find out what happened to the yellow Albatros."

Gunn looked at Pitt across the cramped radio room and thoughtfully jangled some loose change in his pocket. A more hard-headed and determined man he had never seen. Gunn remembered that he had trusted Pitt's judgment on that Delphi Ea affair in Hawaii last year, and he hadn't been let down. If Pitt said he was going to kill every shark in the sea, Gunn mused, he would probably damn near do it. He studied the damp and, by this time, peeling bandages on Pitt's body, jangled the change in his pocket again, wondered what he would be thining about this time tomorrow.

"OK, you win," he said wearily. "I'll no doubt regret this decision at my court-martial. It's a small satisfaction to know what I'll go out with a blaze of headlines."

Pitt laughed. "No such luck, my friend. Whatever happens, you merely ordered a routine hunt to collect marine specimens from a shelf under the cliffs. If we stumble into an embarrassing incident, you can say it was by pure accident."

"I hope Washington will buy that."

"Don't worry, I think we both know Admiral Sandecker well enough to be assured that he'll stand by us regardless of the consequences."

Gunn pulled a handkerchief from his hip pocket and dabbed at the sweat on his face and neck. "Well, where do we go from here?"

"Round up your volunteers," Pitt said briefly. "Assemble them and the equipment on the fantail at noon. I'll explain their mission with a few well chosen words and then we'll go from there."

Gunn glanced at his watch. "It's 9:00 now. I can have them ready to dive in fifteen minutes. Why wait three hours?"

"I need the extra time to catch up on my sleep," Pitt said grinning. "I don't want to doze off sixty feet below the surface."

"That's not a bad idea," Gunn said seriously. "You look like the morning after New Year's Eve." He turned and started through the cabin door, then stopped. "By the way, do me a favor and send that girl ashore as soon as possible. I'm going to be in enough hot water as it is without being accused of operating a floating bordello."

"Not until I return from the dive. It's vital that she remain on board where someone can keep an eye on her."

"OK, let's have it." Gunn said quietly in a defeated tone. "You're holding out on me again. Who is she?"

"Would you believe von Till's niece?"

"Oh no," Gunn looked stricken. "That's all I need."

"Don't work yourself into a coronary," Pitt said softly. "Everything will work out. You have my word on it."

"I hope so," Gunn sighed. He looked skyward and shrugged in helpless despair. "Why me, God?"

Then he was gone.

Pitt stared out the empty doorway for a long moment at the blue uneven sea. The radio operator was bent over the big Bendix set, transmitting, but Pitt didn't hear him. He was lost in the inner silence of concentration and the silence that comes with the blistering heat and its energy sapping partner, humidity. His body was numb—numb from too little sleep and numb from too much mental strain. His nerves were stretched like the support wires of a suspension bridge; if one snapped the rest would part strand by strand until the whole structure swayed and dropped into oblivion. Like a gambler who has bet his last big stake on a ten-to-one horse, he felt his heart pound against his rib cage, driven beyond its regular beat by the deep fear of uncertainty.

"Excuse me, Major." The radioman's low, resonant voice seemed far away. "These communications are for you."

Pitt said nothing. He merely extended his hand and took the messages.

"The one from Munich came in at 6:00." The black man's tone was hesitating and unsteady. "It was followed at 7:00 by two transmissions from Berlin."

"Thank you," Pitt murmured woodenly. "Anything else?"

"This last one, sir, it's . . . well it's really weird. No call sign, no repeat, no sign off, just the message."

Pitt stared down at the top paper. A grim smile slowly moved his lips.

'Major Dirk Pitt, NUMA ship *First Attempt*. One hour down, nine to go. H.Z.'

"Any . . . any reply, Major?" the voice stammered unevenly.

Suddenly Pitt became aware of the sickly expression on the radio operator's face. "You feel all right?"

"To tell the truth, Major, no. Ever since breakfast I've had the worst case of bowel drizzlies in my life, and I've barfed twice."

Pitt could not help grinning. "Compliments of the ship's cook. Is that it?"

The radioman shook his head and rubbed his eyes in one easy movement. "Can't be. Cooky's the greatest—strictly gourmetsville. Nah, it's probably the local version of the flu. Could even be a skunky bottle of beer or something."

"Stay with it," Pitt said. "We need a good man on the radio for the next twenty-four hours."

"You can count on me." The radioman forced a faint smile. "Besides, that chick you brought on board has been clucking over me like a mother hen. With that kind of attention, how much could I suffer?"

Pitt raised an eyebrow. "You must see something in her I don't."

"She's not bad. Not my usual fancy, but not bad. Anyway, she's been bringing tea all morning—a regular Florence Nightingale."

The young black suddenly broke off. His eyes went wide and he threw a hand to his mouth. Then he jumped to his feet, knocking over the chair, ran outside and hung like a dead man over the railing. Animal-like grunts carried back into the cabin, accompanied by low, agonizing moans.

Pitt walked out and lightly patted the ailing radioman on the back.

"I need you by the radio my friend. Hang in there while I send for the ship's doctor."

The radioman slowly nodded his head and said nothing. Then Pitt turned and left, making sure he walked upwind.

After a few minutes spent looking for the ship's physician and asking him to look in on the radio operator, Pitt entered Gunn's cabin and found it dark, the curtains drawn. Cool air flowed from the ventilator, giving the steel cubicle a comfortable, inviting atmosphere, a vast improvement over the intolerable heat of yesterday. In the dim light he made out Teri sitting on the desk. Her chin was resting on a drawn up knee. She looked up at him and smiled.

"What kept you?"

"Business," he replied.

"Monkey business I'll bet." Her face bore a distinct feminine pout. "Where is the big adventure you promised me? Everytime I turn around you've disappeared."

"When duty calls, dearheart, I must answer." Pitt straddled a chair and leaned over the backrest. "A very intriguing bit of apparel you're wearing. Where did you get it?"

"Nothing to it really—"

"I can see that."

She smiled at his remark and went on. "I simply

snipped out a pattern from some pillow ticking. The halter is tied in the back with a bow and the pants are knotted on each side. See!" She stood and undid the knot over her left hip, letting the diminutive cloth dangle teasingly.

"Very, very clever. What do you do for an encore?"

"How much is it worth to you?" she asked seductively.

"How about an old Milwaukee streetcar token?"

"You're impossible," she pouted. "I'm beginning to think you're daft."

He had to force his eyes to ignore her body. "Right now I've got some details that need clearing up."

She stared at him blankly for a few seconds, started to say something, then thought better of it; his face was unsmiling and serious. She shrugged, slowly retied the bikini and settled into a vacant chair.

"You're acting terribly mysterious."

"I'll revert to my old sweet, lovable self after you've answered a few simple questions."

She scratched at an imaginary itch above her left breast. "Ask away then."

"Question number one: what do you know about your uncle's smuggling operations?"

Her eyes went wide. "I don't know what you're talking about."

"I think you do."

"You're insane," she said, glaring at him. "Uncle Bruno owns a steamship line. Why should a man of his wealth and social standing stoop to petty smuggling?"

"Nothing he does can be considered petty," Pitt said. He paused a moment monitoring her expression, and then continued. "Question number two: before you came to Thasos, when was the last time you saw von Till?"

Not since I was a little girl," she answered vaguely. "My mum and dad were drowned when their sailboat overturned in a sudden storm off the Isle of Man. Uncle Bruno was with them at the time. So was I. He saved my life. Since that awful accident he has been very good to me; the best boarding schools, money when I needed it. He always remembers my birthday."

"Yes, he's all heart," Pitt said sarcastically. "Isn't he a bit old to be your uncle?"

"Actually, he was my grandmother's brother."

"Question three: how come you never paid him a visit before now?"

"Whenever I wrote and begged him to let me come to Thasos, he always wrote back and said he was too busy, involved with some vast shipping transaction or something." She giggled softly. "I fooled him this time though. I simply popped in and surprised him."

"What do you know about his past?"

"Nothing really. He talks very little about himself. But I do know he's not a smuggler."

"You beloved uncle is the worst scum that a mother ever dropped." Pitt's voice was tired. He didn't want to hurt her, but he was certain she was lying. "God only knows how many rotting corpses owe their present condition to him; hundreds, thousands more likely. And you're in it with him right up to your lovely little neck. Every rotten dollar you've spent in the last twenty years was soaked in blood. In some cases with the blood of, and yes tears, especially tears, of innocent children. Young girls who were stolen from their parents arms and who finished their adolescence on a filthy, lice ridden pile of straw in a North African whorehouse."

She jumped to her feet. "Things like that don't happen any more. You're lying, you're lying, you're making this up." She was scared now, but playing a magnificent scene, Pitt thought. "I told you the truth. I know nothing. Nothing!"

"Nothing? You knew von Till was planning to murder me at the villa. Your tearful little act on the terrace, I admit, had me fooled. But not for long. You missed your calling—you should have been an actress."

"I didn't know." Her voice was low and desperate. "I swear I didn't—"

Pitt shook his head. "I can't buy it. You gave yourself away outside the labyrinth when we were arrested by the tourist guide. You weren't just surprised to see me, you were goddamned shocked to see me in one piece."

She came over and knelt beside him and held his hands in hers. "Please, please . . . Oh God! What must I do to make you believe me?"

"You might begin by offering me facts." He raised up from the chair and stood directly over her. Then he tore the soggy bandages from his chest and dropped them in her lap. "Look at me. This is what I got for accepting your invitation to dinner. I was set up as the main course for your uncle's man-eating dog. Look at me!"

She looked. "I think I'm going to be sick."

Pitt ached to take her in his arms and kiss away the tears that welled in her eyes, and to softly, gently tell her how sorry he was. Instead, he fought to keep his voice firm and even.

She turned and gazed blankly at the metal sink in the head, wondering if she were going to be sick or not, then she forced her tear-brimmed eyes back on Pitt and spoke in a whisper. "You're a devil. You talk about Uncle Bruno. You're worse, much worse. I wish you would have been killed."

The hate should have been there, but Pitt could only feel a touch of sadness. "Until I say otherwise you'll remain on this ship."

"You can't keep me here, you have no right."

"I have no right, true, but I can keep you here. And while we're on the subject; don't get it in your pretty head to try and escape. The men on this ship are expert swimmers. You wouldn't get fifty yards even if you tried real hard."

"You can't keep me a prisoner forever." Her face twisted with loathing. A woman had never looked at Pitt like that. It made him feel uneasy.

"If my little caper comes off as planned this afternoon, you'll be out of my hair and in the hands of the gendarmerie by suppertime."

Suddenly Teri stared at him speculatively. "Is that why you disappeared last night?"

Pitt was ever amazed at the way her huge brown eyes—her devastatingly beautiful eyes—could run through so many emotions in one blink. "Yes, as a matter of fact, I sneaked on board one of your uncle's ships just before dawn. It was a most instructive excursion. You'll never guess what I found."

He watched her closely, mentally predicting what the next blink would bring.

"I couldn't imagine," she said dully. "The only ships I've ever been on were ferrys."

He walked over and sat down in the bunk. The soft mattress felt good. He leaned back and crossed his arms behind his head. Then he yawned long and slowly.

"I beg your pardon. That was rude of me."

"Well?"

"Well what?"

"You were going to tell me what you found on Uncle Bruno's ship."

Pitt shook his head and grinned. "Female curiosity, once piqued it's insatiable. Since you insist, I found a map to an underwater cave."

"A cave?"

"Of course. Where else do you think your good uncle conducts his slimey business from?"

"Why are you telling me these stories?" The hurt look was back. "None of them can be true."

"Oh good God, get some sense in your head. I'm not telling you anything new. Von Till may have hoodwinked INTERPOL, the gendarmerie and the Bureau of Narcotics, but he didn't fool yours truly."

"You're talking nonsense," she said slowly.

"Am I?" he asked thoughtfully. "At precisely 4:30 this morning your uncle's ship, the *Queen Artemisia,* anchored off the coast below the villa. The ship was loaded to the gills with heroin. Surely you must know about the heroin. Everyone else does. It has to be the worst kept secret of the year. I've got to hand it to your uncle; he's a master of the old magician's routine; dazzle the audience with one hand while you perform the trick with the other. His little act is about to end, however. I have a little trick of my own that will bring down the curtain."

She was silent for a moment. "What are you going to do?"

"What any red-blooded All American boy would do. I'm going to take Giordino and a couple of other men and dive along the shore until I find the cave. It most likely lies at the base of the cliffs directly under the villa. Once we discover the entrance we will enter, seize any equipment and evidence, make a citizen's arrest of your uncle, and then call the gendarmerie."

"You're insane," she said again, only with much more feeling this time. "The whole caper, or whatever you call it, is idiotic. You can't go through with it. Please, please believe me. It won't work."

"It's no use begging. You can kiss your uncle and his rotten money goodby. We hit the water at 1:00." Pitt yawned again. "Now if you will kindly excuse me, I'd like to get a little shuteye."

The tears were back. She shook her head slowly from side to side. "It's idiotic," she whispered over and over, turned and walked into the head, slamming the door behind her.

Pitt lay there, staring at the overhead. She was right, of course, he thought. It did sound like an idiotic caper. But then, what else could she think, she only knew the half of it.

16

The restless sea curled to a tall crest and beckoned like the ominous finger of doom before it rammed into the unyielding gray cliffs. The air was warm and clear and stirred by a faint breath from the southwest. A ghost, or so the *First Attempt* seemed—a white steel ghost—glided at slow speed closer and closer to the boiling caldron, until it looked like disaster was inevitable. At the last instant, no sooner, Gunn spun the helm to starboard, sending the *First Attempt* on a parallel course to the rocky cliff base. He kept glancing warily from the needle, traveling across the fathometer's graph paper, to the surfline, a scant fifty yards away, and back again.

"How's that for curb service?" he asked without turning. The voice was soft and controlled; he was as calm as a fisherman in a rowboat on a placid Minnesota like.

"Your old seamanship instructor at Annapolis would be proud of you," Pitt replied. Unlike Gunn, he was staring straight ahead.

"It's not half as grim as it looks," Gunn said, gesturing at the fathometer. "The bottom is a good ten fathoms below our keel!"

"Sixty feet in less than a hundred yards; that's quite a drop-off."

Gunn lifted one hand from the helm and took off

195

his gold braided Navy cap, swiping a few beads of sweat that hung from his hairline.

"It's not an uncommon occurrence in an area that's free of outer reefs."

"It's a good sign," Pitt said thoughtfully.

"How so?"

"Plenty of room for a sub to maneuver without surface detection."

"At night maybe," Gunn said. "Too obvious during the day. The water visibility is almost a hundred feet. Anyone standing on the bluffs within a mile in either direction could easily look down and spot a three hundred foot hull that was crawling over the bottom."

"It shouldn't be too difficult to spot a diver either," Pitt turned and gazed up at the villa, nestled like a fortress on the craggy side of the mountain.

"You're made to take a chance like this," Gunn said slowly. "Von Till can see any movement you make. I'll bet a dime to a donut that he's had a pair of binoculars trained on us every second since we upped anchor."

"I'm betting on it too," Pitt murmured. He lost himself for a moment in the beauty of the scene. The azure arms of the Aegean encircled the ancient island seascape in a dazzling reflection of sun and water. Only the voice of the crashing surf answered the steady hum of the ship's engines, punctuated occasionally by the shriek of a solitary gull. Above the rocky cliffs, a herd of cattle grazed on a sloping green pasture, like tiny immovable shapes in a Rembrandt landscape. And below, in sheltered coves among the lesser cliffs, piles of sunbleached driftwood lay dead and still on tiny shell-carpeted beaches.

Pitt nearly lingered too long. He tugged his mind back to the job at hand. That mysterious area of calm water was coming up now, only three quarters of a mile away off the port bow. He laid a hand on Gunn's shoulder and pointed.

"The flat pond."

Gunn nodded. "OK, got it. At our present speed we should be alongside in ten minutes. Is your team ready?"

"All set and primed," Pitt answered briefly. "They know what to expect. I've got them stationed along the starboard cabin deck; out of sight to any prying eyes from the villa."

Gunn replaced his cap. "Be sure you order them to leap plenty clear of the hull. Getting sucked into a prop can be a very messy business."

"I doubt that they have to be ordered," Pitt said quietly. "They're all good men. You told me so yourself."

"Damn right," Gunn snorted. He turned to Pitt. "I'm going to keep the ship close-in to the shoreline for another three miles. We might fool von Till into thinking we're on a routine sounding course to chart the shallows. It might work, I don't know. For your sake I hope he's taken in."

"We'll soon find out." Pitt checked his watch against the ship's chronometer. "What time do you make your rendezvous?"

"I'll run a series of doglegs on the return course and arrive back here at 1410. That gives you exactly fifty minutes to find the sub and get out." Gunn dug a cigar out of a breast pocket and lit it. "You and my men be waiting for the ship, you hear me?"

Pitt didn't answer immediately. A broad smile broke across his lips, and his vivid green eyes seemed to be laughing.

Gunn looked puzzled. "What did I say that's so funny?"

"For a moment you reminded me of my mother. She always used to say that when my ship came in I'd probably be waiting at the bus depot."

Gunn ruefully shook his head. "If you don't come back at least I'll know where to look. Well, let's get on with it. You had better climb into your diving gear."

Pitt simply waved in acknowledgment, left the hot confine of the wheelhouse and dropped down the ladder to the *First Attempt's* starboard cabin deck. He found five deeply tanned men waiting for him, probably, Pitt reflected, the five most eager and intelligent men he'd ever known. Like himself, they wore only black bikini swim trunks. All were busily engaged in adjusting breathing regulators and strapping on airtanks; each man rechecked the other's equipment, making certain the tank valves and harness webbing were in their proper position.

The nearest diver, Ken Knight, looked up at Pitt's arrival. "I have your gear all ready for you, Major. I hope a single hose regulator will be OK, NUMA didn't issue us any doubles this trip."

"A single hose will do fine," Pitt replied. He pulled on a pair of fins and strapped a knife to his right calf; then he slipped a mask over his head and adjusted the snorkel. The mask was the wide-angle type that gave the wearer a one hundred and eighty degree range of vision. Next came the airtank and the regulator. He was about to struggle with the tank harness when suddenly the forty pound outfit was swept from the deck and held at his back by two massive, hairy arms.

"How you could ever get through a day without my services," said the voice of Giordino pompously, "is a mystery to me."

"The real mystery is why I put up with your jackhammer mouth and overabundant ego," Pitt said sourly.

"There you go, picking on me again," Giordino tried to sound wounded but couldn't quite pull it off. He turned and looked down at the passing water and, after a long pause, muttered very slowly; "Christ! Look at the clarity of that water! It's sharper than a goldfish bowl."

"So I've noticed." Pitt unsheathed the barbed tip of a six foot pole spear and checked the elasticity of the rubber sling attached to the butt end. "Have you studied your lesson?"

"The old gray matter," Giordino said, pointing to his head, "has all the answers filed and indexed."

"As usual, it's comforting to know you're so sure of yourself."

"Sherlock Giordino knows all, sees all. No secret can escape my probing mind."

"Your probing mind better be well oiled," Pitt said earnestly. "You've got a tight schedule to keep."

"Just leave it to me," Giordino said straight faced. "Well, it's about that time. I wish I was coming along. Enjoy your swim and have fun."

"I intend to," Pitt murmured. "I intend to."

Two chimes from the ship's bell sounded Gunn's one minute warning signal. Pitt, walking awkwardly in his fins, moved onto a small platform that extended over the side of the hull.

"At the sound of the next tone, gentlemen, we go!" He said no more, partly because each man knew what he had to do, partly because there was nothing else to say that had any meaning.

The divers gripped their spearguns a little tighter and silently exchanged glances. One thought and only one thought was on all their minds at this minute: if the jump isn't far enough, a leg could be lost in the whirling propeller. At a gesture from Pitt, they arranged themselves in a line behind the platform.

Before he lowered the mask over his eyes, Pitt took another look at the men around him and for the tenth time studied their identifying features, features he would be able to recognize at a distance under water. The man nearest him, Ken Knight, the geophysicist, was the only blond in the group; Stan Thomas, the short, runty ship's engineer, wore blue fins and was the only member, Pitt surmised, who could probably handle himself in a tough fight. Next came a red bearded marine biologist, Lee Spencer, then Gustaf Hersong, a lanky six foot six marine botanist—both those men seemed to be grinning at each other over a private joke. The anchor man was the expedition's photographer, Omar Woodson, as true a deadpan character as Pitt had ever seen and who genuinely appeared bored by the whole show. Instead of a speargun, Woodson carried a 35 mm Nykonos with flash, swinging the expensive underwater unit over the railing, negligently, as if it were an old used box camera.

Pitt pulled the mask down over his eyes, whistling softly to himself, and gazed once more at the water. It was passing beneath the platform at a much more leisurely rate now—Gunn had cut the *First Attempt*'s speed to a crawling three knots—slow enough, Pitt decided, for a feet first entry. His eyes turned past the bow, looking forward with trance-like fixity at the approximate point in the sea where at any moment now he must dive.

At almost the same instant, Gunn scrutinized the fathometer and the jagged cliffs for the last time. His hand slowly raised, groped for the bell line, found it, paused, then gave one hard pull. The metallic clang burst into the hot afternoon air and carried across the surf to the steep coastal wall, echoing in a muted undertone back toward the ship.

Pitt, poised on the platform, didn't wait for the echo. Holding the mask firmly in place against his face with one hand and clutching the pole spear in the other, he leaped.

The impact shattered the sun-danced water into a blazing diffused pattern of blue brilliance. Immediately after the surface closed over his head, Pitt rolled frontward and kicked his fins as fast, it seemed to him, as a Mississippi River paddlewheeler at full throttle. Five seconds and fifteen feet later, he glanced over his shoulder and watched the dark shape of the ship's hull slide slowly overhead. The whirling twin propellers seemed frighteningly closer than they really were: their thrashing sound traveled at forty-nine hundred feet per second underwater as compared to less than eleven hundred feet through air, and the light refraction magnified their flashing blades by nearly twenty-five percent.

Teeth clenched on the regulator's mouthpiece, Pitt swung around and stared in the direction of the shrinking ship to see how the others had fared. His sigh of relief was answered by the hiss of his exhaust bubbles from the regulator. Thank God, they were all there, and in one piece. Knight, Thomas, Spencer, and Hersong, all in a group within touching distance. Only Woodson had dragged his feet; he hung in the water about twenty feet beyond the rest.

The visibility was startling. The long, purplish tentacles of a jelly-like Portuguese Man O'War were clearly discernible nearly eighty feet away. A pair of ugly looking Dragonet fish swam idly across the bottom, their vivid blue and yellow scaleless bodies topped by high slender gill spines. It was a hidden world, a soundless world, owned by weirdly shaped creatures and decorated by graceful fantasies of form and vibrant hues that defied any attempt at human description. It was also a world of mystery and danger, guarded by a sinister array of weapons, varying from the slaughterous teeth of the shark to the deadly venom of the innocent looking Zebra fish; an intriguing combination of eternal beauty and constant peril.

Without waiting for signs of discomfort, Pitt began snorting into the mask to equalize the air pressure of his inner ears to that of the water pressure. When his ears popped, he slowly dove toward the majestic seascape under him and became a part of it.

At thirty feet, the reds were left behind, and the depths became a soft blending of blues and greens. Pitt leveled off at fifty and studied the bottom. No sea growth or rocks here, just a patch of submerged desert where miniature sand dunes meandered in unbroken snake-like ripples. Except for an occasional bottom dwelling Star Gazer fish, buried with only a pair of stony eyes and a portion of its grotesque, fringed lips protruding above the sand, the sea floor was deserted.

Exactly eight minutes after they had left the *First Attempt,* the bottom began to slope upward, and the water became slightly murky from the surface wave action. A rock formation, covered with swaying seaweed, appeared in the gloom ahead. And then suddenly they were at the base of a vertically sheer cliff that rose at an unbroken 90° angle until it disappeared into the mirrored surface above. Like Captain Nemo and his companions exploring an undersea garden, Pitt began directing his team of marine scientists to spread out and search for the submarine cave.

The hunt took no more than five minutes. Woodson, who had angled a hundred feet out on the right perimeter, found it first. Signaling Pitt and the others by rapping his knife against his airtank, he motioned for them to come and went swimming off along the northern face of the cliff to a point beyond a weed encrusted crevasse. There he paused and held up a leveled arm. And then Pitt saw it; a black and ominous opening just twelve feet below the surface. The size was perfect; big enough for a submarine or, for that matter, a locomotive to have been driven in. They all hung suspended in the clear crystal water, their eyes fixed on the cave entrance, hesitating, exchanging glances.

Pitt moved first, entering the hole. Except for a few dim flashes of light, reflected from the whites of his heels, he disappeared completely from view, swallowed by the yawning cavity.

He leisurely beat the water with his fins and let an incoming swell help carry him slowly through the tunnel. The bright blue-green of the sunlit sea rapidly transformed into a kind of deep twilight blue. At first Pitt could see nothing, but soon his eyes adjusted to the dark interior, and he began to make out a few details of his surroundings.

There should have been a myriad of marine life clinging to the tunnel walls. There should have been darting crabs, winking limpets and barnacles, or crawling lobsters, sneaking about in search of tasty shellfish. There were none of these. The rocky sides were barren, and they were coated with a reddish substance that clouded the water whenever Pitt touched the smooth, unnatural material. He rolled face up and inspected the arched roof, watching in fascinated interest as his exhaust bubbles rose and wandered across the ceiling, like a trail of quicksilver, seeking escape from a vial.

Abruptly the roof angled upward, and Pitt's head broke the surface. He looked around but saw nothing; a gray cloud of mist obscured everything. Puzzled, he ducked his head back in the water and dove, leveling out at ten feet. Beneath him a cylindrical shaft of cobalt light flowed in from the tunnel. The water was as clear as air; Pitt could see every nook and cranny of the cavern's submerged area.

An aquarium. That was the only way Pitt could describe it. But for the fact that there were no portholes in the walls, the cavern could have easily passed for the main tank at Marineland in California. It was a far cry from the tunnel; marine life abounded everywhere. The lobsters were here, and so were the crabs, the limpets, the barnacles, even a heavy growth of kelp. There were also roving schools of brilliantly colored fish. One fish in particular caught Pitt's eye, but before he could get closer, it saw his approach and flashed into a protective rock fissure.

For several moments, Pitt took in the breathtaking scene. Then suddenly, he started as a foreign hand grabbed his leg. It was Ken Knight, and he was motioning toward the surface. Pitt nodded and swam to the top. Again he was greeted by the heavy mist.

Pitt spit out his mouthpiece. "What do you make of it?" he asked. The rock walls amplified his voice to a roar.

"A fairly common occurrence," Knight answered, roaring back matter of factly. "Everytime a swell hits the entrance outside, the force runs like a piston through the tunnel, compressing the air already trapped in the cavern. When the pressure recedes, the expanded, moisturized air cools and condenses in a fine mist." Knight paused to blow some mucus from his nose. "The swells are running at about twelve second intervals, so it should start to clear up at any time."

No sooner had he said it than the mist disappeared, revealing a dim cavern that arched to a dome sixty feet overhead. It was a drowned grotto and nothing more; no traces of man-made equipment. Pitt felt as though he had entered a deserted cathedral whose spires stood in ruined desolation from a World War I artillery shelling or a World War II aerial bombardment. The walls were twisted and broken in jagged fissures, and the shattered rocks at their base showed that another rock fall could come at any time. Then the mist returned and smothered all vision.

Pitt, in the few seconds it took to survey the cavern, was conscious of nothing but the gnawing fear of self doubt. Then came a creeping wave of numbed disbelief, then the chagrin that he had bungled it.

"It can't be," he muttered. "It just can't be." Pitt's free hand curled into a white knuckled fist, and he pounded the water in an outburst of temper and despair. "This cavern had to be von Till's base of operations. God help us from the mess that I've surely caused."

"I'd still vote for you, Major," Knight reached out and touched Pitt on the shoulder. "The geology bears out your hunch. This would seem the most logical spot."

"It's a dead end. Except for the tunnel, there's no openings, anywhere."

"I saw a ledge on the far end of the cave. Maybe if I—"

"No time for that," Pitt interrupted impatiently. "We must get back out as fast as we can and keep searching."

"Excuse me, Major!" Hersong had caught Pitt's arm, an action that surprised Pitt by seemingly coming out of nowhere. "I found something that might be of interest."

The mist went through its cycle and then cleared again, revealing a peculiar expression on Hersong's face that caught Pitt's attention. He grinned at the lanky botanist.

"OK, Hersong, let's make it quick. We hardly have time for a lecture on marine flora."

"Believe it or not, that's just what I had in mind," Hersong grinned back; the glistening water trickled through the strands of his red beard. "Tell me, did you notice that growth of Macrocystis pyrifera on the wall opposite the tunnel?"

"I might have," Pitt answered flatly, "if I knew what you were talking about."

"Macrocystis pyrifera is a brown algae of the Phaeophyta family, perhaps, better known as kelp."

Pitt stared at him, considering, and let him continue.

"What it boils down to, Major, is that this particular species of kelp is native only to the Pacific Coast of the United States. The water temperature in this part of the Mediterranean is far too warm for Macrocystis pyrifera to survive. On top of that, kelp, like its land plant cousins, needs sunlight to provide the process for photosynthesis. I can't imagine kelp thriving in an underwater cave. Nope, if you'll forgive the vernacular, it just ain't done."

Pitt was slowly treading water. "Then if it isn't kelp, what is it?"

The mist was back, and Pitt couldn't see Hersong's face. He could only hear the botanist's rumbling voice.

"It's art, Major, pure art. Without a doubt, the finest plastic replica of Macrocystis pyrifera I've ever beheld."

"Plastic?" Knight boomed, his tone echoing around the cavern. "Are you sure?"

"My dear boy," Hersong said disdainfully. "Do I question your analysis of core samples or—"

"That red slime on the tunnel walls," Pitt cut in. "What do you make of that?"

"Couldn't say for sure," Hersong said. "Looked like some type of paint or coating."

"I'll back him, Major." The face of Sten Thomas suddenly materialized out of the fading mist. "Red antifouling paint for ship hulls. It contains arsenic; that's why nothing grows in the tunnel."

Pitt glanced at his watch. "Time is running out. This *must* be the place."

"Another tunnel behind the kelp? Knight asked in a careful sort of voice. "Is that it, Major?"

"It's beginning to look encouraging," Pitt said quietly. "A camouflaged second tunnel that leads to a second cavern. Now I can see why von Till's operation was never discovered by any native of Thasos."

"Well," Hersong purged the water from his mouthpiece. "I guess we keep going."

"We have no other option," Pitt said. "Are we all ready for another go?"

"All present and accounted for, except for Woodson," Spencer answered.

Suddenly, at that instant, a flashbulb flooded the cavern in a bright blue light.

"Nobody smiled," Woodson observed sourly. He had drifted off to the far wall of the cavern, trying for the widest possible lens angle.

"Next time, yell sex," Spencer joked back.

"It wouldn't matter," Woodson grunted. "None of you know what it means anyway."

Pitt grinned and moved off. He rolled forward and jacknifed, diving to the bottom like an airplane on a strafing run. The others followed, spaced out at ten-foot intervals.

The forest of counterfeit kelp was thick and nearly impenetrable. Thin branches rose from the bottom to the surface, flaring into a wide, spreading canopy. Hersong was right; it was a work of art. Even at arm's length Pitt couldn't have told the plastic from the real thing. He unsheathed the knife and began slicing his way through the brown swaying stems. Working his way forward, stopping only to untangle his air tank, he finally broke into another tunnel. The second had a larger diameter than the first but was much shorter in length. After four stout kicks, Pitt surfaced in a new cavern, only to be enveloped in the unending white mist. Every few moments, the splash of a head breaking the water, announced the arrival of another member of the team.

"See anything?" The voice was Spencer's.

"Not yet," Pitt replied. Mechanically, his eyes strained unblinkingly into the damp gloom. He thought he saw something now, something more imagined than real. Gradually, he became aware of a dark shape, materializing out of the fog. And then suddenly, it was absolutely and concretely there, the smooth, black metal hull of a submarine. Pitt spat out his mouthpiece, swam over to the sub and grabbed hold of the bow planes, pulling himself onto the deck.

Pitt's mind became absorbed in the submarine. At least ten times he'd wondered how he'd react, how he would feel when he finally touched the heroin's underwater carrier. Elation at being proved right—that and more. Anger and disgust flooded over him. If they could only talk, what tales of insidious tragedies these steel plates could relate.

"Please drop your spear on the deck and keep very, very still." The voice behind Pitt was hard, and so was the gun barrel that dug into his spine. He eased the pole spear slowly to the wet deck. "Good. Now order your men to drop their weapons on the bottom. No tricks. A concussion grenade in the water can turn a swimmer into an ugly mass of jelly."

Pitt nodded at the five floating heads. "You heard the man. Drop the spearguns . . . the knives too. There's no sense in antagonizing these nice people. I'm sorry men. It looks like I've blown it."

There was nothing else left to say. Pitt had led these five men into a trap from which they might never escape alive. All emotion left him, he was conscious now only of time. On cue, Pitt raised his hands over his head and slowly turned around.

"Major Pitt, you are an uncommonly aggravating young man."

Bruno von Till stood on the deck of the submarine, grinning like Fu Manchu about to feed a victim to the crocodiles. His eyes were narrowed slits beneath the skin-topped head, and he seemed, at least to Pitt, to radiate a personal and long practiced repulsiveness. But something was wrong, terribly wrong. The old German had both hands in his jacket pockets; he carried no gun. It was the man beside him who held the gun—a mountain of a man with a face of carved stone and a torso like a tree trunk. Von Till's eyes fully opened, and his voice rose in a mocking tone.

"Forgive me for not offering introductions, Major." Von Till gestured toward his companion. "But I understand that you and Darius have already met."

17

"You seem surprised to see me, Major," Darius murmured satanically. "I can't tell you what a great pleasure it is to meet you again under more favorable terms." He jammed the nasty looking Luger against Pitt's throat. "Please do not move and force me to kill you prematurely. Your quick and sudden death would only cheat me out of a great deal of personal satisfaction and pleasure. I said I had an account to settle with you and your ugly little friend; now the hour has arrived to repay my debt for the pain I have suffered at your hands or, more correctly, feet."

Pitt did his damnedest to look casual. "Sorry to disappoint you, but Giordino stayed home this trip."

"Then his punishment shall be added to yours."

Darius smiled pleasantly, then lowered the gun and calmly shot Pitt in the leg. The sharp crack of the Luger amplified to a thunderclap within the rock-walled cavern. A blow—like the thrust of a red hot poker—jerked Pitt sideways and knocked him backward two steps. Somehow, he never really knew how, he managed to remain on his feet. The nine millimeter bullet had torn through the fleshy part of his thigh, missing the bone by a scant quarter of an inch and leaving a neat little reddish hole at the entrance and a slightly larger one at the exit. The burning sensation quickly left, and his leg became numb with shock, the real pain, he was sure, would soon follow.

"Come now, Darius," von Till spoke reprovingly. "Let us not over-indulge ourselves in crudity. We have more important matters to resolve before you pursue your little 'eye-for-an-eye' sport. My apologies, Major Pitt, but you must admit, you have only yourself to blame. Your well aimed kick in such a delicate location will require Darius to limp for at least another two weeks."

"I'm only sorry I didn't boot him twice as hard," Pitt said through clenched teeth.

Von Till ignored him. He said to the men in the water: "Drop your diving equipment on the bottom, gentlemen. Then climb up on deck. Quickly, we have little time to waste."

Thomas raised his mask and threw an if-looks-could-kill stare at von Till. "We're damn well comfortable right where we are."

Von Till shrugged. "Very well, it seems you need an incentive." He turned and shouted into the dim shadows of the cavern. "Hans, the lights!"

Suddenly, a string of overhead flood lights burst on, illuminating the cavern from ceiling to water. Pitt could now see that the submarine was moored to a floating dock that began at a tunnel entrance on the far wall and extended two hundred feet across the water like an enormous wooden tongue. The domed ceiling was much lower in this inner cavern as compared to the outer one, but its horizontal area was several times larger; the square footage would have easily equaled a football field. Along the right wall, on an overhanging ledge, five men stood in frozen immobility, their hands gripped on leveled machine pistols. Each was dressed in the same style of uniform that Pitt had previously seen on von Till's chauffeur. There was no mistaking the business-like manner in which they aimed their weapons at the men in the water.

"I think you'd better do as the man says," Pitt advised.

The mist returned, but the burning lights kept it to a minimum, dooming any chance for escape. Spencer and Hersong climbed aboard the sub first, followed by Knight and Thomas. Woodson, as usual, was last, still clutching his camera in defiance of von Till's commands.

Knight helped Pitt off with his airtank. "Let me take a look at your leg, sir." Gently he eased Pitt to a sitting position on the deck. Then he removed the lead weights from his weight belt and wrapped the nylon webbing around Pitt's wound, stemming the blood flow. He looked up at Pitt and grinned. "It seems as though everytime I turn around, you're bleeding."

"A messy habit I can't rid myself of lately—"

Pitt stopped short. The mist was disappearing again, and the lights had now exposed a second submarine moored on the opposite side of the dock. He surveyed both subs comparing them. The one he and his men rested on had a flush deck from stem to stern, no projections anywhere. The other sub was different; it still retained its original conning tower, a massive structure that sat on its hull like a distorted half-bubble. Three men, backs turned to the drama behind them, were busily removing the machine guns from a shattered airplane that sat on the broad deck.

"Now I know where the yellow Albatros materialized from," said Pitt. "An old Japanese I-Boat, capable of launching a small scout plane. They haven't been in use since World War II."

"Yes, a handsome specimen," von Till said jovially. "I'm honored you could identify it. Sunk by an American destroyer off Iwo Jima in 1945, raised by Minerva Lines in 1951. I've found the combination of submarine and aircraft a most useful method of delivering small cargoes into areas that demand extreme discretion."

"A handy toy for also attacking United States airfields and research ships," Pitt added.

"Touché, Major," von Till murmured. "At dinner the other night you guessed that the plane came from the sea. You were groping blindly, but you came much closer than you thought."

"I can see that now." Pitt shot a quick glance at the tunnel entrance. Two more guards leaned negligently against the walls of the opening, their machine pistols hung carelessly over their shoulders. Pitt started to say: "The antique Albatros—"

"Correction," von Till interrupted. "A replica of an Albatros. For my purposes a slow, bi-wing aircraft was the most efficient means of landing and taking off on short fields, dark beaches, or in water beside a ship; the lower wing can, or should I say could, fold downward in the shape of hydrofoil pontoons. I used the Albatros D-3 design with a more modern engine, of course, because the aerodynamics provided the perfect answer to my requirements. And, an old shabby looking airplane would never be suspected of, shall we say, slightly illegal activities. A pity it will never fly again."

Von Till pulled a box of cigarettes from his breast pocket and lit one. Then he went on.

"My delivery plane was never meant to be armed or flown in combat. It was only after I had no alternative but to assault Brady Field and your precious research ship that I had the guns installed; a drastic move perhaps, but your Commander Gunn refused to be discouraged by my subtle efforts to sabotage his expedition. There was little to fear from a Sunday swimmer or a diving tourist discovering my little underwater modus operandi. However, a trained ocean scientist, that was something else again. I could not take the risk. The raid was, I am still convinced, an excellent plan. Colonel Lewis would have had no choice but to order the . . . its name escapes me, ah yes, the *First Attempt* to evacuate the Thasos coast if the attack had continued unhindered. You couldn't have known, of course, that the Albatros intended to make a token strafing run against the ship immediately after it neutralized the airfield. Inopportunely, Major Pitt, you blundered onto the scene and ruined everything."

"The fortunes of war," Pitt offered sarcastically.

"It is a shame Willie cannot be here to hear you say that."

"Where is good old peeping-Tom Willie?" Pitt asked.

"Willi was the pilot," von Till answered. "When the Albatros crashed into the sea, poor Willie was trapped in the wreckage. He drowned before we could reach him." Von Till's face abruptly became hard and menacing. "It seems you cost me my chauffeur and pilot as well as my dog."

"Gullibility on Willie's part," Pitt said quietly. "I suckered him with the same old balloon trick that the British used on Kurt Heibert. As to the dog, before you sic another one of your hydrophobic bitches on your next unsuspecting dinner guest, I suggest you count your table utensils."

Von Till looked at Pitt curiously for a moment. Then he nodded knowingly. "Remarkable, quite remarkable. You killed my champion hound with a knife from my own dinner table. Most ungracious of you, Major, to say the least. May I ask how you were forewarned?"

"Premonition," Pitt replied. "No more, no less. You should never have tried to kill me. That was your first mistake."

"It is a pity your escape from the labyrinth only prolonged your existence by a few hours."

Pitt nonchalantly glanced past von Till and Darius. The ominous black tunnel was now strangely empty; the two guards had disappeared. Not so the five guards who lined the cavern wall with the machine pistols—they looked as menacing as ever.

"Your reception committee leads me to believe you were expecting us," Pitt murmured quietly.

"Of course we were expecting you," von Till acknowledged matter-of-factly. "Good friend Darius here informed me of your impending arrival. The exact time became apparent when the *First Attempt* began acting suspiciously; no captain in his right mind would run his ship that close-in to the Thasos cliffs."

"How many pieces of silver did it take for Darius to turn traitor?"

"The exact sum wouldn't be of interest to you," said von Till. "The fact is, Darius has been in my employ for ten years. You might say that our association has proved to be quite mutually rewarding."

Pitt stared into Darius' coal-black eyes. "No matter how you slice it, it still adds up to treason. That's your second mistake, von Till. Hiring a slimey cockroach of a bastard like Darius, it's bound to backfire."

Darius shivered in involuntary rage. The Luger protruded from his massive fist as if it were a mutant growth extension, and it was aimed unsteadily at Pitt's navel.

Von Till shook his head tiredly. "Antagonizing Darius will only make you very, very dead."

"What's the difference. You're going to kill all of us anyway."

"Premonition again, Major? It serves you well." Von Till spoke cheerfully. Too cheerfully to suit Pitt.

"I hate surprises," Pitt said caustically. "How and when?"

With a practiced flourish, von Till pushed back his sleeves and carefully studied the dial of his watch. "In eleven minutes to be exact. That is all the time I can afford."

"Why not now?" Darius growled. "Why wait? We have other business at hand."

"Patience Darius," von Till chided. "You're not thinking. We can use the extra hands to load our supplies on board the submarine." He gazed down at Pitt and smiled. "Because of your wound, Major, you're excused. The rest of your men can begin by carrying the equipment you see on the dock into the forward hatch."

"We don't work for butchers," Pitt spoke softly and evenly.

"Very well, if you insist." Von Till beamed at Darius. "Shoot away his left ear. With your next bullet, take off his nose. After that his—"

"Stow it, you sadistic old hun." The words fairly

spat from Woodson's lips. "We'll load your goddamned pigboat."

They had no choice. Pitt had no choice. He could only sit by helplessly and watch as Spencer and Hersong began attacking a small mountain of wooden crates on the dock and passing them to Knight and Thomas on the sub. Woodson vanished into the hatch; only his arms, rising occasionally above the deck to receive a crate, revealed his whereabouts.

The burning sensation returned to Pitt's leg in earnest now. If he hadn't known better, he'd have sworn that a microscopic little man was running back and forth through his wound with a flamethrower. One or twice he nearly blacked out; each time he fought desperately to hold on until the engulfing waves of darkness subsided. On sheer will power alone he kept his voice on a conversational tone.

"You only answered the *when* half of my question, von Till."

"Does the method of your demise really matter that much to you?"

"Like I said, I hate surprises."

Von Till studied Pitt in cold speculation, then he shrugged. "I suppose it does no harm to hide the inevitable." He paused to check his watch again. "You and your men will be shot. A bit barbaric and ruthless, I grant, but I prefer to think of it as a rather humane death, especially when compared to being buried alive."

Pitt thought for a moment. "The loading of supplies and equipment, those men removing the guns from the wrecked Albatros, it all spells get-away. You're folding your tent, von Till, and stealing off into the night. Then after you've left, one minute, five minutes, maybe even half an hour, explosive charges will detonate and seal the cavern under tons of rock, entombing the six of us and erasing all evidence of your underwater smuggling operation."

Von Till looked at Pitt in puzzled suspicion. "Go on, Major. I find your assumptions extremely fascinating."

"You're running on a tight time schedule, and

you're running scared. Under our feet, beneath this dock, rests a hundred and thirty tons of heroin—loaded into the sub at Shanghai and carried across the Indian Ocean and through the Suez Canal by a Minerva Lines freighter. I have to hand it to you; anyone else would have tried to sneak the heroin into the United States through the backdoor without fanfare. Not so Bruno von Till. BBD&O together with J. Walter Thompson and all the other agencies on Madison Avenue couldn't have created a more professional job of advertising the *Queen Artemisia*'s illegal cargo and final destination. It was shrewd thinking. Even though INTERPOL agents have finally unriddled your underwater transportation, it makes little difference. All their eyes are still trained on the *Queen Artemisia*. Do you follow me?"

They stood mute and offered no affirmative or negative reply.

"As Darius has undoubtedly informed you," Pitt went on, "Inspector Zacynthus and the Bureau of Narcotics are currently wasting their time and efforts in preparing a trap for the ship when it reaches Chicago. I shudder to think of the four letter words that will fall on Lake Michigan when they discover nothing but the ship's crew wearing their best actor's smiles and the holds filled with nothing but the cocoa from Ceylon."

Pitt paused and shifted his throbbing leg to a more comfortable position. He noticed that Knight and Thomas had joined Woodson below the hatch. Then he continued.

"It must be a great source of satisfaction to know that INTERPOL has taken your bait, hook, line and sinker. They're totally unaware that the sub and the heroin were dropped here last night in order to be transferred to the next Minerva Line's ship that happens past; which, by the way, should be the *Queen Jocasta*, bound for New Orleans with a cargo of Turkish tobacco and due to drop anchor a mile off shore in approximately ten minutes. That's why you're running scared, von Till. Time has caught up with you, and you have to gamble on a rendezvous with your ship in broad daylight."

"You have a vivid imagination," von Till said contemptuously. But Pitt could see the lines of concern in the old man's face. "There is absolutely no way you can prove your wild theories."

Pitt ignored his words. He said: "Why should I bother? I'm going to die in a few minutes anyway."

"You have a point, Major," von Till said slowly. "I compliment you. Your preception is excellent. I see no harm in admitting that you are correct in everything you have said, with one exception: The *Queen Jocasta* will not dock in New Orleans. At the last minute, it will alter course for Galveston, Texas."

The three men on the other sub had removed the guns from the Albatros and mysteriously dropped out of sight. Hersong stepped off the dock and passed a crate through the hatch to Spencer, who had now vanished into the hull with Thomas, Knight and Woodson. Pitt spoke quickly. He needed every second now.

"One question before Darius gets carried away. Out of old world courtesy, you can't deny me that."

Darius stood there, his evil face masked with murderous intent. He looked like a sadistic kid in a biology class who could hardly wait to dissect a frog.

"Very well, Major," von Till said conversationally. "What is it?"

"How will the heroin be distributed after it's unloaded in Galveston?"

Von Till smiled. "One of my lesser known business ventures is a small fleet of fishing boats; not a financially rewarding venture, I might add, but one that becomes quite useful at times. At the moment, my boats are dropping their nets in the Gulf of Mexico, awaiting my signal. When it comes, they will raise their nets and arrive in port at the exact same moment as the *Queen Jocasta*. The rest is simple: the ship releases the submarine, which is in turn led by the fishing boats to a cannery. The cargo is then unloaded under the building, and the heroin is packed into cans labeled catfood. I must say, it is ironic; all that powder being shipped into every one of your fifty states in catfood cans. The joke is on the Bureau of Narcotics. By the time their suspicions are aroused, it will be too late. The heroin will have already been received and carefully hidden. Admit it, Major, doesn't the prospect of all that heroin being smelled, swallowed, or injected by millions of your own countrymen shock your holier-than-thou Yankee moral standards?"

Now Pitt was smiling. "It might, if it ever came to pass."

Von Till's eyes narrowed. Pitt wasn't acting like a doomed man. Something very definitely was off key. "It *will* come to pass. I promise you that."

"Millions of people," Pitt said wonderingly. "You stand there with a smile on your ugly mouth and openly boast of the misery you're going to extract from millions of people for a few lousy dollars."

"Hardly a few dollars, Major. I think half a billion dollars would be a closer figure.

"You'll never live to count it, much less spend it."

"And who is going to stop me? You, Major? Inspector Zacynthus? Possibly a lightning bolt from the sky?"

"Wishing will make it so."

"I've had enough of his stupid words," Darius said bitterly. "Now—now let him pay for his arrogance." The supremely grotesque face was a cloud of black malevolence. Pitt didn't like the look, he didn't like the look at all. He could almost feel Darius' finger tighten around the trigger of the Luger.

"Come now," Pitt said slowly. "Killing me now wouldn't be sporting. My eleven minutes aren't up yet." Actually to Pitt, it seemed he had been talking for hours.

Von Till stood silent for several seconds and toyed with his cigarette. Then he said: "There is one point that intrigues me, Major. Why did you kidnap my niece?"

Pitt's lips tightened to a sly grin. "To begin with, she's not your niece."

Darius' face went blank. "You—you could not have known."

"I knew," said Pitt evenly. "Unlike you, von Till, I didn't have the benefit of an informer, but I knew. All in all, Zacynthus gave it a good try, but his plan was headed for failure right from the start. He hid the genuine niece away in a safe place in England and found another girl who resembled her. They hardly had to be exact doubles since you hadn't laid eyes on the real Teri in over twenty years. Zacynthus also carefully planned his Mata Hari's cross country vacation to look like nothing more than an innocent surprise holiday visit by a loving relative."

Darius stared at von Till, his massive jaw seeming to grind Pitt's revelation to pieces. Von Till's expression didn't change. He just slowly nodded in apparent understanding.

"Too bad," Pitt said, "it was all for nothing. You weren't the least bit surprised. Darius had seen to that. At that point, you had two choices; you could either expose the girl as an impostor and throw her out, or you could play along and feed her false information. Quite naturally your devious mind chose the latter. You were in your element. You felt like a puppeteer pulling strings. You could now play the girl and Darius on the ends against Zacynthus and Zeno in the middle."

"An irresistible situation," said von Till. "Do you agree?"

"You couldn't miss," Pitt went on calmly. "From the time of her arrival until Giordino and I grabbed her from the villa, the girl's every move was closely watched by your chauffeur. Under the guise of a sort of bodyguard; Willie stuck with her like a leech. It must have been entertaining work, especially when she sunbathed on the beach. At that, her passion for early morning swimming was nothing but a means of making contact with Zacynthus. It was the only opportunity you gave her to pass him information, all of it worthless. How you must have laughed, knowing she was swallowing every bit of crap you fed her. Then something happened and Zacynthus began to get wise. Arriving late for their rendezvous one morning, he probably spotted Willie lurking in the bushes, both eyes unerringly focused on the girl in her bikini. Zacynthus couldn't help wondering if Willie had been there observing all the other pre-dawn meetings. Suddenly he saw his well conceived plan going down the drain. It looked as though you had outsmarted him again."

"We could have regained the advantage," Darius sputtered in pure rage, "except for you."

Pitt shrugged. "Enter our hero, yours truly, who blundered onto the stage, little knowing he would get clawed, beaten and shot before the final curtain. My life would have been far less complicated if only I'd stayed in bed that morning instead of taking an early swim. When Teri discovered me, I was taking a nap on the tideline. It was still dark, and she mistook me for Zacynthus, thinking one of your men had murdered him. She damn near went into shock when my apparently lifeless body suddenly sat upright and started a light conversation."

The pain wave hit him again and he gripped his leg as if trying to squeeze the agony away. He forced himself to go on, his words strained through gritted teeth.

"Something had gone very—very wrong. Zacynthus failed to show, and here was a total stranger who seemingly knew nothing about what was going on—add to that the staggering odds against an outsider accidentally swimming on that particular deserted beach at four in the morning, and you have one confused girl. I'll give her credit, she's a fast thinker. Considering the circumstances, she grabbed at the only conclusion open to her: I had to be on your payroll, von Till. So she went through her carefully rehearsed biography routine and invited me to the villa for dinner, expecting to throw you a curve by innocently introducing you to your own hired man."

Von Till smiled, "I am afraid you cooked your own goose, my dear Pitt, with your ridiculous tale about being in charge of garbage collecting. She didn't really believe it, but oddly enough I did."

"Not as odd as it seems," Pitt said. "No trained agent in his right mind would ever use a cover as hokey as that one. You knew that. Besides, you had no cause for alarm; there was no warning from Darius. It was really only a joke on my part—one that backfired with rather painful results."

Pitt hesitated, adjusting the belt covering his wound.

"When I appeared at your door wearing the oak leaves of a major, you immediately figured I was one of Zacynthus' agents, whom he slipped into the act without Darius' knowledge. Unwittingly I added fuel to your suspicions by damn near coming out and accusing you of enginering the raid on Brady Field. I was getting warm, too warm to suit you, von Till. Your solution was to play Houdini and make me disappear. The risk of exposure was small, the chances were that my body, or what was left of it, would never be found in the labyrinth. By this time the girl caught onto the fact that she had made a terrible mistake. I *really* was an innocent bystander who *really* happened to be swimming on that particular beach at four in the morning. It was too late, the damage was done. She could do nothing but stand by helplessly and keep her mouth shut while you disposed of me."

Von Till looked thoughtful. "I think I see, I see indeed. You still assumed the girl was my niece, and you kidnaped her out of revenge."

"You're half right," Pitt came back. "Information was my other motive. When someone tries to kill me, I like to know why. Except for you, my only source for the answer was the girl. But Colonel Zeno appeared outside the labyrinth and put a crimp in my plan before I had a chance to question her. Even so, as matters turned out, I did Inspector Zacynthus a big favor."

"I fail to understand," Darius said icily.

"For Zacynthus the abduction was made to order; the girl's usefulness was over, and, as long as she continued to play the role of your niece, her life wasn't worth two cents. Somehow, he had to discreetly slip her away from the villa and off the island. As it turned out, I played into his hands and laid her at his feet on a silver platter. However, Zacynthus wasn't out of the woods yet. A new and totally unexpected pair of problems faced him: Giordino and myself. He knew we were out to get your scalp, and, as much as he liked the idea, he still had to stop us. Legally, he had no jurisdiction and couldn't detain us by force. So he did the next best thing and asked us to cooperate with INTERPOL. That way he could watch us like a hawk."

"You are quite correct, Major." Von Till ran a hand over his hairless pate, wiping the moisture from the gleaming skin. "I had every intention of killing the girl."

Pitt nodded. "I wondered why Zacynthus was so insistent that I keep Teri on board the *First Attempt*. She'd be safe from you, and could keep an eye on Giordino and me. It didn't dawn on me until this morning what game the girl was playing and whose side she was on."

Darius stared at Pitt in bleak puzzlement. "What goes on here, Major Pitt? You could not possibly have known all this."

"Nice girls don't carry twenty-five caliber automatic Mausers taped to their legs," Pitt said. "That's a sure sign of a professional. Teri wasn't carrying a gun when I met her on the beach—Giordino discovered it when he snatched her off the couch in the villa's study. Obviously, she feared someone inside, not outside the villa."

"You are even more perceptive than I gave you credit for," von Till said bitterly. "I may have slightly underestimated you. But it makes little or no difference on the outcome."

"Only slightly underestimated?" Pitt asked consideringly. "I wonder. If I've been wise to the girl's deception, why do you think I'd stand by and allow her to drug the *First Attempt*'s radio operator so that she could sneak off a message to Inspector Zacynthus, announcing my intention to explore the cavern?"

"The answer is simple," von Till said smugly. "You didn't know Darius was working for me. He received the girl's message, but, unfortunately for you, neglected to pass it on to Inspector Zacynthus. Face it, Major, you got involved with matters far above your head."

Pitt didn't reply immediately. He sat quite still, absorbing the pain that burned in his leg, wondering if now was the right moment. It would be impossible to go on much longer—his vision was beginning to blur around the edges—yet he couldn't overplay his hand. He turned his head slightly and stared dully up at Darius. The Luger still aimed at Pitt's navel. This had to be it, he told himself—he hoped to God his timing was right.

"I agree," he said casually. "It just goes to prove, you can't win them all, can you, *Admiral Heibert?*"

At first von Till didn't respond. He stood there, his face without expression. Then the sheer incredibility of Pitt's words began to register. He took a step toward Pitt, his mouth barely moving.

"What—what did you call me?" he asked in a tight whisper.

"Admiral Heibert," Pitt repeated. "Admiral Erich Heibert: Commander of Nazi Germany's transportation fleet; fanatical follower of Adolph Hitler; and brother of Kurt Heibert, the World War I ace."

What little color was left drained from his face. "You—you have lost your senses."

"The U-19, that was your final mistake."

"Nonsense, utter nonsense." The tight lips spoke low and unbelieving.

"The model in your study. It struck me as strange at the time; why would an ex-combat pilot display a replica of a submarine instead of the aircraft he flew during wartime? Pilots are as sentimental about those things as sailors. It didn't figure. The ultimate irony is that Darius, not knowing your true identity, used Inspector Zacynthus' radio to contact the German naval archives in Berlin at my request."

"So that was what you were after," Darius said, his eyes still watchful.

"It was handled as a routine inquiry. I asked for a crew list of the U-19. I also contacted an old friend in Munich—a World War I aviation buff—and asked him if he knew of any flyer by the name of Bruno von Till. The replies were most interesting. A von Till actually flew for the German Imperial Air Service all right. But you claimed to have flown with Kurt Heibert in Jasta 73 out of the Xanthi aerodrome in Macedonia. The real von Till flew with Jasta 9 in France from the summer of 1917 until the Armistice in November of 1918; he never left the Western Front. The next intriguing tid-bit was the first name on the U-19's crew roster—a Commander Erich Heibert. Being an inquisitive cuss, I didn't stop there. I radioed Berlin again, this time from the ship, and asked them to send all available information on Erich Heibert. That did it—I couldn't have created a bigger stir with the German authorities if I'd resurrected Hitler, Goering and Himmler all in one swoop."

"Sheer babble—he's delirious." The shrewd, calculating Fu Manchu look had returned to the old German's face. "No one in their right mind would believe such a ridiculous fairytale. A model submarine—hardly a valid connection between me and Heibert."

"I don't have to prove anything. The facts speak for themselves. When Hitler took power you became his devoted follower. In return for your loyalty, and in recognition of your previous valuable combat experience, he promoted you to Officer Commanding Transportation Fleet; a title you held throughout the war until just before Germany's surrender when you seem to have vanished."

"That has nothing to do with me," von Till said angrily.

"You're wrong," Pitt returned. "The real Bruno von Till married the daughter of a wealthy Bavarian businessman who, among other interests, owned a small fleet of merchant ships—ships that sailed under the flag of Greece. Von Till knew a good thing when he saw it. He took out Greek citizenship papers and became Managing Director of Minerva Lines. Financially the company was a loser, but he built it into a first class carrier fleet by smuggling arms and essential war materials into Germany in direct violation of the Versailles Treaty. That's how you knew him, you helped engineer the operation. You both had a good thing going, but von Till was no mental retard. He figured the Axis powers would lose in the end. So he threw his lot with the Allies early in the war."

"You fail to make a connection," Darius said. Pitt had his interest, but it could just as easily fade at any moment.

"Now comes the good part. Your boss, Darius, isn't a man to leave anything to chance. A less clever man would have simply tried to vanish. Not Admiral Erich Heibert. He was much too cunning. Somehow he made his way through the Allied lines to England, where the bonafide von Till was living, murdered him and took his place."

"How was it possible," Darius demanded.

"It wasn't only possible," Pitt said to Darius, "it was accomplished to the letter. They were both roughly the same size and build. A few alterations here and there by a skilled surgeon, a few gestures and speech mannerisms, practiced until perfect, and the man who stands before you became a dead ringer for the original Bruno von Till. Why not? There were no close friends, von Till was sort of a loner, no one knew him well. His wife had died childless. There was, however, a nephew who had been born and raised in Greece. Even he didn't catch on to the switch till years later. Then it cost him his life. Mere child's play for a professional killer like Heibert. The nephew and his wife were murdered in a faked boating accident. Teri, their young daughter, was spared. No benevolence on Heibert's part I assure you. The public image of a considerate and protective grand uncle was too good to pass by."

Pitt stole another encompassing look at the guards, the tunnel and the Japanese I-Boat. Then he turned back to von Till.

"After the switch, smuggling was merely a sideline for you, Heibert. The inventive creation of a submarine attached to the keel of a ship came natural for an old U-Boat commander. To the outside world, Heibert, alias von Till, had it made. Minerva Lines was thriving, the money was rolling in. But you were worried, things ware going *too* well. The more prominent you became, the better your chances of being exposed. So you moved to Thasos, re-built the villa and played the role of an eccentric millionaire recluse. Business as usual was no problem. A high power shortwave radio was installed so you could operate Minerva Lines without ever setting foot on the mainland of Europe. But your perverted past was too strong. You let the company fleet run down to a fourth rate freight hauler, and turned your talents almost entirely to smuggling—"

"Where is all this talk leading?" Darius interrupted.

"The *fait accompli*—the pay-off," Pitt explained. "It seems that Admiral Heibert here was conspicuous by his absence at the Nuremberg War Trials. His name is right up there next to Martin Bormann on the wanted war criminals list. A real sweetheart this one. While Eichmann was burning the Jews, Heibert was emptying the POW camps by driving Allied prisoners into the holds of old merchant vessels and setting them adrift in the North Sea, trusting to British and American bombers to do the Nazi's own dirty work. In spite of the fact that he had disappeared at the end of the war, he knew what was in store if he stayed in Germany. He was convicted *in absentia* by the International Military Tribunal at Nuremberg and sentenced to death. It's a pity he wasn't hung before now, still it's better late than never."

Pitt had played his last card. There was nothing left for him but to hope, he could stall no more.

"Well there you have it. A few facts, a few educated guesses. The story's a bit sketchy I admit. The Germans could only radio a brief outline of the information they had in their files. The exact details may never become known. No matter, you're a dead man Heibert."

Von Till looked at Pitt in cold speculation. "Pay no attention to the Major, Darius. His whole make-believe tale is nothing but the clever stall of a desperate man—"

Von Till paused, listening. At first the sound was faint—it seemed like an eerie thumping. Then Pitt recognized it as the heavy tread of hobnail boots moving closer along the wooden deck. The mist was back, and its moist atmosphere cloaked any shape or form, while at the same time it amplified the approaching footsteps into a kettledrum beat. It sounded as though the unseen noisemaker was lifting his feet and dropping them with much more force than necessary. Then a ghostly and faceless figure, dressed in the uniform of von Till's bodyguards, grew out of the mist. Barely discernible, the figure stopped several feet back and clicked his heels.

"The *Queen Jocasta* has dropped anchor, sir." The voice spoke in a low guttural tone.

"You idiot!" von Till snapped, angry at the interruption. "Return to your post."

"No more delays," Darius snarled. "Just one bullet in the Major's groin so he can linger in agony." The Luger's muzzle fell to Pitt's lower torso.

"Whatever's fair," Pitt said quietly. He had a strange expressionless stare that was more disturbing to von Till than any show of fear ever could have been.

Von Till arched forward in a curt, precise bow. "I'm sorry, Major," the old German said slowly and very deliberately. "Our interesting little chat has come to an end. Please forgive me if I fail to provide the traditional blindfold and last cigarette." He said nothing more, the evil, venomous smirk on his face spoke for him, and Pitt braced himself for the almost certain blast from Darius' gun.

18

A gun roared: not the sharp bark of a Luger, but the
heavy, ear-stunning roar of a big bore, forty-five Colt
automatic. Darius shouted in pain as the Luger flew
from his hand into the water. Giordino, in a uniform at
least two sizes too large, nimbly leaped off the dock
onto the sub deck and shoved the Colt into von Till's
left ear. Then he turned to admire his marksmanship.

"Well, what do you know, I even remembered to
remove the *safety*."

"Nice going," Pitt said. "Errol Flynn couldn't have
made a more dramatic entrance."

Their faces confused and uncomprehending, von
Till and Darius stood frozen in mute shock. The hot
floodlights glared through the mist, burning it away
completely, and the guards on the ledge could see that
something totally unexpected had occurred on the sub's
deck. As if drawn by one string, all five men raised
their machine pistols and aimed them directly at Pitt.

"Keep your fingers off the triggers." Giordino's
voice boomed against the rock walls. "Shoot Major Pitt
and I splatter your boss's brains half way to Athens.
Shoot and you all die. There are guns trained on your
hearts—I'm not bluffing. Look at the tunnel."

If there was one thing in the cavern whose supply
outdistanced its necessity, it was the machine pistol.
There were ten more of them in the hands of the tough-

est bunch of men Pitt had ever seen. They were grouped in loose formation around the tunnel entrance, four in the prone position, three kneeling, and three standing. Pitt almost had to look twice to make them out clearly; their black and brown camouflaged field dress blended perfectly into the craggy shadows. Only their maroon berets, the hallmark of an elite outfit, betrayed their presence to the casual eye.

Giordino continued: "Now please turn your attention to the submarine at my rear."

It wasn't exactly the straw that broke the camel's back, but it was the ugly, air cooled machine gun, gripped by a fiendishly grinning Colonel Zeno on the I-Boat's conning tower, that broke the bodyguards' will to fight. Slowly they lowered their guns and raised their hands in the air; all except one, he hesitated and paid the price.

Zeno fanned the trigger of his weapon. Two bullets, no more, spat from the aircooled barrel in one brief blast. The unthinking, unfortunate guard slumped soundlessly to the ground and rolled limply into the water, staining the brilliant cobalt blue with a growing cloud of red.

"Now walk, don't run to the nearest exit," Giordino said casually, "your hands clasped on your heads."

Pitt, the tired expression on his face reflecting the gnawing pain in his leg, said to Giordino: "You sliced your timing pretty thin."

"The capital of Italy wasn't constructed in twenty-four hours," Giordino paraphrased pontifically. "After all, swimming ashore, finding Zacynthus, Zeno, and their roving band of commandos, and then leading them through that godawful labyrinth on the run wasn't the most leisurely of chores."

"Did you have any trouble with my directions?"

"No problem. The elevator shaft was right where you said it'd be."

Von Till moved close to Pitt, his eyes cold as ice. "Who told you about the elevator?"

"No one," Pitt replied tersely. "Wandering through the labyrinth, I accidentally took a side corridor that

ended at a ventilator shaft. I heard the sound of generators somewhere beyond the opening. Their purpose
came to me when I was sure of the sea cavern. Your
villa sits on a near vertical line above the shoreline
cliffs. An underground elevator had to be the only
means of moving from the villa to the cavern without
detection. The shaft, the cavern, and passageways were
a made to order arrangement for smuggling, courtesy of
the Phoenicians over two thousand years ago."

"Wait a minute," Giordino cut in. "Are you suggesting that somebody was smuggling out of here before
Christ?"

"You didn't do your homework," Pitt grinned. "If
you'd read the brochure that Zeno handed out before
we started on the tour of the ruins, you'd know that
Thasos was originally settled by the Phoenicians to ex-
ploit its gold and silver deposits. The tunnels and shaft
are part of an ancient mine. Eventually it was worked
out and abandoned. The Greeks discovered it a few
hundred years later and thought it was some kind of
mysterious labyrinth built by the Gods."

A movement on the dock attracted Pitt's attention
and he looked up.

Zacynthus appeared seemingly out of nowhere and
stood, staring down at Pitt for several long moments.
Finally he asked:

"How's the leg?"

Pitt shrugged. "It'll probably smart a bit when the
barometer drops, but it shouldn't slow up my sex life."

"Colonel Zeno sent two of his men after a
stretcher. They should be here in a few minutes."

"Were you able to overhear any of our enlighten-
ing conversation?"

Zacynthus nodded. "Every word. The acoustics in
here would do credit to Carnegie Hall."

"You'll never prove any of it," von Till said in
contempt. His lips curled in a sneer, but there was a
trace of desperation in his eyes.

"As I've said," Pitt murmured tiredly, "I don't
have to prove anything. At this minute, four war criminal investigators are flying here from Germany, cour-

tesy of the United States Air Force, who were only too happy to lend a helping hand after your little shooting party at Brady Field. Each one of those four men is a specialist. They know every hidden identity trick in the book. Plastic surgery, a different voice, your advanced age, nothing will fool them. I'm afraid it's the end of the voyage for you, Admiral."

"I am a Greek citizen," von Till said arrogantly. "They have no legal right to abduct me to Germany."

"Cut the masquerade," Pitt lashed back. "Von Till was the Greek citizen, *not* you. Colonel Zeno, will you please explain the facts of life for the Admiral."

"With pleasure, Major." Zeno had left the conning tower of the Japanese I-Boat and was now standing next to Zacynthus. He grinned broadly under the big, flowing moustache and eyed von Till with piercing scrutiny. "We take a dim view of anyone who enters our country illegally and we greatly dislike playing host to a wanted war criminal. If you are indeed Admiral Erich Heibert, as Major Pitt claims, I shall personally see to it that you are turned over to the war criminal investigators and placed on the first plane back to Germany and the gallows."

"A most appropriate and convenient ending," Zacynthus said slowly. "It saves the taxpayers the expense of a long, drawn out trial for narcotics smuggling. On the other hand, we lose the opportunity to bag half the illegal drug buyers in North America."

"Aren't you forgetting that opportunity makes the thief," Pitt grinned.

"What do you mean by that?"

"Simple arithmetic, Zac. Now you know how the heroin drop is made and where. It would be an easy matter to take over the *Queen Jocasta,* keep the crew incommunicado, and deliver the goods in person. I'm certain the proper authorities could hush-up Heibert's capture until you can spring your trap at the cannery in Galveston."

"Yes," Zacynthus said consideringly, "yes by god, it just might work. Providing I can find a crew to operate the ship and submarine on short notice."

"The Mediterranean Tenth Fleet," Pitt offered. "Use your influence and make an urgent request to our navy for an emergency crew. They can be airlifted into Brady Field. Timewise, it shouldn't set the *Queen Jocasta* off schedule for more than five or six hours. If you push the old tub you can make that up in a day and a half."

Zacynthus surveyed Pitt with mixed curiosity and admiration. "You certainly don't miss much, do you?"

Pitt shrugged, retaining his grin. "I try."

"There is one thing I wish you'd explain."

"Name it."

"How did you know Darius was an informer?"

"I smelled a rat when I searched the *Queen Artemisia*. The transmitter in the radio cabin was set on the same frequency as the set in your office. I must confess, at the time I thought it might be any one of you. The field narrowed down to Darius after I swam ashore and met Giordino. He said that Darius had been stationed on your radio during the entire time between the arrival and departure of the *Queen Artemisia*. It was a cozy arrangement. While you and Zeno were on a wild goose chase, keeping an eye on the villa and battling mosquitos, Darius was comfortably sipping his Metaxa and notifying Heibert of your every move. That's why I had the ship all to myself. The crew members were all busy down in the bilges, releasing the sub. The captain hadn't bothered posting a lookout because Darius had ssured him all was clear. What Darius didn't know, and even you didn't know, Zac, was that I intended to swim out and scout the ship from the water. You suspected nothing when Giordino and I volunteered to watch the ship from the beach. It was only at the last minute, when I saw no sign of the *Queen Artemisia's* crew, that I decided to sneak on board for a closer look. My apologies for not clearing my actions with you, but I was certain that you'd have raised hell and tried to stop me."

"I'm the one who should offer apologies," Zacynthus said. "I deserve the dunce award of the year. God, how could I have been so blind? I should have guessed something was wrong when Darius was never able to intercept any messages between the passing Minerva ships and the villa."

"I could have relayed my suspicions to you on the road this morning," Pitt said. "But it hardly seemed the right time or place, particularly in front of Darius. Secondly, without one hundred percent proof I doubt seriously whether you or Zeno would have believed my accusation."

"You were quite right," Zacynthus admitted. "Tell me this. Where did you find out about the *Queen Jocasta*?"

"The Air Force has a funny habit about loaning out their vehicles; sooner or later they want them back. After Giordino and I left you, we stopped off at Brady Field and returned the truck to the motorpool. Colonel Lewis was waiting for us. It was he who alerted me to the *Queen Jocasta*. One of his morning patrols sighted her cruising north toward Thasos. The next step was to check the ship's cargo and destination with the Minerva Line's agent in Athens. His reply added to an interesting coincidence. Not only were two Minerva ships passing by the villa within twelve hours of each other, but both were headed for ports in the United States. I began to get the picture—von Till, or rather Heibert, intended to switch the sub and the heroin from the *Queen Artemisia* to the *Queen Jocasta*."

"You might have let me in on your secret," Zacynthus said with a noticeable trace of bitterness. "I came within a hair of locking Giordino up when he bounded into my headquarters, demanding that I, together with Colonel Zeno's men, follow him into the labyrinth."

Pitt studied him. The inspector's face was grim. "I considered it," Pitt said honestly. "But I figured the less everyone concerned knew, the less chance there was for Darius to get suspicious. I also purposely kept the girl in the dark because it was essential that her message, warning your headquarters of my plans to search for the cavern, reek with serious intentions when Darius intercepted it. My actions were devious, I admit, but my reasons were valid."

"To think that the Bureau's finest investigator was shown up by a rank amateur." Then Zacynthus grinned and there was a warm hint in the smile that removed the acid from his words. "But it was worth it, well worth it."

Pitt was greatly relieved. He didn't wish to make an enemy of Zacynthus. He turned and looked at von Till. The old German stared back at Pitt with a contempt in his eyes that went far beyond mere hate. The only feeling that suddenly welled within Pitt was one of disgust. He spoke quietly, but his cold voice carried to every inch of the cavern.

"You would have to die a hundred thousand deaths, and then some, to repay all the lives you stole, old man. Most men are born and go to the grave without killing anyone, but your list stretches endlessly from the helpless prisoners you condemned to the cold waters of the North Sea to the schoolgirls you sold into slavery in the scum infested back alleys of Casablanca. How ironic that a man who caused so many other people to die in agony should die horribly also. My only regret is that I won't be there to see your neck stretched, Heibert; see your withered old body jerk and bounce when it hits the end of the rope. They say the shock forces the bladder and the bowels to move. That's a fitting end for you, old man. Thrown in an unmarked pauper's grave to rot through eternity in your own filth."

Muttering incoherent words, his face distorted in blind anger, and entirely oblivious to the surrounding guns of the gendarmerie, von Till hurled himself at Pitt. It was the mad gesture of a hysterical man. Giordino's forty-five clubbed him on the back of the neck before he took the second step. He fell awkwardly to the deck in a crumpled heap and lay as if dead. Giordino didn't even look down as he holstered his gun.

"You cracked him a bit hard," Zacynthus said reprovingly.

"Vermin don't die easily," Giordino replied impassively, "especially when they're as mean as that old bastard."

Darius had not moved or spoken since Giordino

shot him. Any other man would have gripped a
wounded and bleeding hand; not Darius. The huge
brute let his hand hang limply to one side, indifferently
allowing the blood to splatter on the sub's deck. The
lost expression on his face reminded Pitt of a newly
caged gorilla he had once seen in the San Diego Zoo, an
ugly misshapen monster who could not grasp the meaning of the barred walls and the strange looking animals
beyond that stood five deep, observing his every movement. Pitt was very happy indeed that at least five of
Zeno's gendarmerie had their guns trained between
Darius' cold black eyes.

Pitt nodded toward Darius. "What happens to
him?"

"A fast trial," Zacynthus answered. "Then the firing squad—"

"There will be no trial," Zeno interrupted. "The
gendarmerie have never admitted to a traitor in their
ranks." His voice was grave, yet his eyes were filled
with sadness. "Captain Darius died in the performance
of his duties."

The cavern suddenly became silent. Pitt, Zacynthus and Giordino all exchanged puzzled glances over
Zeno's use of the past tense.

Darius said nothing. He displayed no emotion, no
sign of fear, only a resignation to a fate that precluded
even the remotest possibility of hope. Slowly, very carefully, like a man who hadn't tasted sleep in days, he
climbed from the sub onto the dock and stood before
Zeno, his head bowed.

"It seems I have known you for many years, Darius," Zeno sounded very tired. "Yet I haven't really
known you at all. God alone knows why you came to be
what you are. It is a pity, the gendarmerie lost a good
man . . ." Zeno hesitated, groping for words, but he
could think of nothing else to say. Carefully, almost to
the point of meticulousness, he withdrew the cartridge
clip from his gun and removed all the shells except one.
Then he reinserted the clip and held out the gun, butt
first, to Darius.

Nodding, as if in secret understanding, and searching Zeno's eyes for a sign that never came, Darius took the gun, turned slowly towards the tunnel, and began walking numbly across the dock.

"No goodby, no regrets, no *to hell with you*," Giordino said uncomprehendingly. "Just like that, he wanders off and blows his brains out. Ten will get you one that Darius makes a break for it."

"His life ended when he became a traitor," Zeno said quietly. "Darius knew it then—he knows it now. An early death was his fate when he dropped from the womb, there was no escaping it. Five minutes to talk with his God and prepare his soul—then he will squeeze the trigger."

Giordino watched Darius fade into the blackness of the tunnel and said nothing. The finality of Zeno's words shattered all his doubts over Darius' intentions. Until the day he, himself, died, Giordino would never understand how anyone could let loose of life so unquestioningly.

He turned back to Pitt. "Time's a wasting, we're running out of the money. Gunn is probably having a spastic fit wondering what happened to his precious scientists."

"Can't say as I blame him." The voice came from Knight, who was climbing out of the deck hatch, a sly smile across his face. "Great intellect is hard to come by these days."

"An egghead comedian," Giordino groaned. "What has science come to?"

In spite of the pain in his leg, Pitt couldn't help but laugh. "Maybe some of Knight's intellect will rub off on you when you escort him and the other eggheads back to the *First Attempt*. I'm holding you responsible until they're safely on board."

"Talk about appreciation," Giordino groaned again. "After all I've done for you."

"It's better to give, than to receive," Pitt said soothingly. "Now hop to it. If you expect to swim out through the submerged tunnels, you and the others will have to retrieve the diving gear from the bottom."

Woodson crawled from the hatch and walked over

to Pitt. "Maybe I better stick with you, Major, until you're bedded down."

"No thanks," Pitt answered, mildly surprised at the look of genuine concern on Woodson's otherwise expressionless face. "I'm OK. Zac here is going to take me to a hospital full of nymphomaniac nurses, right Zac?"

"Sorry," Zacynthus smiled. "Not unless the Air Force has changed its enlistment policy. I'm afraid the base hospital at Brady Field has the only decent facilities on the island for plugging bullet holes."

The litter-bearers arrived and immediately eased Pitt onto the stretcher. "Oh well," he said, "at least I travel first class." Then he sat up. "Damn! I almost forgot. One last thing. Where's Spencer?"

"Here, Major, right here," The red-bearded marine biologist stepped from behind Woodson. "What can I do for you?"

"Relay my compliments to Commander Gunn and give him a present for me."

Spencer paled visibly at the sight of Pitt's bloody leg. "Consider it done."

Pitt leaned over the side of the stretcher and rested on one elbow. "In the outer cavern, twenty feet down, there are several small fissures along the base of the north wall. One has a flat rock over the entrance. If he hasn't already muscled his way out, you'll find a *Teaser* inside."

Spencer's face registered total surprise. "A *Teaser!* Are you serious, Major?"

"I ought to know a *Teaser* when I see one," Pitt replied jokingly. "See to it that you don't drop him."

Spencer let out a long whistle. "Well what do you know. I was beginning to think no such creature existed." He paused a moment, deep in thought. "Christ, I don't dare damage him with a spear shaft. A net bag, if only I'd carried a net bag."

"There's only one way to catch a *Teaser*," Pitt grinned. "Grab him by the fin."

The pain was going away now. Pitt's leg felt like it was no longer part of him. The floodlights fused together in one massive blur, hurting his eyes. Everything seemed to slow down, and the voices became far away. Then the stretcher bearers picked Pitt up from the dock, moving, it seemed to him, as though they were wading through glue. He raised his head for the last time that day.

"Zac, one more request." Pitt's voice was down to a bare murmur. "What is the girl's real name?"

Zac looked down at Pitt and smiled with his eyes. "Her name is Amy."

"Amy," Pitt repeated. "Never knew a girl by the name of Amy before." He relaxed and fell back against the stretcher, closing his eyes. The last thing he remembered before the soothing blanket of darkness fully covered him was the sound of a single shot, echoing from somewhere within the depths of the labyrinth.

TALLY

The sky was a brilliant ceiling of blue as far as the eye could see. The summer air was hot and dripping with unseen humidity encouraged by burning waves from the blazing sun. In blinding radiance, tall white buildings stood like small chiseled mountains and reflected the heat onto the black asphalt pavement below; the traffic was heavy, and the sidewalks were crowded with scurrying office workers on lunch break as Pitt pushed aside the wide glass doors and limped stiffly into the air conditioned lobby of the Bureau of Narcotics building.

For a bachelor, he thought, one of the wonderful things about Washington, D.C. is the overabundance of girls. They come in every size, age, and disposition and swarm like chattering locusts throughout every government office in the city, providing the hungry male with all the advantages of a rich kid running amok in a candy store. Pitt selected his most charming, devil-may-care smile and offered it to a trio of giggling secretaries who exited the elevator. They returned his smile, accompanied with the usual combination of cursory and demure glances that women are prone to allow for strange men, and then wiggled past him into the lobby, sneaking an additional peek at him over their shoulders.

A moment later, playing the role of the wounded warrior to perfection, Pitt leaned heavily on his cane and limped from the elevator onto the thick carpet of the eighth floor. In the center of the anteroom a dozen girls, displaying an unrestricted forest of nyloned legs, sat at a dozen desks and furiously assaulted a dozen typewriters, never once hesitating to look up at him. He moved slowly over to a well-bosomed blond whose desk top contained a small rectangular sign: "Information." Then for a moment he stared down at her, admiring the view.

"Excuse me."

She didn't hear him over the din of the clacking machines.

"Excuse me," Pitt repeated loudly.

She turned and noticed him. "May I help you?" The voice was cool, the big hazel eyes unfriendly. Pitt admitted to himself that he had to go along with her icy greeting. The white turtleneck sweater, the green California sport coat, the handkerchief casually fluffed from the breast pocket hardly categorized him as an executive or important Washington bureaucrat.

"I would like to see the Director of the Bureau."

"I'm sorry," she said, turning back to her typewriter. "The Director is extremely busy and cannot see anyone."

Contempt and anger began to mount in Pitt. "Inspector Zacynthus made an appointment for me—"

"Inspector Zacynthus' office is on the fourth floor," the girl droned mechanically.

A gun shot couldn't have received more attention than the resounding bang from Pitt's cane as he slammed it on top of the receptionist's desk. The typists' eyes burst wide, and their hands froze above keyboards, sending the anteroom into a sudden dead silence. Her face drained of all color, the large-chested blond stared up at Pitt, a fear mushrooming inside her.

"OK, dearheart," Pitt said menacingly. "You get up off your well rounded little bottom and you go and inform the Director that Major Dirk Pitt is waiting to keep the appointment set by Inspector Zacynthus."

"Pitt . . . Major Pitt from NUMA," The blond gasped. "Oh I'm sorry, sir. But I thought—"

"Yes, I know," Pitt offered. "I'm out of uniform."

The blond jumped from her desk, snagging a stocking in her haste. "Right this way, Major. They're expecting you."

Pitt grinned at her, grinned at the other girls sitting awed in their chairs, felt self-satisfied at the admiring expressions from all twenty-four eyes, the bovine, adoring gaze reserved for celebrities and movie stars. It inflated his male ego.

"Keep typing girls," he said good-naturedly. "Mustn't keep the Bureau waiting for all those letters and reports."

The blond led him down a long hallway, slowing her pace every so often to allow him to catch up. She halted and rapped on a walnut stained door. "Major Pitt," she announced, and then stood aside to let him pass through.

Three men rose as he walked into the room. The fourth, Giordino, remained comfortably anchored to a long leather couch.

"I thought I'd never see the day," he said. "Dirk Pitt hobbling around on a cane."

"Just practicing for my senile years," Pitt retorted.

A short, red-haired man with a zeppelin-shaped cigar stashed jauntily between his lips came over and shook Pitt's hand. "Welcome back, Dirk. Congratulations on a great job in the Aegean."

Pitt stared into the griffin-featured face of Admiral James Sandecker, the crusty chief of the National Underwater Marine Agency."

"Thank you, Admiral. Any word on the *Teaser* yet?"

"Only that it's alive and still swimming," Sandecker answered. "Since Gunn had it flown over last week in a special tank, I haven't been able to get near the goddamn thing—a horde of scientists have been crowded around it, ogling their damn eyes right out of their sockets. They promised me a preliminary report by morning."

Zacynthus came across to greet Pitt. He seemed younger, much more relaxed than when Pitt had last seen him, three weeks previously.

"Good to see you walking again," Zacynthus said smiling. "You look as mean and nasty as ever."

He took Pitt by the arm and led him over to a tall man standing by the window and introduced them. Pitt studied the Director of the Bureau and was studied in return by hard gray eyes that peered intently from a high-cheeked, pockmarked face; it was a face straight out of a police lineup. Pitt amusingly reflected that the Director looked more like a narcotics smuggler than the chief administrator of several thousand federal investigators. The Director spoke first.

"I've looked forward to meeting you, Major Pitt. The Bureau is deeply grateful for your assistance." The voice was low and very precise.

"I didn't do much. Inspector Zacynthus and Colonel Zeno carried most of the load."

The Director met his eyes evenly. "That may be, but you carry the scars." He motioned Pitt to a chair and offered him a cigarette. "Did you have a good flight from Greece?"

Pitt lit the cigarette and inhaled deeply. "Air Force cargo planes aren't exactly famous for their cuisine and royal coachman service, but I must admit that it was considerably more relaxing than the flight in."

Admiral Sandecker gave Pitt a puzzled look. "Why the Air Force? You could have flown from Athens on Pan Am or TWA."

"Souvenirs," Pitt laughed. "One of my mementos of Thasos was too bulky to fit in the luggage compartment of a commercial airliner. Colonel Lewis came to my rescue and helped me hitch a ride on a half-empty Air Force cargo plane that was headed stateside."

"Your wound," Sandecker nodded at Pitt's leg. "Healing all right?"

"It's still a bit stiff," Pitt answered. "Nothing a thirty day medical leave won't cure."

The Admiral eyed Pitt shrewdly for a moment through a blue haze of cigar smoke. "Two weeks." The tone reeked of cool authority. "I have more faith in your recuperative powers than you have."

The Director cleared his throat. "I've read Inspector Zacynthus' report with a great deal of interest. There is, however, one point he didn't cover. It isn't important, but out of personal curiosity, I wonder if you could tell me, Major, how you came to the conclusion that Minerva Lines ships had the capacity to carry submarines?"

Pitt smiled with his eyes. "I guess you might say, sir, the secret was written in the sand."

The Director's lips curled in a humorless smile. He wasn't used to indirect answers. "Very Homeric, Major, but hardly the answer I had in mind."

"Strange but true," Pitt said. "After finding no sign of the heroin on board the *Queen Artemisia*, I swam to the beach and began doodling with a stick in the sand. A detachable submarine seemed like an abstract idea at first, but the more I doodled, the more concrete it became."

The Director leaned back in his chair and shook his head sadly. "Forty years, a hundred agents from twelve different nations, all struggling under the most adverse conditions imaginable to break von Till's smuggling operation. Three of those agents gave up their lives in the struggle." He looked gravely across the desk at Pitt. "Somehow it almost seems a tragic joke that our efforts overlooked a solution that was so apparent to someone standing on the outside looking in."

Pitt stared at him in silence.

"By the way," the Director continued suddenly cheerful, "I don't suppose you've had a chance to hear the results of our Galveston stakeout?"

"No sir." Pitt carefully tapped an ash in an ashtray. "Until five minutes ago, I haven't seen or talked to Inspector Zacynthus since we parted on Thasos, nearly three weeks ago. I've had no way of knowing whether my small assist paid off for you in Galveston or not."

Zacynthus looked at the Director. "May I fill Major Pitt in, sir?"

The Director nodded.

Zacynthus turned to Pitt.

"Everything went according to plan. Five miles outside the harbor we were met by a small fleet of von

Till's fishing boats—a bit tricky at this point, not knowing the proper identification signals. Luckily I persuaded the *Queen Jocasta's* captain—with the threat of castration with a rusty knife—to desert the enemy and join our side."

"Did anyone come aboard?" Pitt asked.

"There was no danger of that," Zacynthus replied. "A boarding party would have looked too damned suspicious to a passing patrol boat. The fishermen merely stood off and signaled us to detach the sub. Interesting piece of machinery, that sub. The Navy engineers who studied it coming across the Atlantic were quite impressed."

"What made it so unique?"

"It was fully automatic."

"A drone?" Pitt asked incredulously.

"Yes, another one of von Till's clever innovations. You see, if the sub had an accident or was detected by the Harbor Patrol before it reached the cannery there was no way in hell it could be traced or connected to Minerva Lines. And without a crew there would be no one to interrogate."

Pitt was intrigued. "Then it was controlled by one of the fishing boats."

Zacynthus nodded. "Right up the middle of the harbor's main channel and under the pilings of the cannery. Only this trip the sub carried several uninvited stowaways: myself and ten marines on loan from the Mediterranean Tenth Fleet. I might add that the cannery was surrounded by thirty of the Bureau's best agents."

"If Galveston had more than one cannery," Giordino said thoughtfully, "you'd have been in big trouble."

Zacynthus grinned knowingly. "As a matter of fact, Galveston boasts a total of four canneries, all located on pilings over the water."

Giordino didn't have to ask the obvious question. It was written all over his face.

"I'll put your mind at ease," Zacynthus said. "The Bureau's Gulf Ports Department had each cannery under surveillance for two weeks before the *Queen Jocasta*'s arrival. The tipoff came when one of them received a shipment of sugar."

Pitt raised an eyebrow. "Sugar?"

"Sugar," the Director offered, "is often used to adulterate the heroin and boost the quantity. By the time pure heroin is cut by the middle man and cut again by the dealer, the original supply is increased by a substantial amount."

Pitt thought for a moment. "So the one hundred and thirty tons was only a beginning?"

"It could have been the beginning," Zacynthus answered, "if it wasn't for you, old friend. You're the only one who saw through von Till's plan. If you and Giordino hadn't arrived at Thasos when you did, the rest of us would be sitting up in Chicago about now, forming a daisy chain and kicking each other into Lake Michigan."

Pitt grinned. "Write it off to luck."

"Call it what you will," Zacynthus retorted. "As things stand at the moment, we have over thirty of the biggest illegal drug importers in the country waiting for indictment, including everyone connected with the trucking company that transported the goods. And that's only the half of it. When we searched the cannery office we found a book with the names of nearly two thousand dealers from New York to Los Angeles. For the Bureau it was comparable to a prospector discovering the mother lode."

Giordino let out a long whistle. "It's going to be a bad year for the addicts."

"That's right," Zacynthus said. "Now that their main source is dried up, and the local law enforcement agencies are rounding up the dealers, the users are about to face the worst drug famine to come along in the last twenty years."

Pitt's eyes left the room and gazed out the window, seeing nothing. "There is just one more question."

Zacynthus looked at him. "Yes?"

Pitt didn't reply immediately. He fiddled with his

cane a moment. "What became of our old friend? I've seen no mention of him in the newspapers."

"Before I answer you, take a look at these." Zacynthus pulled a pair of photographs from a briefcase and laid them in front of Pitt side by side on the desk.

Pitt leaned over and studied them carefully. The first was a snapshot of a light-haired man who wore the uniform of a German naval officer. He was caught in a relaxed pose, standing on the bridge of a ship and peering out to sea, his hands resting carelessly on a pair of binoculars that hung around his neck. The face in the second photograph stared back at Pitt with the familiar leer of a shaven-skulled Erich von Stroheim. A huge white dog stood at the lower half of the picture, crouched as if ready to spring. An involuntary chill crept through Pitt's body as he remembered— remembered all too vividly.

"There doesn't seem to be much of a resemblance."

Zacynthus nodded. "Admiral Heibert did a remarkable job—scars, birthmarks, even his dental fillings matched von Till's."

"What about fingerprints?"

"Impossible to prove anything. There were no known records of von Till's prints, and Heibert had his altered by surgery."

Pitt sat back puzzled. "Then how can we be sure—"

"The uninvited detail," Zacynthus said slowly. "No matter how exhaustingly they try or how diligently they plan, all criminals get their tails pinned to the wall by the uninvited detail. In Heibert's case it was von Till's scalp?"

Pitt shook his head. "I don't follow you."

"When von Till was a young man, he contracted a skin disease called *Alpecia areata* which caused complete baldness. Heibert didn't know this. He thought von Till had shaved his head in the Prussian tradition, so quite naturally he took to the razor. It didn't take the War Criminals Investigators long to spot the growth. There was, of course, later evidence that confirmed Admiral Heibert's identity, but the hair was the first nail in the coffin."

Pitt suddenly felt a vague mixture of relief and satisfaction. "Has he swung yet?"

"Four days ago," Zacynthus said matter of factly. "You saw nothing in the newspapers because there was nothing. The Germans kept his capture and death quiet. They're sick and tired of having the mud of their Nazi past rubbed in their faces every time an old war criminal is ferreted out. Besides, Heibert didn't have the same notoriety as Bormann and a few others of Hitler's personal clique."

"Makes you wonder how many more are scattered around the world," Pitt murmured.

The telephone on the desk buzzed, and the Director picked it up. "Yes . . . yes, I'll pass along the good news, thank you." He replaced the telephone in its cradle, his pitted face split in a wide grin, and he turned to Sandecker. "That was your office, Admiral. Allow me to be the first to offer my congratulations."

Sandecker rolled the cigar to one side of his mouth. "What in hell for?"

The Director, still grinning, stood up and laid his hand on the Admiral's shoulder. "It seems that your marine oddity turned out to be a viviparous female. Consequently, you, sir, are now the proud papa of a bouncing baby *Teaser*."

The steaming heat was beginning to fade, and the lengthening shadows were stretching far behind the late afternoon sun when Pitt limped out onto the sidewalk. He paused a moment and looked at the city. The streets were busy with homeward bound traffic, and soon all the surrounding buildings would be mute and deserted. He looked toward the Capitol building in the distance, its white dome transformed into a blazing gold tint from the falling sun, and he remembered another scene on a faraway beach and a white ship and a vibrant blue sea. It seemed so long ago, nearly an eternity.

Giordino and Zacynthus came down the steps and joined him.

Zacynthus spoke jovially. "Gentlemen, I suggest that since we are all single, debonair men-about-town we combine forces and engage in a bit of fun and frolic."

"I'll buy that," Giordino volunteered.

Pitt shrugged in mock sadness. "It wounds me deeply, but I must decline your intriguing invitation. I already have a previous engagement."

"I think this is where I came in," Giordino moaned.

Zacynthus laughed. "You're making a big mistake. I happen to possess a little black book which contains the phone numbers of some of Washington's fairest—"

Zacynthus suddenly stopped in midsentence and stared at the street, his eyes wide in blank astonishment.

A gargantuan black and silver car rolled silently up to the curb and stopped. Elegant in design, majestic in appearance, the regal coachwork seemed out of place beside the more modern mechanized traffic, like a queen of the realm amid a bustling crowd of foul-smelling rabble. And as a fitting touch, the *piece de resistance,* a lovely dark-haired girl graced the steering wheel.

"Good lord" Zacynthus gasped. "Von Till's Maybach." He turned to Pitt. "How did you get it?"

"To the victor belong the spoils," Pitt grinned slyly.

Giordino raised an eyebrow. "Now I see what you meant by a bulky souvenir. I might add that your other souvenir isn't half bad either."

Pitt opened the front door of the car. "I think you both know my ravishing chauffeur."

"She reminds me of a girl I once met in the Aegean," Giordino said smiling. "But this one is much better looking."

The girl laughed. "Just to show that flattery has its reward, I forgive you for that rough ride through the labyrinth. Only next time give me warning so I can put on some decent clothes."

Giordino looked genuinely sheepish. "I promise."

Pitt turned to Zacynthus. There was a faint smile in Pitt's eyes. "Do me a favor, will you Zac?"

"If I can."

"I'd like to borrow the services of one of your agents for a couple of weeks. Do you think you can arrange it?"

Zacynthus looked down at the girl and nodded. "I think so. The Bureau owes you that much."

Pitt climbed into the front seat and closed the door. Then he handed his cane out to Giordino. "Here, I don't think I'll be needing this anymore."

Before Giordino could make an appropriate reply, the girl engaged the clutch, and the big town car slipped into the moving line of traffic.

Giordino watched the high-roofed car until it rounded a distant corner and was lost from sight. Then he turned and looked at Zacynthus.

"How are you at whipping up scallops with mushrooms in white wine sauce?"

Zacynthus shook his head. "I'm afraid I've never graduated beyond frozen TV dinners."

"In that case, you can buy me a drink."

"You forget, I'm only a poor civil servant."

"Then look upon me as an item on your expense account."

Zacynthus tried to look serious but failed. Then he shrugged. "Shall we?"

"Lets."

So arm in arm, much to the amusement of passerbys, the tall Zacynthus and the short Giordino, looking all the world like Mutt and Jeff, began walking down the sidewalk in the direction of the nearest bar.

ABOUT THE AUTHOR

CLIVE CUSSLER lives the same sort of adventurous life as his hero, Dirk Pitt. Tramping the Southwest in search of gold mines, diving in isolated Rocky Mountain lakes for missing aircraft, heading an expedition to salvage John Paul Jones' ship, the *Bonhomme Richard*. Most recently Cussler discovered and excavated a sister ship to the *Monitor*, as well as finding artifacts from its famous nemesis the *Merrimack*. A noted collector of classic automobiles, Cussler lives in the foothills overlooking Denver, Colorado. Here he writes his bestselling thrillers: RAISE THE TITANIC!, ICEBERG, THE MEDITERRANEAN CAPER, VIXEN 03—and most recently, NIGHT PROBE!

<u>SAVE $2.00</u> ON YOUR NEXT BOOK ORDER!

BANTAM BOOKS ❧
Shop-at-Home Catalog

Now you can have a complete, up-to-date catalog of Bantam's inventory of over 1,600 titles—including hard-to-find books. And, you can <u>save $2.00</u> on your next order by taking advantage of the money-saving coupon you'll find in this illustrated catalog. Choose from fiction and non-fiction titles, including mysteries, historical novels, westerns, cookbooks, romances, biographies, family living, health, and more. You'll find a description of most titles. Arranged by categoreis, the catalog makes it easy to find your favorite books and authors and to discover new ones.

So don't delay—send for this shop-at-home catalog and save money on your next book order.

Just send us your name and address and 50¢ to defray postage and handling costs.

BANTAM BOOKS, INC.
Dept. FC, 414 East Golf Road, Des Plaines, Ill. 60016

Mr./Mrs./Miss/Ms. _____
(please print)

Address _____

City _____ State _____ Zip _____

Do you know someone who enjoys books? Just give us their names and addresses and we'll send them a catalog too at no extra cost!

Mr./Mrs./Miss/Ms. _____

Address _____

City _____ State _____ Zip _____

Mr./Mrs./Miss/Ms. _____

Address _____

City _____ State _____ Zip _____

FC—2/83A